PiNS

Christine Todd

RED ANEMONE
BOOKS

RED ANEMONE BOOKS

First published in Great Britain in 2010
First published in United States in 2012
by Red Anemone Books

ISBN: 978-0-9831888-3-4

Interior Design by Chandler Book Design
Cover Design by Dotti Albertine

RED ANEMONE
BOOKS

redanemone.com

FOR JEAN-MICHEL AND EMILY

1

A t 8:13 a.m. Friday, the phone startles me out of a dead sleep. I bolt upright. My grab at the receiver sends the cradle flying onto the floor. It skitters across the carpet and lands with a clatter on the exposed wood bordering the room. The line stays open.

"Hi, it's Shirley."

The sound of her voice jolts me wide awake. "Yes."

"Is Bob there?"

"Why, is something wrong?"

"I'm running late. Cameron just called to say that Bob isn't in the office yet either. And Jane is on vacation, so there's nobody there to run the place."

I glance across at my husband, "He's still in bed." I'm surprised. It's not like him to forget to set the alarm. He must be exhausted from all of his extracurricular activities.

"In *bed!*" She sounds aghast, no doubt wondering what we've been up to all morning.

I want to banish any question about the Makepeace-Jamison's sex life from that ditzy head of hers. Bob will have lied to her about that. I yawn, and make a long O sound, as if luxuriating in the afterglow. I murmur, "I'll get him up right away."

"The meeting is at eight-thirty," she cries. "He'll never make it. I'll have to put Cameron in charge of everything. Hopefully, he knows what he's doing. At least the client knows him, so we're sort of covered. I'll get in when I feel better. Right now my head feels like a pincushion."

I'm staring at Bob. Throughout our conversation he has not moved, even to breathe.

My husband's bloated face lies pale against bright blue sheets; his empty brown eyes stare at the wall. I stand over him, astonished at the sight, and envision his pin-festooned Voodoo doll. My heart hammers out shock. I shriek, *"What have I done?"* His cheek is cold, and feels denser than normal. I shout, *"Bob!"* even though I know he's gone.

I dial 911, my teeth chattering so hard I sound as if I'm shivering. I remember that when people die, they are said to leave their bodies and hover over the room. My head bows and my eyes examine the floor.

The dispatcher is efficient and kind, asking questions with admirable empathy. After doing my best to quake out my answers, she finally says, "It's all right, ma'am, the paramedics will arrive in a few more minutes. I'll stay on the line with you until they arrive."

"No!" My brain hops about in fright. I have to get the Voodoo dolls stashed, the evidence hidden. Talking to her during all of that would make me feel even crazier.

"What is it, Ms. Jamison? Are you okay?"

I hardly recognize the mad green eyes reflecting back at me through the mirror. Squeezing them shut, I force myself to slow down. "I want to get dressed before they arrive."

"I prefer to stay on the line and keep you company."

"Thank you, but I need a little time alone to pull myself together."

"Weeeell, if you're sure—"

"I am, thank you."

"Please call me back if you need anything at all."

Shaking like mad, I raise my eyes to the mirror. I am a ghoul. *I have killed my husband.*

I see Bob's old smile, feel his lips brush my cheek.

Deep within, my tears feel stuck.

I pull on jeans and a t-shirt. Bolting downstairs, I snatch both of the Voodoo dolls off the windowsill and rummage around my kitchen desk drawer for the box of pins. Flinging open the hall closet door, I toss them onto the top shelf.

I am an actress in a murder movie. I hover at the open front door, nervously awaiting help like a distraught wife ought to. Sirens sound nearby. Within seconds, the paramedics, the police, the fire truck, and god-knows-who-else arrive. Do they suspect that something out of the ordinary has happened to Bob?

My legs threaten to fold up like concertinas. I think: Maybe Woodside's emergency services people get bored sitting around waiting for things to happen. After all, Woodside is not Chicago. Chicago's dispatchers have heard everything. Chicago's paramedics have seen everything. Bob's death would be mighty unexciting to any of them. They'd just send a couple of people over to sort things out. In Chicago, I would be *safe*.

Vehicle doors slam shut, startling me to my senses.

I can't move.

A gentle voice says, "Ms. Jamison?"

I nod.

"I'm Detective Jonathan Wilson. I understand your husband is upstairs?"

"Yes."

He signals to the rushing horde. They race through the foyer carrying black bags and a folded gurney. Caught up in their wake, I start flying close behind.

Clustered next to the bed, the paramedics snap out instructions to each other. Detective Wilson says. "Would you allow Donna to take you out of the room now, Ms. Jamison?"

The female paramedic barely looks up. She and her three male counterparts are yanking out a load of paraphernalia. They're going to try and resuscitate Bob.

"No!" I cry in bewilderment, avoiding my husband's marble face, trying not to picture the impending assault to his poor, empty body. "Can't you see he's already gone?"

"It's required by law," someone says. "We have to do this."

"I need to be alone," I whisper, fleeing for the door.

When the detective places his hand on my shoulder I'm numb-brained, staring out into the back yard without seeing it.

"I'm so sorry, Ms. Jamison," he says, "but I have to ask you a few questions."

My heart bumps about. "Questions?"

"It's standard procedure. You were the only witness to your husband's death."

"But I didn't actually witness anything."

He sits across from me, facing into the room. I can feel his stare, and wonder if he might like to pin a homicide on me. I hope he doesn't look in the hall closet. I focus on the wide red vase that adorns the kitchen table. It's filled with daisies, each one a round, yellow sun radiating delicate white petals.

"Did Mr. Jamison have any serious medical problems that you know of?"

"No. Although, last year he was once checked for heart pain."

"What kind of mood was your husband in when he went to bed?"

"Mood?"

"Did he seem upset?"

"He seemed … tired."

"Did you and your husband eat dinner together last night?"

To avoid his eyes, I give his forehead my full attention. "Bob didn't eat dinner. He just came home, drank a martini, and went to bed."

I'm certain the detective is scrutinizing me. He takes in a large breath. "You will, of course, want to know what has caused your husband to die so unexpectedly. I'm sure the autopsy will give us the answer."

My pulse pounds in my ears and I fight to stay upright. I picture thirteen pinpricks on Bob's skin. I hear the pathologist saying, "Looks like Voodoo to me."

"I know this is upsetting, Ms. Jamison."

I can't believe this is happening.

Noise filters more loudly into my head as people begin to leave. I hear the paramedics directing each other as they wheel Bob out of the bedroom and down the stairs.

I stand in the downstairs hall, waiting for him for the last time.

The gurney's wheels rumble across the foyer's slate floor. Bob lies on his back, zipped up like a business suit inside a travel bag, ready to be removed from his dream house by strangers, and without benefit of ceremony.

It doesn't seem right. "I want to stay with my husband for as long as I can."

"Of course," says Detective Wilson, "Donna will accompany you. We're taking your husband to Woodside hospital."

The female paramedic steps forward. "Come with me," she says. Getting a firm hold of my arm she deftly ushers me outside.

The heat is stifling and the sun shines so harshly my eyes cannot stand to stay open. I fumble through my purse for sunglasses. They're not there. I hear the crunch of tires against our graveled driveway as vehicles drive away, and catch the faint odor of diesel fuel as it wafts into my nose. I sneeze, and search for a tissue.

"Yikes," says Donna, "It's like a sauna out here." She shades her face and squints at me. "You all right?"

I blot my eyes. "I'm hanging in."

She puts her arm around my waist, "We'll soon be on our way."

We stand off to one side as the men hoist Bob into the back of the ambulance and strap him down. I feel a stab of grief. But when I look back at our empty house, a sudden, shameful morsel of relief pops up in my mouth.

The ambulance lurches forward. Donna sits beside me, holding onto my hand as though it might run away. She peers at me through sharp, violet-blue eyes, her motherly face solemn. Light brown curls surround her head in rows of bubbles that bob around whenever we hit bumps in the road. She's probably wondering if shock is taking hold.

Since Bob was officially proclaimed dead, we're spared the sirens and high speeds. Even so, we arrive at the hospital's emergency entrance within ten minutes. Once there, everyone leaps into action.

I stand aside as Bob and his gurney are swiftly lifted out of the ambulance, keep up a brisk pace as it's wheeled into the hospital, and then watch as he and the paramedics disappear down a hallway without a second glance. I imagine they needed to get Bob out of the way in pronto style. The emergency room staff won't want their patients to think that they have anything to do with a dead person in a body bag.

"Is there anything more I can do for you, Ms. Jamison?" asks Donna.

I shake my head. "No, thanks."

"I'm so sorry for your loss." She hugs me hard. "Take good care of yourself," she advises, before trotting off in search of her co-workers.

Suddenly alone, I stand bewildered. My nose has latched onto the hospital's cocktail of clean smells—a splash of lemony disinfectant mixed with a dash of antiseptic. It masks the underlying odor of things bitter and soured. Almost.

Pressure grows in my throat so hard it makes my eyes tear. Old sorrows surface. I see myself, years ago, huddled next to my mother's hospital bed listening to her lungs wheeze and rattle like a set of flabby old bellows, my own breathing tight and shallow, my body stiff with fear. I didn't recognize her at first, this skeleton with tangled blond hair and yellowed skin, this shrunken woman with grimaced mouth and square white teeth too big to be real. But when I picked up her hand, her eyes opened—dazzling blue, lighting up at the sight of me—and I knew that this dying woman was my mom.

"Don't leave us," I cried. But she was already adrift, lying on her side, a tiny curled shape beneath a white blanket. That terrible night's sky held a silvery full moon and hosts of pinprick stars that shimmered an eerie, magical light around her like a shroud.

Dad leaned against the wall, his eyes on the door. He muttered something to my mother, and then disappeared from her bedside as she faded away, calling to her on the way out, "I'll be back shortly."

He stayed away for three hours. If I had not flown back to Vancouver to be with her, my mother would have died alone, waiting for him. She waited away her life.

"Molly!" Bob's cardiologist and part-time friend, Jim Burdick, is striding toward me, his straight chestnut hair flopping up and down, his face tight and drawn. "Are you all right?" he says, urgently. "I was in the hospital when the paramedics called in. I've been waiting for you to get here."

He grabs my hands tightly in his and looks down at me with large, sad eyes. Since I'm five feet ten, it's not often I look up at a man, but Jim is six feet two—an inch taller than Bob. Although, perhaps not now, I puzzle, since I seem to remember that when people die, they manage to elongate by about an inch. For all I know, Jim and Bob are now the exact same height. Hair is supposed to keep growing after death. At least, so they say. I envision Bob grown longer in every way. He's lying in the crematorium oven, his skin melting from the bone like molten plastic.

"Molly? Molly?" Jim's hands hold my shoulders as if to steady me, "Are you all right?"

His voice creeps into my head from miles away.

"You've had a terrible, terrible shock," he says. Putting one arm around me, he motions toward empty chairs off in the corner. "Let's go over there where we can sit you down and talk."

He's so focused on my needs; he doesn't seem to notice the two women whose eyes fix on him as we pass by. Since last March—when his pretty violinist wife ran off with a cute percussionist from New York, flooring everyone who thought they knew her—he's been available. But despite his handsome looks, I've never known what to make of him. Adonis Jim charms anything that moves.

"How are you holding up?" Jim asks, settling me into a chair.

"I'm operating on automatic pilot."

"That's understandable, Molly. It's to be expected under these circumstances." He sits down next to me, and picks up my hand. "Tell me what happened."

"Bob went to bed fine and woke up dead."

"That's it?"

"That's all anyone knows."

Jim puts his arm around my shoulders and draws me close. I want to lay my head on his chest and feel his arms encircle me. My eyes begin to close.

"We have to remember that, last year, Bob experienced chest pain, Molly."

I pull slightly away and sit straighter in my seat. "But he had those stress tests or whatever they're called. He said he sailed through them. He was fine, wasn't he?"

"Just because he tested fine, does not necessarily mean he was fine." He pats my hand. "We rely a bit too much on EKGs and stress tests. Frankly, they're not always accurate; they're just the best tools we've got to work with." He shakes his head and sighs. "It's a damn shame. Bob was such a great guy."

He glances at his watch. "I'd like to check in with pathology right away and see what's going on with Bob. Will you be all right, Molly? How are you getting home?"

"Home?" I've been so busy protecting Bob from having to make his hospital journey alone; I never even considered my own round trip needs.

Seeing my confusion, Jim squeezes me tighter. "Would you like me to phone Jane?"

I picture Jane lounging on a white sand beach. She's smiling at her husband and their precious little daughter who splash about at the water's edge. She's holding a tall, cool drink with a festive paper umbrella stuck in it. I say, "She's in Acapulco with Bernie and Bernice. They haven't been away together in ages. I'm not spoiling it for them."

"Is there someone else I can call?"

My mind zips through its list of names. There are Bob's colleagues, our clients, our work-related associates, and a neighbor or two; lots of people to keep me busy, but, except for Jane, I can't think of a single close friend. I'm on my own. How did I end up so isolated?

"Molly, are you really all right? Would you like me to prescribe something for you? Sedatives will help you relax and get some sleep. They'll help you keep up your strength and get through this."

My college pals scattered everywhere, and I didn't make enough of an effort to keep in touch. Bob didn't like a single one of them. My roommate, a brainy, witty feminist was consistently under attack. "She's so unlike you, Molly. She comes across as a man hater. Is she a lesbian?" Nobody in my group could please him. "They're nice enough, I guess, but they're not like you," he said, "You're all ten years younger than me, but they're a bit too immature and unworldly." Of course, none of them claimed to like him either, which made it easier for me to let go.

"Molly?"

Picking up my purse, I slowly rise to my feet. "Actually, a friend is on her way. She should arrive any minute." I avoid his stare.

"You're sure?"

"Yup. I should get going."

"How about I write that prescription?"

I shake my head.

He hesitates, before giving me a final hug. "Take care, Molly, and call me anytime you need to talk. I'll keep in touch with you."

When I walk down the hallway leading to the front entrance, I know he's still watching.

•

The front steps of the hospital bake in blinding sunshine. Lazy, humid air wraps itself around me like a steamy, heavy blanket, the weight of it wearing me down in an instant. I wobble down to the sidewalk and look toward the taxi stand through bleary eyes. First in line sits a flashy, purple Park Avenue. I'm grateful when it pulls up to me, its air conditioner blasting. Sinking into cool, white leather seats, I marvel at my good fortune. This taxi puts most limos to shame. Its tinted windows dim the interior, keeping out the sun's worst rays. A woven wool carpet of the deepest black-purple lies soft underfoot, pure luxury against my sandaled feet. Immaculate white leather lines the doors and ceiling, wrapping the interior in quiet comfort. This is the cleanest, fanciest cab I've ever seen.

"Hi. My name is Mohammed." The cabbie is a handsome, stocky man with strong features and dark eyes. "Where would you like me to take you today?" His hand appears as he grasps the back of his seat and pulls himself further around to watch me. His nails gleam, spotless.

I cough to rouse my voice.

The cab's engine whispers and its shock absorbers work their magic as we float away from the hospital and dead Bob.

I think that Jim Burdick might already have his hand on the body bag's zipper, might be opening it up to check on his ex-patient and sometimes friend, might be looking into

Bob's vacant eyes. Someone once told me that doctors never operate on friends or family because too much emotion is at work and so much is at stake. I wonder if Jim will stand and watch the pathologist perform surgery at Bob's autopsy or if he will deem Bob too close a friend and decline the gory viewing experience.

I don't know if I can bear this.

Mohammed's eyes flash a worried look through the rear view mirror.

"You are OK? Yes?" he asks, in charming, stilted English.

"Yes, thank you," I say politely, even though I'm none too sure of it.

"Today is most hot. Sometimes it makes us feel bad, right?"

I'm slumped in the seat and now struggle to sit up straighter. My head is too heavy. I let it fall back onto the headrest, close my eyes, and then quickly open them.

What will Jim and the pathologist think after doing all of their tests? What happens if an autopsy produces nothing at all, or worse, thirteen mysterious red pinpricks?

"It's too warm in here, maybe?" The cabbie leans forward to fiddle with the air conditioning. "Are you too warm?"

"Really, I'm fine. Thank you." My energy wanes further.

Again, Mohammed glances at me in the rear view mirror. I sit like a lump all the way home.

At the house, I still don't think to move. Mohammed springs out of his seat and opens the door for me, his eyes relaying concern. I start rooting through my purse for cash. I have thirteen cents.

I take the stairs to our bedroom two at a time, praying that Bob's wallet is in his nightstand drawer with his keys, as usual. Relieved to find it looking fat and healthy, I grab it, and rush back outside.

Mohammed stands beside his cab. "Thank you, nice lady," he says, tucking my big tip into the pocket of his pristine white shirt.

A slip of paper escapes from Bob's wallet and flutters to the ground. Mohammed picks it up and hands it back to me. It's a receipt from The O-K Hotel. According to the amount paid, it's nothing more than a cheap motel. In fact, it's likely to be the cheap motel used for Bob's womanizing business; Monday's date, August 13th, is stamped across the top, proof of his illicit nooner with Shirley.

My brain shoots me back to Monday night. Bob is undressing with uncommon exuberance. He's tossing his socks and infamous jockey shorts into the laundry basket. He's flicking off the light. He's kissing me, thrusting his tongue into my mouth. *I can taste her.* My gag reflex is gathering strength and I swallow three times, hard.

There should be a way for a person's bad behavior to show up amongst their innards, like a black cinder, grown in direct proportion to their capacity for dishing out grief. Then, the pathologist could detect Bob's cruelty and report on that.

> *"Bob Jamison, aged 45 years, died from a huge overdose of his own indifference. He did not care whether his good wife lived or died, did not care whether or not he hurt her. He used her until she was all used up, and when she finally rose*

to her own defense, he complained that she was becoming a paranoid bitch. The cinder of his bad behavior grew so large there was no room left in him for anything else. It squeezed out his lungs, damaged his liver, rotted his kidneys, mangled his bowels, and hardened his heart. Ultimately, his indifference killed him."

"Perhaps the heat is too much for you," Mohammed says quietly. "Please, allow me to walk you to your door."

I wonder if he treats his wife with such consideration.

The house envelops me in welcoming coolness. Leaning my back against the closed door, I listen to the taxi glide away.

Ten years ago, I heard a similar purr as my taxi pulled away from the Chicago Hilton Hotel's curb. I was happy and excited arriving for my very first American Women in Radio and Television luncheon. By chance, Bob and I were seated next to each other. My stomach had fluttered. He looked like the hero I once yearned to meet, someone who could lift me up to where I wanted to be. He was paying no attention to the *Radio Advertising Today* speaker, a curvaceous blond with a dusty voice who had other men riveted to their seats. Instead, he gazed at me. "So, you're a recent Columbia University graduate, you're starting up your own ad agency, and you're from Canada," he whispered, his voice coiling around me like a sensuous, living thing. "I sure hope you're planning to stay in Chicago."

My heart flopped about. I thought: This sophisticated, older man likes me. I secretly called him Mister Perfect.

He was everything I was looking for: tall, dark, handsome, intelligent, funny, successful, and well off. He was living The American Dream. He was Prince Charming to my Cinderella.

At the end of the luncheon, he grasped my hand and said softly, "Let me take you out tonight." He didn't even care that people were watching.

Aware of the smiles around the table, I grew flustered.

"Come on," he smiled. "It's Friday. We'll have fun. No strings attached. I promise."

At eight o' clock, he stood on my doorstep right on time, his arms filled with long stemmed red roses, the promise of mischief crackling the air. (My heart still pulses at the thought.) After dinner at Gibson's Steak House we sipped B&Bs on the 95th floor of the John Hancock Building, well-heeled people all around us, the city at our feet. "I want to see you every night," he said at midnight, sweeping me away completely.

He told people he fell in love with me at first sight. He asked me to marry him after one week and kept it up until I did. He wined and dined me and showered me with gifts, even after I asked him to stop.

I fling down my purse and kick off my sandals. In the laundry room, I turn the washer's water temperature up to hot, tear off my clothes, and throw everything in. Then, I strip the bed, and prepare to launder all of the bedding, eliminating anything of Bob's that might try to cling onto life; the smell of him, any thread from his pajamas, any flake of skin, any hair that's escaped his body will be washed, bleached, and rinsed away.

Under a stream of warm water in the shower, I scrub

my skin raw with a new, stiff loofah lathered up with my favorite Miracle soap, and then wash my hair twice. Only then, do I start to feel clean.

2

This nightmare began just before breakfast yesterday morning, when the Road to Hell ran clear through our laundry room. Still in my pajamas, I unwittingly stood on it, busily sorting through dirty clothes, separating pale colors from bright, black from white, my mind seeking ideas for magazine articles, tackling my writer's block, and lining up rows of good intentions. Without warning an invisible force, a serpent, delivered headline news about bites taken from apples. On the front of Bob's pure white jockey shorts sat a dime size drop of menstrual blood. The truth about my husband was shockingly sealed. In one bizarre split second, our marriage was confirmed as the stuff of tabloids and daytime TV.

It took me a little while to grasp this fact. Embarrassment and grief surged through me, unhinging my logic. I thought: This blood must belong to me! My brain began to whip through my menstrual cycle calendar, pinpointing times that didn't add up.

Jane's words echoed loudly in my ears. "You really need to keep both eyes on Bob, Molly. Right in front of everyone, Shirley's suddenly acting as if his agency is her dynasty, and he's letting her get away with it."

Aside from being my best friend, Jane was Bob's executive assistant. She'd been watching them, alerted by Shirley's growing officiousness toward the staff and my husband.

"Shirley's always done that!" I retorted, my mouth dry with fear. "She's always acted as if she owns the place. She's an idiot. Bob has said so himself!"

"He can call her an idiot all he wants, but I know what I see and it doesn't look good."

"That's because of the way *she* acts!"

"It's also because of the way *he* acts. They disappear from the office more than ever—"

"She is his vice president. They *have* to work closely together. They *have* to go out and see clients, and all the rest of it."

"That's true to a point. But, if you could see the way she flirts with him now," Jane persisted, "it's way beyond a joke. And—"

"Shirley flirts with all the men. I've seen her do it for years."

"They are up to no good," Jane said gently. "If I didn't believe it, I wouldn't say it."

"Just because you believe it doesn't make it true."

I kept on arguing—recycling the very excuses Bob had fed to me over the years—until she gave up, stung by my refusal to listen. Jane had risked her job to enlighten me, only to discover that the more precarious my life with Bob grew, the harder I held onto it.

Yet, Jane had read the signs correctly. I believed her now.

"You're paranoid!" whispered Bob. I heard him say this even though he was trying to scrub himself clean in our shower upstairs and I was stultified on the ground floor below. In fact, I heard it clearly. He'd repeated it so often, it felt lodged in my brain, entwined around its wiring, ever ready to interfere with contradictory thoughts. According to Bob, I saw things that weren't there. I heard things that weren't said. I knew things that weren't true. He told me this with eloquence and with authority, he being the owner of a successful advertising agency, me being the owner of not much any more.

Yet, a blood-red polka dot mocked me from its site of sin, refusing to be dismissed as an innocent thing, an unexplainable fluke, a god-knows-what. Bob's lies had become manifest. This time, I believed what my eyes and gut told me.

Leaning on my elbows against the dryer, my forehead resting in the palms of my hands, I realized that should my life end right there on the laundry room floor, the washer towering over me like a gravestone, Bob would not care.

I thought: Why has this happened? *What have I done wrong?* I wanted him back, loving me like he used to.

I felt hot and faint. My hands did a St. Vitus' dance as I flicked the air conditioning up to frigid blast levels. I thought: If I should go up in flames of anguish, he won't be faced with the cost of my cremation. He'll just get out the dustpan and brush.

Dizziness struck. I stood still as stone in the center of our cheery, red-walled utility room, the scent of Wild Flowers soap tickling my nose, the radio droning softly through the intercom system. A raspy-voiced woman was singing a song I'd never heard before, something like, *"I stay true to myself and you ain't gonna change it."*

I bent over and rested my head on my arms.

What was I going to do?

I felt like a devastated child. My mother died when I was twenty-seven, my grandmother when I was eighteen. Dad lived two thousand miles away in Vancouver with his wife Denise and hardly bothered to keep in touch. Bob was all I had left. My bare feet assaulted the washer and dryer, their soles conducting a staccato of thunks against the metal. I had to stop myself from shouting, "I want my mom! I want my grandmother! I want my life back! I want to not have this awful thing happening to me."

I tried to think, but my brain wouldn't let me. Groaning loudly, so as to hear my voice above the piercing whine of the washer's final spin, I slowly straightened up. Our house looked just as perfect, but it felt like a wasteland.

•

I lay rigid on top of our bed staring at the ceiling, listening to the splash of Bob's shower. My voice wouldn't rouse itself. My lips stayed pressed together. Like Chicago car doors in winter, I was frozen shut.

I caught myself desperately wanting to be wrong about Bob, falling into the old coping patterns, fashioning all sorts of excuses to save him. Perhaps he had a dread disease concerning his family jewel. Or was it just a dark red paint spot? Did I look at the dot that carefully? Didn't we recently use red paint around the house? Did Bob shower at the gym and mistakenly pick up identical jockey shorts, ones that belong to that vile man who uses the locker next to his? Doesn't that guy brag about doing the rounds with his friends' wives?

"Moll?" Bob was picking up my hand and planting a light kiss on my mouth. "What's wrong, honey?"

My eyes refused to look at him. "I've been hit with a major headache."

I imagined dangling his jockey shorts in front of him, and pictured the wide-eyed innocent face he would flash. After a moment of silence, during which he'd formulate his best approach, his mouth would turn tight-lipped or petulant-pout. "I don't know how it got there, Moll," he'd declare, in an angry or sulky way. "Maybe *you* have a small cut on your hand or something?"

"Poor honey." Bob carefully donned his business suit. "What's for breakfast?"

My heart knotted up. "Cereal, toast, whatever."

He sighed, and left the door wide open as he strode out of the room.

I bet he'd done this to destroy my solitude and quiet. I must have been thinking too much again.

He started banging about in the kitchen. Drawers opened and clashed shut. Silverware clattered and scraped against stoneware dishes. He wasn't happy. The bedroom intercom burst out with loud music sending my heart into an uproar. A male voice shouted, "This is WBUZ, the buzz, Chicago's favorite radio station!" Bob had switched it on in the kitchen and it blasted through our entire intercom system. "Coming up is Crazi-O Band's number one hit," the disc jockey bellowed, "the hottest song going for all you Voodoo gals out there. It's the 'Voodoo Woman's Antheeeeeem.'"

"I'm a Voodoo Woman, and don't you forget it." I tried to block it out. *"I stay true to myself and you ain't gonna change it."*

I struggled to my feet and turned off the bedroom speaker. I closed the door. I crawled back onto our bed and lay flat and still. I felt as clean as dirt.

The phone rang once. Bob grabbed it downstairs and said one of his loud hellos. My grandmother's English voice piped up in my head, "Good heavens! It's like Kings Cross Station around here." In spite of my misery, I smiled. And then, the part of me that is just like her did something outrageous. Carefully picking up the receiver, I began to eavesdrop.

"What was that sound? Is it her?" whispered a familiar female voice. She must have thought that by speaking softly she could prevent a covert interloper like myself from overhearing.

Bob brought on his big boss voice. "Let's talk about this later. It can wait."

"But—"

"You can tell me as soon as I get in, right before the staff meeting."

"But—"

"I told you, Shirley, I'll see you then."

After she snorted and hung up, Bob stayed silent on the open line. I held my breath. Finally, he dropped the phone down with a bang. When he walked into the bedroom, I was flat on my back, my eyes closed.

"Cheer up, Moll." He sat on the bed and nuzzled my cheek. His hand slid under my shirt and squeezed my breast.

"Don't!"

Back in the kitchen, he cranked up the radio to floor-shaking levels. I curled into a ball and tried to contain my fury.

I couldn't move until I heard his car carry him away to his meeting and to her. I couldn't face the laundry and sorting through our clothes. I didn't want him in my bed any more.

But I knew that I did. I still wanted to please him. I thought: If I stay, I can start to fix whatever it is that needs fixing. Then, the best part of Bob will want to blossom, the ugly part will fade away, and we'll be as happy as we were when we first met and he was satisfied with me.

My pain started to lift.

My mother nodded, yes.

My grandmother shook her head. "Remember Molly, if you always do what you always did, you'll always get what you always got."

I was like the woman in the old joke. When her psychologist asked, "Would you describe yourself as being indecisive?" she answered, "Well … yes, and no."

My head ached, a sure sign that I was running low on caffeine. In the kitchen, I reached for a cup. Standing side-by-side on the highest shelf sat our two unused John Hancock Building coffee mugs, bought in remembrance of our first date. I stretched for one. It jiggled on the shelf as I eased it toward the edge. I barely caught it as it tipped toward me. Leaning against the counter, I felt weak, woozy.

The mug slid through my hands and dropped like a bomb, shattering into a zillion pieces.

I stared up at the lonely mug still on the shelf, and then down at the broken one on the floor. "Which one is mine?" I asked, before the tears came.

•

Dropping my pajamas down the laundry chute I wondered where people go when they die. Perhaps the afterlife was lived behind a one-way mirror that we humans couldn't see through. Was Mom standing on the other side watching my failures play out? Was Grandmother? My face flamed at the notion.

"Where are you two?" I wanted to shout. "I *need* you!"

My mother would tell me to keep trying to work things out. My grandmother would advise the opposite. "No point in throwing good years after bad." I could rarely please one without disappointing the other.

I flipped on WBUZ and turned up the volume before stepping into the shower. I wanted to hear music that would raise my spirits. Maybe then I could think clearly. Water splashing over my head, I stood akimbo, my left foot tapping out a tattoo on the mosaic tile floor. I pictured the one-way mirror and cried out to the other side, "How do I get through this without you?"

"Voodoo Woman's Anthem" fired up the radio, Crazi-O's lead singer's gravely voice blasting out her message.

"I'm a Voodoo Woman, hurt me and you'll regret it."

My hips started swaying in a circular fashion, my arms made sensuous, curving motions, and my feet turned me around two or three times. Water washed over my head and down to my toes like a blessing. Suddenly, I knew what I was going to do. I was going to get Bob for doing this to me.

Panic rose. We had already merged most of my agency business into Bob's. He would be desperate to keep it. I thought: No matter what I come up with, he'll somehow thwart me. I won't have a dollar to my name. I'll end up on the corner of Michigan Avenue and Oak Street with my hand out for nickels and dimes.

I imagined Shirley Bills catching me at it. She was smirking and rooting around her pockets for a penny or two. She was wearing a baby pink mink, full length. She looked like a French poodle on steroids.

> *"I stay true to myself, and you ain't gonna change it.*
> *Whatever you try to do, I'll have a spell to rearrange it,*

I told myself to shut up. Of course I could come up with a foolproof plan; it was just a matter of applying brainpower. Willing myself to calm down, I slathered shampoo onto my hair and gave my head a deep massage. Clues collected together in the base of my brain before journeying into view.

I needed to research divorce lawyers.

I thought: Oh my God, not that! I've got nine years invested into this marriage. Nine years! How can I give up on us now? When Bob is happy with me life is wonderful. I have to find a way to keep him happy, because I don't know how much more of this I can take.

My mother's gaunt face rose up to meet me, her blue eyes on her hospital room door as she waited in vain through her pain and grief for one last sighting of Dad. Sorrow and anger enveloped me. Was Mom's waiting gene embedded in my DNA?

What happened to me? Where was Molly Makepeace, the clever, eighteen-year-old girl who drove her tiny sports car all the way from Vancouver to Chicago so many years ago? Where was the accomplished, twenty-four-year-old single woman with her two degrees and her own snazzy advertising-slash-writing business? Was she all used up? Long since gone?

Grandmother would be more outrageous than this. She'd light a few candles and wish him gone. She'd thwart him in every way. If I'd acted more like her, I might have left Bob years ago. The shower shot a sudden sharp spray at me needling my skin so hard I nearly jumped out of it. I thought: There'll never been a better time to follow Grandmother's lead.

> *"Cuz, my magic will bring you down, will bring you down."*

I realized that throughout my anguish, Crazi-O's message had kept me spellbound. In fact, I was still humming along with "Voodoo Woman's Anthem." Turning off the shower to catch the song's every last word, my head nodded yes, yes, yes, in time to the beat.

> *"Yes, my magic will put you down, on the ground."*

If "Voodoo Woman's Anthem" had been around when Grandmother was alive, she'd have cheered me on with it. "One day, Molly, you'll have a metamorphosis," she once predicted, "and you'll become a strong, magical woman."

> *"Yes, I'm a Voooooooooooooooodoo Woman*
> *I stay true, true, true to myseeeeeeeeeeeeeeeeeeeelf*
> *Before anyone else."*

Like a target inviting the sharpest of darts, the circle of blood centered on Bob's white jockey shorts flashed into my brain. A smile worked its way up from my lowest depths, tweaking my mouth and hardening my eyes.

I growled, "That's it!"

And Grandmother gave a nod from the corner.

•

At noon on the dot I stood firmly inside the door of Chicago's Old Town's Spiritual Magic Shop, breathing in the sweet smells of incense and blinking black blotches out of my eyes as they adjusted from the sunny outdoors to the shadowy interior. An old voice creaked, "Can I help you?" Turning toward the sound, I faced an ancient, silver-haired woman, her carved golden face a map of deep lines running east, west, north and south like darkened pathways. Draped in a blood-red silk robe, she sat on a high seat behind a tall counter surrounded by slender black candles that flickered a halo of light around her head. She looked an unlikely angel.

"Just shopping for candles," I stammered, feeling foolish,

not daring to admit why I was really here.

She smiled, showing off startling white teeth. "Straight ahead to the far wall. You'll find most of our collection there."

I could see now that the store was quaint and slightly shabby with high ceilings, varnished floors, and black matte walls. A huge crystal chandelier hanging above three long aisles spread dusky light into corners. Red velvet curtains pulled across the store's small display window blocked out natural light. The place looked deserted. Fixing a studious gaze onto the far wall, I set off towards it, a flurry of goose bumps flying across my shoulders and down my arms. When she spoke again, I jumped. "If you want to find what you're looking for you must take time to look around," she said. "Try aisle three."

Discombobulated about why she was making that recommendation, I seized a large shopping basket and made a fast turn into the candle aisle, where I almost ran over Mary Murphy, my nervous neighbor who lived two houses away from me in good old boring Woodside.

On account of her large bottom, poor Mary was often the butt of Bob's jokes. Whenever we saw her power walking through the neighborhood, he'd secretly jeer, "There she goes again. Here's my head, my ass follows." Yet, despite her bulbous posterior, Mary was a well-toned athlete with shining blond hair, sky-blue eyes, and clear, tanned skin. By any measure, the woman was a stunner.

I hadn't seen her since mid-July, when she and her super jock husband, Ivan, were power walking past my driveway with such speed, I feared they were under pursuit. Lucky for me, I was in my car with the top down and so rode alongside them to shout my hello. Ivan grinned and shouted back, "Hey! What's up, Molly?" Red-faced Mary practically hid behind him, a sturdy damsel in distress, her handsome prince shielding her from the big, bad world. I felt so awkward I blushed just like her.

Had I arrived at the store five minutes earlier, she might have caught me buying Voodoo supplies, not just candles. Unnerved by the idea, I babbled, "Oops! Sorry, Mary, I didn't see you. What a nice surprise to find you here. How are you doing these days?"

Mary turned crimson. "Hi. Fine. You?"

I thought: I'm quite in the mood to throttle Bob, and his company vice president, Shirley Bills. But I said, "Great. Just looking for my favorite candles."

She nodded.

No one could ever accuse Mary of talking too much.

"Actually, I was just leaving." She dropped the candles she was holding back on the shelf as if they were lit firecrackers. "I have a dental appointment."

Relieved that she was getting out of my way, I joked, "It doesn't get much worse than that." But I pictured my husband bopping the help, and I felt my throat constrict. My legs began to weaken and my stomach contents wanted to make a public exhibition of themselves. I took a deep breath to help keep them in place.

Mary gave a small smile. She still hadn't met my eyes. Watching her fly out the door empty-handed, I wondered what had really brought her here. Perhaps inside their four walls, Prince Ivan was arrogant, like Bully Bob. Maybe she too heard "Voodoo Woman's Anthem" on the radio that morning and—hoping to give him a prick or two of the pain he'd pinned onto her—came here for her supplies. For all I knew, zillions of women like me were out searching for something nice and sharp to stick into their husbands' effigies. Who could blame them?

I fixed my attention back onto the candles. Which ones should a Voodoo Woman choose? Picturing the majestic old woman at the front of the store—and taking into consideration the color of her candles, her robe, and her teeth—I decided to grab a box of black, a box of red, and for good measure, a box of white. Each box contained a "Marie's Voodoo Dozen." Thirteen.

As if on cue, and in perfect harmony with the flute music that began drifting up, over, and around the aisles, the mysterious woman up front started to sing a soft chant in a voice that quavered with age, and raised the hair on my arms.

Slinking over to aisle three, wincing whenever the worn wood floor squeaked loudly underfoot, I was astounded to find a display of Voodoo dolls, all kinds of them. Fright flashed cold across the nape of my neck, making me shudder so hard, my hand grabbed onto the top shelf to help keep me balanced. This store's "gift shop/spiritual items" listing in the Internet Yellow Pages was a bit of a misnomer.

The mystical woman's chant grew stronger. Feeling quite wicked, I hid a smile and focused on the large black sign that sat on an easel beside me. Looping silver lettering fell across the paper in a slightly upward path.

MARIE'S MAGICAL PRICES
August 13th thru 16th
Select Voodoo dolls – $26.26 each
(suitable for all-purpose spells)
Pin boxes - $13.13 each (large pins included)
Robes - $39.39 (silk/cotton blend)
FREE Authentic Spell Book
(With purchase of $65.65 or more)

Who was Marie? Was she the Voodoo Woman up front? How did *that* woman know I was looking for Voodoo dolls? And look at the date. Today marked the end of the sale. Was that just a happy coincidence?

"Coincidences are life's signposts," Grandmother once told me. "Ignore them at your peril." I thought that if I had the courage to listen, I might hear lots more wisdom from the grave. Now that I was going to leave Bob, I must get brave enough to prick up my ears like a set of antennae.

I studied the sale's magical price numbers, each one of them divisible by thirteen, which felt strangely pleasing. I'd always been drawn to that number. Back in the day, carrying my new MA degree like a lifeline, I moved into apartment number 1313 on the thirteenth floor of a fine Chicago mid-rise. It was the cheapest spot in the building.

So many people were afraid of that number. Yet it brought me my first clients, people in small businesses, kind people willing to hire inexperienced me for their media buying and marketing needs. From my home office I bought advertising space, wrote print ads and radio commercials, and built business plans. I met Jane. I pitched editor Alex Fox from *City Gardener,* who published my first freelance article. Aside from meeting Bob while living there, it was the luckiest time of my life.

The chanting ceased as I gravitated toward two nine-inch Voodoo dolls. One had crinkled yellow hair and a pale, thin face that wore a surprised look. The other was chunkier, with short black hair and suntanned complexion. It stared at me, eyebrows raised, its expression superior. Together, the dolls personified Bob and Shirley. I snatched them up. Without hesitation, I threw in a large box of the longest pins I could find, and an ankle length black flowing robe, which I imagined was something a novice Voodoo priestess might wear. Red robes, I presumed, would be worn by high priestesses, like the regal woman in front.

A silver nameplate with MARIE printed on it shimmered from the counter beside the cash register. Candle flames seemed to expand their glow. Marie the mystical queen checked out my chosen items and added the free spell book, beaming her dazzling smile as she stroked the dolls. "Oh yes," she nodded her approval, "these are ideal."

Embarrassed by the flush of pleasure that warmed my face and neck, I clutched my bag of supplies and moved quickly toward the door. A sense of otherworldliness hummed in my brain and my skin tingled.

"Understand your powers," she called after me. "Know yourself."

•

Turning my car onto my street, I caught a glimpse of Mary Murphy's unfortunate backside disappearing around a curve. After dumping her candles in the store and rushing

home, she was setting off for another of her power walks.
What happened to her dental appointment?

Was there something about me that bothered her?
Engulfed in gloom, I parked in our pristine garage, energy
pouring downward from an aching head, draining out
through stiff feet and rigid toes, cold enough to make me
shiver. Legs of lead heaved feet of stone out of the car
and onto the cement floor. I felt dwarfed by everything
around me. Even my tiny two-seater looked a size larger.
As I leaned over the gear stick to hoist the shopping bag
from the passenger side floor, a brutal ache lodged itself
into my innards.

Hadn't we been happy *sometimes?* Had I imagined our
laughter, Bob's generosity, his passionate lovemaking, and
the tenderness he poured over me when my mother died?
Had it been true, or just a foil to keep me around? Was he
the cat? Was I the mouse?

In the kitchen, I dumped out the contents of the Old
Town's Spiritual Magic Shop bag and sorted out my stock
of Voodoo tools, lining them up on the island like soldiers.
I threw my priestess robe over my head and searched the
pantry for matches. I shoved candles into holders. Hair
at the nape of my neck rose like hackles on a wolf as my
brain replayed last Saturday night's fight like a scene from
a movie trailer.

We had been dressed in our finery, faces glum, driving
toward home after what should have been a fun night
out. 'We've actually left a client's wedding reception early
because of your vice president,' I hissed.

"You're the one who wanted to leave." Bob stared at the
road, one hand on the steering wheel, performing his calm

and reasonable routine.

"I wanted to leave because that woman made us all look like fools."

"Shirley stood next to us beside the dance floor, Moll."

"We stood in a row staring at the dancers like three frozen stooges."

"That's your opinion."

"She made sure you were stuck in the middle. She never even acknowledged my existence."

"Oh, we can't have that, can we? Anyone who doesn't notice you must have a real problem."

"She acts like a woman who is tired of waiting."

"You're doing that paranoid thing again."

Fury flailed me like a cat-o-nine tails as I arranged everything on the kitchen island's makeshift altar. Shirley Bills' face weaseled its way into view. I thought: If I die, she'll come to my funeral shedding crocodile tears. She'll comfort broken-hearted Bob in front of everyone. She'll plan a garish decorating of this house before my ashes hit the ground.

Wearing my yellow rubber gloves, I picked up Bob's underpants and placed them on top of the empty shopping bag. Slapping Bob Doll on the counter to the right of them and Shirley Doll to the left, I wailed to the walls, "Why wasn't I enough for him? Was it something I did that made everything go so wrong?"

The pain beneath my ribs grew. Around me, the room glowed with ethereal light. Unearthly silence stole into my ears. Hands steady, I lit three candles, one in each color—black, white, red. Next, I stuck four pins into each doll: one in the head, one in the heart, one in the stomach, and one in the neck, which was exactly what hurt on me. A fifth pin was strategically added to Shirley Doll, because she was such a pain in the ass.

I arranged them into sitting positions on the kitchen windowsill, above the sink.

I folded Bob's underpants and left them on top of his dresser, spot side up.

And I waited.

●

"Hi sweetie," Bob piped into the empty kitchen. "It smells great in here."

Robe flowing behind me, I walked down the stairs and swept past him. "It's chicken curry. A *hot* one." Across the room, piquant steam rose from the simmering pan, permeating the air.

"What's that you're wearing?"

"A priestess robe."

"A *priestess* robe? Why? Is there some kind of costume event tonight?"

"Nope."

"Then why are you dressed like that?"

"It's comfortable."

I noticed his eyes roll as he leaned over to give me a kiss.

He headed for the bar. After pouring a couple of martinis, he handed one to me before settling down with a sigh onto his chair at the kitchen island. "Mmmm." He smelled the air and watched me measure rice.

He looked pale, and bloated. Too much booze? Too much partying with Shirley? I envisioned the two of them pulling their illicit nooner, primly hanging up their business suits before falling onto a cheap motel's bed. I bet they even had stupid pet names for each other, like Shirley-Whirly and Bobbly-Wobbly.

Bob's pet name for me was Moll.

Moll: noun (slang)
1. The female companion of a gangster
2. A female prostitute

The idea that it defined my situation plagued my head. I squished the notion and told myself that Bob must never have known what moll meant. Surely?

I zeroed in on Moll Shirley. She had come to our house for parties, and dinners and drinks after work, sitting at the kitchen counter while I made our meals, sipping the martinis my husband stirred for her, smiling at him with sly eyes. "You're getting to be such a Betty Homemaker," she declared during her last visit, making me feel like a frump.

The Voodoo dolls gazed at Bob.

"What are those?"

"What are what?"

"Those doll things. What are they?" His eyebrows looked like one long, black furry caterpillar.

"They're dolls."

"I know they're dolls. But those are pretty weird dolls, aren't they?"

"What do you mean, *weird*?"

His mouth tightened the way it did when he started to

get frustrated. "I mean they're strange. Strange looking rag dolls with … what the hell is that?" He walked over to them for a closer look. "What's going on?"

"What do you mean?"

"Stop it, Molly"

"Stop what, Bob?"

"You're playing games."

I stuck a surprised look on my face, the way he did whenever he willfully refused to admit the obvious to me. "What games?"

He reminded me of the handsome British actor I saw in a costume drama, who displayed anger via the flaring of his nostrils. Bob's nose was working overtime. Picking up Bob Doll, he turned it every which way, checking out the pins' locations. "This isn't funny," he muttered.

I sniffed my drink. Bob hadn't insisted that I explain myself fully—as though Voodoo dolls stuck through with pins were a normal, albeit irritating, sight in our house.

"I'm going to get changed." He headed toward the stairs, his dark hair neat and tidy, his Armani suit jacket laid in precise folds over one arm, his Italian silk tie holding firm to its Windsor knot, his black shoes shining like mirrors. From this angle, his shoulders looked broad and slightly stooped. He appeared as vulnerable as a forlorn child.

I wilted, and blabbed, "Are you feeling okay? Have you cut yourself lately?"

"Cut myself?"

"Your hand? Your stomach? Anything at all?"

"No." Bob started examining the front of his extra-starch white shirt, lifting his tie and examining his hands and fingers. "Why do you ask?"

I stirred the curry and started the rice, angry with myself for offering him that hint, for wanting to believe that he could still, somehow, redeem himself.

"What's wrong with you, Moll?" His voice sighed with disapproval. He was twisting the problem away from himself, working to make it all about me, as usual.

"Wrong?" I echoed.

Thwarted in his attempt at spin, he shook his head as if to suggest that he was wearying of dealing with an imbecile like me. Then he plodded away, a badly-done-to man. I knew he was flummoxed. Where was his Molly Makepeace, the Peacemaker?

Whistling softly, I drubbed out "Voodoo Woman's Anthem," jabbed a pin into Bob Doll's groin, and then added eight more pins to each doll's head for a total of thirteen apiece. Now they were equal.

After a great clattering of dishes and banging of cupboard doors, I sang up the stairs like a good wife should, "Hurry Bob, dinner is just about ready." No response. I bet he'd found the offending item, and was sorting through his list of lies.

I set the patio table, berating myself for feeling a bit sorry for him. Flopping onto a chaise longue, I vowed to stay focused. The deep azure sky contained a hint of pink, and the promise of good weather tomorrow. It was a comfort.

Over an hour later, I awoke with a start. Where was Bob? I slid open the patio doors and peeked inside. The house appeared deserted. For all I knew he was in his car heading over to Shirley's for a strategy meeting. He might already be there. I snuck through the house and up the stairs. Our bedroom door was open. Facing the wall, pretending to sleep, Bob lay stiffly on his side. His undies were gone from the dresser.

I thought: He doesn't know how to talk his way out of this one. Either that, or he already has an exit strategy of his own in effect, a stealth divorce that's creeping up behind me. I panicked. I wouldn't let him do that to me. Ready or not, I'd have to act. I'd beat him at his own game. I needed to show him that our ending was my choice.

Under a full moon, I slowly cleared the table. Our untouched food went into the refrigerator. I forced my feet to climb the stairs. I dreaded lying next to Bob all night, but knew I had to. In the dark, I slid into my pajamas. Keeping as far away from him as possible, I climbed into bed and faced the door.

3

'm an accidental murderess, sitting as though stiffly starched in Bob's chair at the kitchen island. The fresh ginger tea that I hoped would settle my gurgling stomach is working. I inhale its bite and try to think.

I need to get rid of Bob Doll. I consider Bob's Mount Everest compost heap, which is half way down the back yard at the far edge of the flower garden. This enormous eyesore of a pile came into being five years ago, after I told Bob that high heaps have been known to burst into flames. To prove me wrong, he made a big production of piling onto it every ounce of garden refuse, every mowed blade of grass, every fallen leaf, and each dead flower. He'd saunter down the yard like a waiter, tray held aloft piled high with potato peelings, carrot scrapings, lettuce leaves, coffee grounds and breadcrumbs. He'd say, "This just goes to prove you shouldn't believe everything you read in the papers, Moll."

Just last Sunday, before setting his emptied tray down with a flourish, he bragged that he'd soon need a ladder to reach the top of his creation. "Mount Everest," he guesstimated, "must be close to six feet high." He didn't mention whether or not it was as hot as hell. Surely, it has to be by now?

Standing on my desk chair searching the hall closet's top shelf, I fish out Bob and Shirley Doll and the pin box from behind stacks of scarves and gloves and set them on the island. I pull pins out of Bob. I can't look at his face.

I envision Shirley as a black widow spider, hanging belly upward on her sticky web, her red dotted spinnerets spinning an ever-expanding net while she waits for the kill.

What did Bob see in her that is missing in me?

It's a disappointment to find that although Mount Everest feels somewhat hot, it seems to be doing its job quite well. Bob was right after all.

Picking up our large garden fork, I position it tines forward—the way Sir Lancelot might have held his lance while doing a charge that would help him skewer his opponent. I poke and shove Bob Doll into the center of the pile, before throwing down my weapon.

Shirley Doll, still bedecked with pins, gazes at me dim-wittedly. I arrange her on the window ledge where I can keep an eye on her, and poke at pins whenever the urge hits me. I tell myself that this is just venting.

•

She needs to know about Bob. I light a black candle, and call her cell phone. She answers with a trill, "Hellooow, Shirley speaking."

"It's Molly."

"What's up? I heard that Bob never made it in today. I didn't either."

"He's in the hospital."

"Oh my God! What happened?"

"Come over to the house and I'll fill you in."

Falling onto the couch, I curl up as small as my height allows. I've come to hate Shirley with such a passion there's no room in me for anything else. My toes, fingers, earlobes, each strand of hair, each eyelash, every nook and cranny feels full of it. I wonder if it's killing me from the inside out, setting fire to my organs, creating within me an enormous black cinder from which I'll never recover.

Snatching *City Gardener* magazine from the coffee table, I fix my attention on an article about a woman who bemoans the number of weeds growing in her organic garden. Staring across the room at Shirley Doll, I consider what to do with the biggest remaining weed in my life.

I first met her ten years ago at Bob's firm's annual summer picnic in Woodside Park. Even the sweltering August weather cooperated that day by dropping its temperatures to eighty degrees and giving us humidity levels below forty-five percent. Hand in hand, Bob and I walked through the park between trees thick with foliage. Spectacular red Cannas, almost as tall as we were, grew in masses along the way. Dahlias—orange, yellow, purple, pink—waved over blue Lobelia borders. Perky Gerberas smiled in scarlet. I can still smell their sweetness.

Twice, Bob stopped to nuzzle my face. "They're all gonna love you, Moll. Who couldn't?" After an idyllic six months with my Mr. Perfect, I floated along in a happy daze, wondering how he could love me so much, loving him back because of it.

In the Rose Garden, his clients and staff clustered around tables beneath green and white striped tents. Ice clinked in glasses as bartenders hopped back and forth behind the bar. White plates stood stacked on buffet tables next to polished silverware and green linen napkins. Waiters plied cheerful guests with fancy hors d'oeuvres. Everywhere, deep pink orchids bowed from tall, narrow vases. I was completely bowled over.

Of course, Bob never did anything half measure. He guided me from table to table, introducing me to everyone, acting besotted, making me feel the same way about him.

Shirley arrived late. She wore a tight, yellow, tank top that didn't quite reach the waistband of her low cut, short-short, white shorts. She was a woman who just missed being pretty. Her brown eyes were a little too pale, her nose a bit on the long side, her upper lip too thin, her chin a tad small. With her bleached hair and dark tan, she looked to me like a film star caricature. She sauntered over and parked herself in front of Bob, her pale eyes looking me up and down. "So, *this* is the mysterious Molly." With shoulders back and breasts held high in their push-up, push-out bra, she tilted her head and gazed up at him.

My insides dipped when I saw his face. He was giving her the same smile and admiring eyes that swept me off my feet and made me want to believe in him. "Molly, this is Shirley Bills, our new receptionist."

She stuck out her hand for a limp handshake; her little ragged-edged teeth showing for an instant, her gaze resting back on him before her hand left mine.

"Nice party, Bob." As she talked, she stretched a shoulder here and swayed a hip there, but her gaze never shifted. She did everything but shimmy her shoulders.

I thought: Bob must think this woman is an idiot.

But when I turned to him, he was grinning at her. I froze, my head trying to compute what my eyes were seeing. They appeared to share a private, sexy joke, or an amusing secret of some sort that separated me from them.

Something dark and painful rose from my gut.

Bob's arm slid around my shoulders and he pulled me close. "How about a wine, Moll?" he whispered.

One of his clients, a large woman with big hair and mauve lips said, "You are so lucky to have him." An unsettling pang shook me. But I smiled and said, "Yes, I know."

For the rest of the afternoon, I mixed and mingled, picked at elegant hors d'oeuvres, pushed down filet mignon with broiled mushrooms, drank tall gin and tonics with large lime wedges, and acted as if I hadn't a care in the world.

I was in the ladies' room when I ran into the mauve-lipped client I had met earlier. She shook her head sadly. "Wanna swap guys?" she moaned. "My husband never treats me like a queen."

"Sorry," I smiled, "Bob's already taken." And something scary inside of me slid around.

Tonight, these memories surface with perfect clarity—the punch to my heart and the taste of Pinot Noir, the twist to my gut and the smell of garlic tinged beef, the insult to every bit of me as I stood alone in a crowd amongst the roses.

Waiting for Shirley, I hide behind the *City Gardener* centerfold, humiliation hot on my cheeks.

"I'm such a flaming idiot!" I yell to our empty house.

I go over to Shirley Doll and twist the pins, every one of them, hard. Reaching beneath my desk, I pull out my wastebasket and hide her beneath a load of crumpled papers. Nobody will find her in there. My breath comes in great, painful gasps. I drag myself into the living room to watch for the woman who has made my life miserable. It's past six o' clock. She'll arrive any minute. I'd better get myself together.

4

Watching Shirley and her shiny new SUV trundle toward the house, I steam afresh. I used to wonder how she could afford so many expensive things. Now I imagine Bob provided whatever it took to make her happy and keep her mouth shut.

Sliding out of the driver's seat, Shirley's stiletto shod feet work to get a grip on the graveled drive. She faces the house, smoothing down her pink skirt and straightening her flowered blouse, licking her lips and rubbing them together.

Unused to taking orders from me, she looks annoyed. Clinging onto her oversized, faux snakeskin purse, she totters to the front door. I savor the vision of her standing on the step waiting for me to act, and count out a full minute before opening up to let her in.

Heels click-clacking, she follows me into the kitchen and sits down in her usual spot at the counter. Her shocking-pink toenails match her skirt and sandals. Fastened into her pixie ear lobes are half-carat diamond studs. During our Independence Day bash, she first showed them off to me, turning her head every which way so that they caught the sun's rays and flashed their authenticity in a blinding Morse code.

Now, she's sitting in front of me with her nose turned up. Since she was left standing alone on the edge of that dance floor, she's no doubt been in a constant waiting snit.

"So how's Bob? What is it? What's happened to him?"

I pour tea and hand her a napkin. "I asked you to come over, Shirley, so that we are face-to-face while I tell you what's happened."

"Riiiight," she drawls, wary now.

"Bob died this morning."

She opens her mouth and closes it. Her hands clasp her chest. "No! It's not true."

For the first time, I hear the tick of the clock on my desk.

Shirley's eyes are starting to tear, her face slowly turning puce. "Oh God," she whispers.

Watching her root around her faux snakeskin purse for a faux cotton hanky, I feel no sympathy. I picture the O-K Hotel receipt, and push her teacup over to her.

"What *happened* to him?"

"Nobody knows."

"Where was he?" she says. "Did it happen here? Was he in his car on his way to work?"

"He was in bed," I say, "with me."

I don't know if she's even listening. She's dabbing at her eyes, careful to keep her mascara in place. I wonder if she is reliving their lives together in memory flashes—him and her sneaking here, her and him sneaking there. Her face is turning a peculiar shade of yellow. "I feel sick," she peeps.

I rush to help her off the chair and along the hall. She sticks her head in the toilet just as her retching begins.

Waiting at the counter, I look out across our secluded backyard, and consider the years of work I've poured into it. When we were married, Bob insisted we build his dream house out here. "My folks left me this land," he pleaded. "It's all I have to remember them by." It didn't matter to him that my dream was to live at the top of a Chicago skyscraper in an apartment with wraparound windows, a balcony, and spectacular views of the city and Lake Michigan. I finally caved to his wishes, feeling mean spirited by my constant refusals. "Molly wanted to get high," Bob joked, at my expense, "but this house brought her down to earth." Under the earth seems more like it.

I take in the large open kitchen and family room. Pale oak floors and colorful carpets lie underfoot. Whimsical artworks hang on walls. This house is mine now, I realize, surprised that it didn't dawn on me sooner.

No wonder Shirley feels sick. Her hopes and dreams are dashed to dust. Without Bob this house will never be her home, despite all of her efforts to get it. She wasted a lot of years.

The toilet flushes and she staggers back, looking a bit green around the edges, carrying her shoes. "What do they *think* happened to him?"

I wait until she sits back down, takes a sip of her tea, and meets my eyes.

"The autopsy will soon tell us."

"Oh God."

We sit quiet, each with our elbows on the counter, teacups resting between both hands. I'm suddenly too tired to want to fight, to shout my pain and anger, to tell her what I think of her.

"I haven't been able to really pull myself together since my hysterectomy," she says, "let alone handle this."

"Hysterectomy?" All I can see is the spot of blood on Bob's undies. If she's had a hysterectomy, it cannot belong to her.

"In June," she nods, her eyebrows hovering high above beige eyes like a pair of sparrows over two mud puddles. "I was off work for four weeks."

"But...you were on vacation in Colorado."

"I didn't want anyone to find out. You know how it is in this business. I'm only thirty-five like you, but they'd all be calling me old. So, right after I got rid of a huge fibroid tumor and my uterus, I went to visit my sister and sit in the mountains." She mops her brow with a length of toilet paper. "It's a good thing I hate children."

I want her out of my house so that I can think. "I don't feel well myself, Shirley. I need to lie down."

"Of course you do." She jumps up and air kisses my cheek, acting nicer than she ever has. When she pulls back, I look into her face and catch a shadow of fear. "I'll take care of everything, Molly. I'll call around from home tonight and let the staff know what's happened." She finds her putrid pink sandals, pushes her feet into them and adjusts the straps. "This will be such an awful *shock* for everyone. Next week I'll have my work cut out keeping the staff rolling, and the clients' confidence in the agency up." She pats my hand. "I'll make sure we manage, so don't worry about that."

"I'll contact Jane," I say, knowing that I won't until she is safely home late Sunday night.

Shirley straightens her skirt with slow movements, her palms flat and fingers spread wide as they slide down the sides of her hips. The solitaire diamond ring on the third finger of her right hand sparkles. Her diamond earrings flash.

"Poor Molly," she sighs, collecting a tissue from my desk and dabbing at her nose. "Don't move, sweetie, I'll see myself out."

I sit at the counter until I hear her car start. Lugging myself onto my feet, I dump the last of the tea down the sink and begin to tidy up the kitchen. I rinse cups and put them in the dishwasher. I wonder if I should eat something, and decide it's too much trouble. Ignoring the flashing message light on the phone, I shuffle down the hall to the foyer.

Shirley's story about Colorado digs me with warnings. Why did she share such a personal secret with me? Before now she's done nothing but tell me lies. Did she suspect I set her up for an ambush? Besides, even if her story is true, hysterectomies don't stop people from having affairs. Shirley may not have been the woman Bob bopped on Monday, but that doesn't mean he didn't bop her at all. He might have had it going on with her and lots of other women.

It occurs to me that I forgot to ask the paramedics for Bob's wedding ring; I suppose that somebody will return it to me, even though I don't want it. How proud my husband was about never taking it off, even to swim or wash or shower or sleep. "I put this on for keeps," he said. "I don't want to jinx us." I used to think that was so endearing.

The stairs seem steeper than usual. I collapse into my stripped-bare bed and disappear into a dead sleep.

•

I dream that I'm a little girl in a white party dress, red bow in my hair. I'm in a deserted cafeteria with my grandmother and mother. The food counter's highest shelf displays spectacular deserts. My taste buds spurt at the sight of a glorious slice of lemon meringue pie, which stands tall between a chocolate mousse, and a slab of carrot cake. On the shelf below lie white bread sandwiches with scant fillings, their crusts curled.

Grandmother nods toward the display. I am to make my choice.

I have a secret weakness for lemon meringue, which offers tartness and sweetness topped in white clouds that carry a hint of darkness around their edges. Mom would take the chicken sandwich. Grandmother would choose chocolate mousse. Whom do I please? I search one solemn face and then the other, but receive no hint. There's nothing left but to please myself. I stretch high to reach the lemon meringue pie.

Mom and Grandmother smile.

5

Saturday morning, my brain crawls out of sleep mode with grave reluctance. Curled up tight, facing the vacant side of the bed, I wonder at the quiet house. Tuning in half an ear, I listen for familiar bathroom noises—the heavy splash of hot water pelting away at Bob's razor, or the splatter of shower spray hitting his skin. Arms pressed tightly across my stomach, I roll over, blink my eyes, and catch sight of his smiling face staring at me from a framed photo on the dresser.

I think: Oh my God, this really is happening! I lift myself onto my feet and hobble across the floor like an arthritic old woman to turn it face down.

•

I wonder what Jane is doing right this minute? Eating

an exotic breakfast? Swimming in glassy seas under clear Mexican skies? I stick myself into her vacation pictures and float alongside her, the sun hot on my face. I wedge myself between her and Bernie at their patio dining table, Bernice on my lap counting seashells, the beach spread out white and clean before us. I want some of their happiness to rub off on me.

What would my best friend think if she could see me now? Would she stick by me? Would she turn away? Would she call up the men in their little white coats?

Coffee poured, I sit nervously at my kitchen desk and switch on my computer. Trembling hands type in "Voodoo." Pages of information pop up.

> *VOODOO: Spirit. Divine Creature. Serving the spirits.*
> *In the United States and throughout the Caribbean nations, the ancient African Voodoo religion is melded together with Roman Catholic teachings and beliefs. Voodoo practitioners (mostly women) use spells, potions, and rituals to heal, help, or hinder people, and to communicate with ancestors and the spirit world.*

My eyes run further down the list of links, and halt on "Marie Laveau." Remembering the elegant Marie at the Old Town's Spiritual Magic Shop, I feel a tiny ripple of fear, but then an intense curiosity takes hold of me. Positioning the mouse, I click through.

> *Voodoo Queen Marie Laveau, 1801–1881, was*

*born in New Orleans to a wealthy Caucasian
father and free Creole mother. French speaking,
she was a respected Voodoo high priestess, devout
Catholic, and freedom fighter for enslaved women
and their children. Regal in bearing, she was
intensely beautiful, her luminous, light Creole
skin a pale fusion of colors—shades of black from
Africa, hues of white from France and Spain,
and burnished reds from Native Americans.
During Voodoo rituals she was known to dance
hypnotically within the boundaries of her own
small Voodoo circle, invoking the spirits, her
snake, Zombi, coiled around her body. When
permitted, other women would join her to form
larger Voodoo rings.*

Picturing the solid red circle I found on Bob's laundry
yesterday morning, I think: *Circles! Rings! Coils!* Picturing
the mysterious Marie at the store, and the candles I bought,
I think: *Black! White! Red!*

*Madame Laveau was married for just one year
when her husband, Jacques Paris, mysteriously
disappeared and was presumed dead.*

Grandmother experienced something similar to Madame
Laveau. Right after she threw him out, her husband
mysteriously disappeared too. My mother never really
forgave her for that. "I never had a father, but you certainly
will," Mom would say, which made me feel guilty about the
quality of her life with Dad.

> *She later lived with Cristophe Glapion until*
> *his death in 1835. She produced fifteen children*
> *(some argue it was five) and named all three of*
> *her daughters Marie. One of them looked just*
> *like her. This Marie would follow in the footsteps*
> *of her mother to become a Voodoo high priestess*
> *of great renown.*

Thank God for birth control pills, I think, seeing myself collapsing under the weight of such a brood. But I consider Marie's look-alike daughter and feel the rise of tears. If Bob hadn't put off having the child he claimed to want, or if I'd refused to take years of birth control pills to shut down my mothering system, turning back every opportunity to grow a new person, how different would my life be? Might I have delivered a daughter? Would she have green eyes and black curls? Would she be tall and slender? Would people say, "Look at Molly's little girl, she looks exactly like her?"

Waves of sorrow on the rise, I blink at my computer screen and click on another link. It occurs to me that my grandmother kept her own family name, and also named her daughter after herself. She and my mother were each called Victoria Plant. It turned out well since they both loved gardening.

I click through to the next page and read further.

> *During the Battle of New Orleans, Marie Laveau*
> *used her magic to care for the wounded. She visited*
> *city hospitals to cure the sick. She helped victims of*
> *the 1850s Yellow Fever epidemic. Using her spells,*

*potions, and charms (gris-gris) to manifest her
wishes, she saved a young Creole man from being
found guilty of murder (despite the preponderance
of evidence against him), demonstrating her powers
to one and all.*

I picture myself arrested for murder, standing in the
docks of a packed court in front of people who thought
they knew me. "This can't possibly be true!" they'd say.
"Molly doesn't have a bad bone in her body." Before
Thursday, I used to believe that myself.

I guzzle my coffee and traipse across the kitchen for a
refill. Back at the computer, I scroll down to catch the last
sentence.

*Yet, Marie Laveau could be ruthless and
intimidating, casting spells to cut down anyone
who turned on her.*

Voodoo Woman Marie Laveau would never put up
with a man like Bob. I have to admire that. She seems
fair-minded and ethical (in her own way). She raised five
or fifteen children in sweltering New Orleans, without
benefit of air conditioning, a washing machine, stove or
refrigerator. She helped free women from slavery. She saved
a young man from being hanged. Throughout it all, she
saved herself.

My heart swells with inspiration. I want to emulate this
amazing Voodoo Queen. Just like her, I'm a free woman.
Just like her, I will save myself because I have to. She would
never tolerate bullies like Bob and Shirley. There's nothing

wrong with that.

But, Bob is dead, and guilt prickles away at me like a scratchy Voodoo tickle. My Voodoo dabbling is over. I've already had enough.

My head is aching and my heart feels leaden. I'm standing at the kitchen sink swilling down a couple of aspirin when the first flowers arrive, a bouquet of long-stemmed white roses and delicately branched baby's breath, arranged to perfection in a cut glass vase. My throat tightens. Someone wasted no time in getting this sent out; they paid a bundle for the express delivery alone. Peeling away the cellophane wrap, I snatch out the card.

> *"Dear Molly,*
> *Please accept our deepest sympathy.*
> *Bob will be deeply missed by us all.*
> *Take care,*
> *Shirley and the gang at the office."*

My mouth drops. Suspicious that she includes "the gang" on her large, personal expenditure, I reread the message for clues. Something isn't right. It's not like her to want to share the limelight, particularly on her dime. Tapping the card hard against the counter, I attempt to think like Shirley.

She'll have shopped at exclusive Blooming Norah's on her way home last night. I envision her swishing about the store choosing the vase, the bouquet, and the card. At the cash register, she's opening her bottomless purse to lift out her wallet—a rarely-opened pouch inhabited by moths. There she keeps her long-lived dollar bills … a few coins

… her insurance cards … and … her … *company credit card!*

My body heat soars. Has she charged the roses to her expense account? Have I just paid for my own expensive sympathy flowers? I lift my hair and fan my face and neck with the card. Does she think I'm *that* stupid?

Since I already know the answer to the question, I tip out the wastebasket, get a firm hold of Shirley Doll's legs and smack her head against the side of the sink a few times, sending pins scattering across the floor. *"Shit!"* I yell, *"Shit, shit, shit!"* I throw her across the wood floor, which only makes things worse. Pins lie out in the open, hide under chairs, and get lost in the carpet. *"Shiiiiiiiit!"*

Outside, the town's sirens blast, shocking me into silence. Either Woodside is about to be hit by a tornado, or it's just testing its emergency system. I check the clock. It's exactly noon—a respectable time to open a bottle of wine. I fill my glass to the brim with a British Columbia Pinot Noir from my dad and Denise, and take a big swig, glad that I didn't serve it to Shirley and Bob during one of our dinners together, right here in my home.

Crawling around the floor picking up Shirley Doll's pins doesn't improve my mood. Two pins draw blood; one of them scratches my right knee, the other buries itself into my big toe. Tears lie hot on my cheeks. I keep going. Within a few minutes, every pin found (except those sporting my blood) is pushed back into the doll, which is then reburied amongst the waste paper. I don't care if this is crazy.

6

It's mid-afternoon, and I haven't left the couch. Bob's history is vivid in my head, sparking all of my protective instincts. When he was eight and Clarence was twenty-three, their parents were smashed to bits in their Toyota on I-94, run over by a jack-knifing semi that was carrying tons of frozen chicken to Wisconsin. When he was thirty-eight, Bob had too many martinis and surprised me by suddenly talking about it.

"So…social services moved me in with my brother. The first thing Clarence told me was that Mom and Dad never wanted me. He said that if I'd never been born they'd have never been on the expressway going to see me in the school play.

"He left me alone in the house at night, Moll, even though I begged him not to. I never knew what to expect. He'd promise to be home, but he never was. He blamed his theology studies, said he was at the library or whatever. I used to wake up in the dark, crying for Mom and Dad, begging them to come back. I'd call out for my brother, but he never came back either.

"One night, Clarence walked through the front door and heard me shouting and crying upstairs. He damn near knocked my bedroom door off its hinges bursting in like the crazy ass he is. He yelled, 'Don't you ever dare call our parents back from their heavenly home. They're a lot happier there than they were here with *you*.' He forced me onto my knees. 'Pray for forgiveness. Pray you'll learn to become a decent man like me and Dad.'

"Another night, after he left me alone, I heard weird noises. I figured there was a monster in my closet. I looked out the window and saw a dim light coming from his office shed. I ran to hide next to it, desperate for Clarence to save me. I heard this noise, you know, like somebody's getting strangled.

"I couldn't breathe. I looked through the shed window. Clarence's bare ass was facing me thumping up and down on the floor like mad, like he was having a fit or something. I bust in to save my brother. Then I saw this naked blonde underneath him. It was Mrs. Schultz from next door.

"Clarence smacked me so hard, I was out cold. When I woke up, I was in the dark again."

I helped undress and put drunken Bob to bed that night. I tucked him in and kissed him goodnight the way his mother would. And I stayed.

I have to call Clarence to tell him that his only relative, his baby brother, is dead.

I still can't do it.

For the past two years, the brothers haven't contacted each other. As always, their rift started over religion. Bob told Clarence to quit preaching at us. Pastor Clarence the Bulldog persisted the way evangelical ministers sometimes do: after being warned to stop, he pushed even harder.

"Go to church, Bob," he prodded for the umpteenth time that weekend, "you just might learn something." He sat in our red armchair, his fingers clasped together as though he was giving himself a handshake.

"You just can't help hunting for sheep to scare into your flock, can you, Clarence? Keep those pews filled and the money rolling in, right?" Bob's voice took on a ministerial timbre. "Keep your coffers overflowing by draining some poor sap's not-so-expendable income. Promise him Heaven. Doesn't matter to you if he can't afford to live on Earth. Tithing away the grocery money will keep him and his starving family out of Hell, and you out of the unemployment line. Won't it?" Bob didn't wait for an answer. "You're nothing but a bunch of thieves. Pastor Prey-ers, parading as Pastor Prayers." He took a deep sip of his double martini to further jab his teetotaler brother.

"You don't know what you're talking about," Clarence sniffed.

"Behold, the truth doth hurt," Bob roared. "You keep people so damn busy with all the let's-avoid-hell eating and drinking rules and all kinds of other made-up sins, they don't have time to think, let alone live. And *you* dare call *me* a sinner! Jezzuzz!"

Clarence's face was a patchwork in pink. "You need new material, Bob, yours is stale."

"The fact is I already go to church. We go every Sunday

morning, don't we Moll?"

"Stop it, both of you!" I snapped.

"You go to church?" Clarence stole a look at me from beneath lowered lids. "Which church would that be, exactly?"

"Saint Mattress," Bob drawled, "Where else would we go?"

"Don't ever expect to see me back in this godless house!"

"Don't ever expect to see me back in your godless church!"

•

It's now eight o'clock. The phone rings five times before Clarence answers. At the sound of his voice, I burst into tears.

"Who is this?"

"It's Molly," I sob.

"Oh my God! What's happened?"

"It's about Bob. When I woke up yesterday morning, he had … he had … died … in bed. I'm so sorry, Clarence … so sorry … so sorry … so—" I clamp my mouth shut with my free hand.

"Dear God! What have you done?"

"Done?"

"Why are you saying you're so sorry over and over like that?" His voice cracks.

"You're Bob's brother. I'm sorry to have to tell you this news. That's all."

"How could he just die like that? Was he ill?"

"He seemed fine—"

"It's not supposed to be this way. He's fifteen years younger than me. *Fifteen years!*"

"It's shocking, I know."

He sucks in a long breath. "What happens now?"

"They're doing an autopsy. Woodside hospital. It's one of the best."

"Dear God."

"They said it should be viewed as routine under the circumstances."

"When will we get the results?"

"I don't know. Soon, I hope." I press the speakerphone button, grab a tissue, and blow my nose with shaky hands.

Clarence is silent, digesting the news. I wonder if he'll shed tears or not.

My theory is that Bob had lots of unshed tears in him, on account of never being allowed to cry them away as a boy. When he could no longer contain them, when he was sloshing about full to the brim and could not swallow them down any more, the dam would break, releasing a flood. It could happen over what seemed the most trivial of things, like getting another speeding ticket, as he did a while back. His dam burst right on the shoulder of I-94, much to the surprise of the burly state trooper who pulled him over. (I wondered if he was near the scene of his parent's crash.) Bob told me this in confidence. I took it as a sign of his love for me.

I see us last winter, leaving Jane and Bernie's house right after dinner, citing bad weather. We were driving along icy roads. Snowflakes as big as lace doilies kissed our windshield. Snow flurries morphed into a blizzard, turning the black sky white. The trees along our road formed a snow-laden canopy and the way ahead sparkled like silver. We could hardly see where we were going.

At home, we lit the fire and curled up with steaming mugs of cocoa, so comfy in our pajamas we practically purred like cats. "What a night!" Bob groaned, but he was smiling.

"I'm glad we're home." I stretched and yawned, loving this time.

We watched the flames, the Beatles' "Norwegian Wood" playing softly from our CD player. Bob nudged me and sang along with John Lennon, his eyes full of mischief. We both loved the same music, an important thing, I thought.

"Hey Moll, want to hear something weird?"

"How weird?"

"Assuming a woman isn't a lesbian, what does she get from a man that she can't get from another woman, aside from sex?

"That's *very* weird!"

"Go on. Give it a try."

I said, "Companionship?"

He said, "She can get that from another woman."

"Financial support?"

"She can get that from another woman."

"Children?"

"That involves sex, so it doesn't count."

Finally, I admitted, "Jeez! I really don't know."

"That's because women don't need men."

I tried to dismiss the idea. "Well, assuming a man isn't homosexual, what does a man get from a woman that he can't get from another man, aside from sex? Doesn't the same principle apply?"

Bob gazed at the fire, "No, it doesn't."

"It doesn't?"

"Nope."

For a moment, his face appeared to crumple. I moved closer, reaching for his hand, afraid of knowing what he was about to tell me.

"Men don't talk to each other, Moll. A man needs a woman to *talk* to."

"When I preside at Bob's funeral, there'll be people or situations he'd want me to mention. You'll need to give me information on that sort of thing."

I jerk upright, wondering if Clarence has had to repeat himself because I tuned out.

"You know how it was with Bob." I soften my voice to almost a whisper. "You know he would never agree to a religious ceremony."

"I have a duty to see that he has a Christian burial." He's turning up the volume on his evangelical voice.

"I promised Bob that I would have his body cremated."

"That's not Christian."

"In today's world cremation is considered Christian."

"Not in my church."

"I promised him. Please respect his wishes. He wants no religious ceremony, or minister, or burial either."

"He's my brother. He gets a *Christian burial!*"

I imagine him thumping his Bible, making enough noise to drown out all dissent. "Bob was not religious, Clarence. You of all people know that."

"Molly, I *insist!*"

"He asked me to cremate him, have a non-religious

memorial service, and scatter his ashes. We promised each other the same thing. He even listed his favorite music for both occasions. It's all written into our Last Will and Testament."

"You two always were a pair of pagans."

Neither Clarence nor Bob believed they resembled each other at all. Yet, in one way they were alike. They were blood bullies. Neither one of them seemed to care much about anyone else. Not even each other. Not really.

"I'll let you know about the memorial service as soon as Bob's body is released."

I hear the click as Clarence hangs up the phone.

•

Dad's wheedling voice sounds freshly oiled, excuses sliding off his tongue in a checklist. "You understand don't you, sweetheart?" he says, "I've had this three-month Australia trip booked since February. I wouldn't know how to tell Denise it has to be delayed. She's only been home twice since we got married. She hasn't seen her family since they visited us two years ago. Everyone there is expecting us."

I imagine him with his suitcase already open, his clothes half folded, his eyes on his watch. I feel like telling him that Denise has seen her family more than I've seen mine over the last seven years. Instead, my peacemaker self takes over.

"I understand," I say.

"You take care of yourself now, Molly. We'll be thinking of you."

My grandmother pipes in with, "That man is enough to make a vicar swear."

"Bye sweetheart."

"Bye Dad."

7

This first weekend has stretched before me like a hated task. I expected that unwanted people would show up to voice grief over the loss of their colleague and friend, and didn't know how I'd cope. Instead, I've been left quite alone, which confuses and saddens me. I suppose that on Saturdays, people have errands to run, houses to paint, gardens to prune, groceries to buy, and children to entertain. For some, Sundays inspire church attendance, brunches in family-style restaurants or at grandma's house, golf for the men, games for the children and work for the women. Important things like that take precedence over a man dead and gone. I spend both days lying around the house, lost in a fog, eating crackers, olives stuffed with blue cheese, dill pickles, and other foods that can be easily lifted out of a jar.

Sunday evening's downpour brings rolling thunder, high winds, blackened skies, and furious, magical lightening bolts, which make me feel that at least the weather and I are in step. Gunning the engine of my bright red 1976 Triumph Spitfire, I shoot out of the garage and into nature's glorious tantrum. Reckless on lonely roads, I zip around curves and speed along stretches, reveling in its nimbleness, loving the earthy smell of its new black leather seats. My car has been updated, painted, and refurbished so often Dad tells people it's like the antique hammer that received three replacement heads and five replacement handles during its lifetime, and still looks brand new.

I bought it from a used car dealer on my eighteenth birthday. My grandmother had just given me a six thousand dollar check, saying she wanted to see me enjoy my inheritance before she died. "Buy whatever makes your heart sing," she advised, "and it had better not be something sensible."

I didn't let her down. Before the ink dried on the paperwork, she struggled to get into the passenger seat, trusting me as I lowered her into it, catching her breath as cancer gnawed pain into her bones. I drove us all the way to West Vancouver, detouring through downtown for a slow drive past her old haunts, flying each way across Lion's Gate Bridge, admiring the sunshine sparkling on the water, taking Marine Drive's curves and corners at fast speeds, laughing so hard my tears spilled out and I had to pull over.

"I love your *Spitfire*," Grandmother murmured. "I love your *Triumph*. You must learn, Molly, that sometimes you have to do both."

I scan the Triumph's polished walnut dashboard and look out over its long, low front end as it eats up the road, its motor rumbling like a race car's, bittersweet memories of Grandmother's life and death pushing me along from behind.

•

On Monday, I'm up and dressed early. Between collecting the steady stream of delivered flowers from a variety of florists, I try to gather up my lost logic and figure out what must be done next.

Perhaps I should share my burden of guilt, and tell Jane about my Voodoo dalliance.

My grandmother's voice rises, "If you want nobody to know your secret, tell the same person. Nobody!"

My mother's voice is silent. Those two are agreeing on more than usual.

At noon, Jane stands on the stoop dressed in a forest-green silk suit and cream silk shirt, holding an armful of wrapped flowers and a large brown carrier bag. She's already in tears.

"Oh my God, Molly," she says, dropping everything to hug me. "I still can't believe this."

I stare at the empty driveway. "How did you get here?"

"I caught a cab that was sitting right outside the office building." She wipes her eyes and points toward the carrier bag. "I'm too upset to drive; besides, the lunch I promised includes wine."

When I called her late last night, she was so shocked by the news Bernie had to take the phone from her to find out what was going on. Then, I had to stop them both from rushing over. Instead, Jane agreed to go into the office this morning to help the staff cope, which was more than I could do.

She gives me a worried look, "How are you managing?"

"My famous robot control is in fine fettle."

"That's not always a good thing, Molly."

"How's Bernice taken Bob's death?"

"She acts worried and asks if Aunt Molly is leaving too."

I choke up.

Jane passes me the tissues and takes another herself. "So, when does your dad arrive?"

I fumble with the scissors against the wrap on the flowers. "He's not coming."

"What?"

"He's taking Denise to Australia for three months to see her family."

For once, Jane is speechless.

"Of course, he said he was sorry about ten times, but their trip was already arranged. They're on their way as we speak."

"Un-bee-leev-able!"

I wield my less-than-sharp scissors against the bouquet's contrary wrap, and tear away the last of it. In vivid purples, reds, and pinks, a dozen anemones speak to the notion of life lived large. With heads held high on eccentric stems that curve this way and that, they journey toward uniqueness, their lacy, black centers presenting feminine images of strength like iron. No wonder I've always loved anemones. They're perfect for the Voodoo Woman in me.

Unable to squeak out a thank you, I grasp her hand.

"I still can't believe Bob is gone," she says. "I can still see him sitting at his desk, wheeling and dealing with media reps and clients. He never *looked* ill. This morning, when

I went into his empty office, it broke me up. I can't even imagine how you feel."

I carry the anemones over to the kitchen table and position them dead center. "I mostly feel disconnected. My head is all over the place. The air looks weird, almost as if I'm peering through clouds all the time. I can't face Bob's office yet. Maybe once the autopsy is over, and the memorial is behind me. I just can't *think.*"

"Shirley and I can deal with the office. You have enough to deal with right here." She looks around the room. "This place looks like a flower shop." She's awed by a spectacular arrangement of long-stemmed peach roses from David and Rachel Rose of Rose Manufacturing, a couple whose account I began working with during my days in apartment 1313, until we moved them into Bob's agency three years ago.

Jane sticks her nose into the exquisite stargazer lilies, gerbera daisies and red roses bouquet, the most colorful and scented arrangement of all. "These are beyond gorgeous," she says, "I see they're from Jim Burdick. He's always had a soft spot for you."

"He left me a voice message over the weekend, wanting to get together and talk. I didn't call him back. I just can't deal with people right now. Present company excluded, of course."

"Of course."

"Do you think there's power in names, Jane?"

"Well … I once met a doctor called Doctor Doctor. Did his birth name power him into a medical career? Who knows?" From the brown carrier bag, she's produced a bottle of Chianti, Italian bread, and three white cardboard boxes stamped across the top with Stefano's logo, my favorite Chicago restaurant. "What brought this on?"

"The two Victoria Plants. I've wondered if my mother's growth slowed when she gave up the name Plant for Makepeace."

"I'm not sure I know where you're going with this."

"Did my mother's peacemaker role begin with the name Makepeace?

"Well—"

"I think I fell into that peacemaker role myself. Now, the only *peace* I want to *make* is with myself."

"What is it? What are you trying to say?"

"You were right about Shirley."

I hear her sharp intake of breath.

"You tried to tell me a long time ago, and I shot you down."

"I should have stayed out of your business, Molly. You must have felt ambushed."

"I found a receipt from the O-K Hotel. It was for a nooner on August thirteenth." I say.

"How do you know it was for a nooner?"

"Why else would Bob be in a cheap motel?"

"Shirley's condo is in the Hancock Building," she says gently. "Wouldn't they do nooners there?"

"That building is full of ad agencies. It's crawling with media people."

"Too risky," she bites her lip. "That's true."

Jane carefully pops open the wine. She spoons chilled pasta salad onto plates. Pale rotini, chopped tomatoes, and tiny capers glisten in their coat of vinaigrette. Topped with see-through lemon slices and basil leaves, it sits in heaps next to crusty bread. She plunks a slab of butter on a plate and sets it right in front of us.

We're sitting at the kitchen table, facing the sliding glass doors that open onto the patio. She's treating me the way she treats Bernice. "You have to eat to stay strong." She butters bread and balances it on the edge of my plate. She says, "Eat, eat." She fills my water glass. "Drink, drink."

I am a mechanical woman.

She clinks her wine glass softly against mine. "To courage," she says.

"I'll drink to that."

I remember the courage Jane displayed after her ordeal with Freddie Hare, the man she was living with when I first got to know her. She thought they were happy until she came home one night and found that he and his belongings had vanished. "He's got more balls than the NFL," she cried. "He even took our photo album." I picture Freddie Hare running to his new burrow like a frightened rabbit, leaving Jane to face barren closets and empty drawers, and a bathroom cabinet containing only her things.

"How has Clarence taken the news?" Jane speaks deliberately, bringing me back to the present and what needs to be done.

I shrug. "It's hard to say what bothers him the most. Having a dead brother or having a cremated brother."

"He needs a damned good thump about the head."

"This is true."

"You're sticking with Bob's wishes, aren't you? I mean *everyone* knows how Bob felt about religion and burials."

"He always threatened to come back and haunt me if I let Clarence bury him."

"I've heard him say it."

"So, my feet are planted … no pun intended. I just hope Clarence leaves me alone. You know how he goes on."

"You've told him the news. Under the circumstances, you owe him nothing more."

"I suppose that's true."

"It's definitely true."

Jane is tired, the slope of her shoulders and the dark smudges under her eyes attest to it.

"How were things at the office this morning?" I ask. "Are you managing all right?"

'We brought everyone in for a one hour staff meeting, and then sent them all home for the day. Everyone's terribly upset.'

"And the clients?"

"A number of Bob's long-term clients often worked with Shirley and her account executive, Cameron—who always manages to save her ass and make her look good— and not just with Bob and me. Hopefully, their clients will stay put. The clients you brought into the company are likely to hang in with us, because they've had success working with you in the past."

"But?"

"Some clients will believe that an advertising agency can't continue without its president, particularly new clients like Murphy's Landscaping, who worked exclusively with Bob. They'll take more reassuring."

I freeze. "Bob picked up Murphy's Landscapes?"

"Last month. You didn't know?" Jane stares at me, stopped by this uncomfortable surprise.

My voice sounds as if it's coming from somewhere else,

"I just saw Mary Murphy in ... a downtown Chicago store. She acted embarrassed and ran." I point across the room to a cluster of white lilies in a black pot. "She and Ivan sent me those."

"I don't get it." Jane looks nervous. "Bob should have told you."

"Who makes Murphy's advertising decisions, Mary or Ivan? Who meets with Bob?"

"Mary," she whispers.

Something thrashes about in my gut. "How like Bob to want me to find out from someone else that our neighbors are also his clients. Then, he'd pretend he just forgot to mention it and call me paranoid for questioning him."

"He made fun of Mary's ass all the time," says Jane. "He didn't think she was too bright."

"Shirley is hardly the brightest bulb in the chandelier and he bopped her."

She takes a steadying breath. "Once or twice I caught Mary looking a bit gaga over him. I never saw Bob look at her that way though. I just can't see him with her..." Her voice trails off.

"She acts so shy," I murmur. "But, remember how she was at our Independence Day bash? She was having that animated conversation with Jim Burdick. When she caught us watching, her face caught fire. Remember?"

"I do. Doctor Jim definitely has a way with women."

My chest tightens. "I can't think about this. I need to get focused on keeping the agency's doors open."

Jane ushers me outside to loll about on the patio with the last of the wine. A flock of birds lands on the lawn, picking at it with their beaks, chasing one another away from anything tasty, squabbling up a storm. They make such a racket we laugh. We lie back in our chairs, eyes closed, the sun sprinkling us with light through breeze-ruffled leaves.

Since the day we met, I've counted Jane high on my list of blessings. She was a senior account executive at WBUZ, the buzz, when my new agency landed on her account list. She taught me all there was to know about buying effective radio advertising schedules, which helped bring success to my tiny list of clients. "I enjoy helping women get started," she declared. She introduced me to other media people, and included me in station events where I'd meet local advertisers. "I'd like you to meet the president of Makepeace Advertising," she would announce like a proud big sister, creating a flurry of interest in me. Because of her, whenever I consider buying airtime, I still think of WBUZ first.

When Bob's executive assistant position opened up eight years ago, Jane asked me to recommend her. "I'd love a job like that," she said. "I'm ready for a change."

Bob hadn't known we were personal friends, believing Jane to be merely an excellent networking opportunity and a great business contact for me. If he'd known how close we were becoming, he might have found ways to dislike her. As it stood, he always thought he'd developed her friendship first.

He hired her after just one interview. "She's about thirty-five, single, no children," he reported back to me, as if I didn't know already. "No worries about her having to take off work because of sick kids, or whatever. Plus, at her age, it's not likely she'll *ever* get married so she'll probably *never* have kids." One year later, Jane married Bernie. One year after that, she presented the world with their adorable red-haired Bernice. Jane stands as one more testament to Bob's flawed reasoning.

Her chair scrapes against the patio brick. "As much as I'd like to take a nap right now the office awaits. I'm just going to make a quick call to the woman that we loathe, and make sure all is well." The patio door slides open with a soft whoosh as she steps inside.

My eyes shoot open. Jane's back on the chaise longue, smoothing down her silk skirt, making sure that she's presentable before heading back to work and a desk piled high with projects.

"Did Shirley have surgery in June?" I blather.

"What kind of surgery?"

"A hysterectomy."

"At her age?"

"It happens."

"If it happened, I think I'd know. For starters, it would have been advertised from one end of Chicago to the other."

"That's true. There are few secrets in this industry."

"What made you think she had a hysterectomy?"

I shake my head and sigh, "Seems like I'm confused about a lot of things these days." But I'm imagining Bob in our bedroom that night, holding his infidelity jockey shorts in one hand and his cell phone in the other. He's talking to Shirley, warning her that they have been found out. No wonder she made up that nonsense.

"What do you think would happen, Jane, if I let Shirley go?"

"I hate to admit it, but I think we'd be in a more precarious position."

"Do you think some clients might feel there's no captain steering the ship, even with us there?"

"Some might. Not all."

"Can we stay afloat without her?"

"I'd like to say yes, Molly, but I really don't know. We have to prove to our clients that even without Bob, we're still stable. But until then," her voice trails away.

I know it's true. If the agency loses its vice president as well as its president, clients will trample over each other in a race for the exits.

I hear myself hiss, "I can hardly stand knowing that I *need* Shirley Bills."

We sit in the sunshine, staring up at white clouds edged in darkness. Rain is on the way. "I want you to keep me posted on everything that goes on in that agency until I can get in."

"It's a given."

At the sound of the doorbell, Jane shouts, "Oh my God! He's here already!" Jumping up, she runs into the house to find her purse and lipstick. "Please tell Mohammed I'll be right there."

Mohammed?

I open the front door and there he stands in his deep purple pants and pure white shirt. "Hello lady. You better today?"

There are thousands of taxis in the Chicago area, yet Jane walked right out of the office building and into Mohammed's.

"I come to pick up your friend?"

"Jane will be right out."

"Now you and Jane will become my best customers."

"Please, call me Molly."

Behind him, his rich purple cab shines to perfection. Emblazoned across the doors in white are the words "JC Cabbs."

Mohammed follows my gaze. "My company. I own it."

I think: *Jesus Christ Cabbs? Surely not!* I recently discovered that there are groups of Christian Jews in the world, but there's no such thing as a Christian Muslim. Perhaps he's a Christian Arab. That's quite possible, I suppose, although, he might be a Christian Persian ... or would that make him Assyrian? I really should know more about the world. I once visited London with my grandmother, where there happen to be an amazing number of Middle-Easterners with Cockney accents. Now that Bob's dead, I ought to travel more. He never wanted to, whereas I always wanted to see the pyramids. Of course, they're in Egypt. Egyptians are Muslim, but then again—"

"Where are you, Molly?" Mohammed peers into my eyes. "You see your husband maybe? Jane told me. Very sad."

"Why isn't your company called Mohammed's Cabbs?" I blurt, wondering too late if it's rude to ask.

"JC means, justa come. It's clever English! I justa come here three years ago from Iran and started Justa Come Cabbs." Mohammed grins. "Get it?"

I laugh, "Very clever English."

"Hi Mohammed!" Jane comes up behind me, waving her purse. She stops to whisper, "If you change your mind about staying with Bernie and me, we'll come over right away to pick you up." She gives me a quick, hard hug, and then sets off toward the cab at a good clip.

Mohammed doesn't budge. "There's something else," he says. "Someone is bad to you. Yes?" He has a gentle look about him, a certain charm, a kindly sort of nosiness that's impossible to resist.

"Something like that."

"There is a saying," he thunders, his expression dark, his right forefinger pointing skyward, "Trust your Higher Power!" His eyes glitter as they fix onto mine. "But tie up your camel!"

"Does that mean—?"

"No matter our faith, if we walk into traffic we will be knocked down. If we sit on an anthill, ants will torture us. This is the way of the world." He takes a big breath. "Do what you can to *protect* yourself. Be wise. Tie up your camel."

The truth of it bowls me over and for a few seconds, I can't speak. I've left untied camels all over the place, all of my life. They're trotting about everywhere, taking up my headspace, confusing my brain and preventing me from focusing on what's important and what's not.

There's my Dad and Denise. There's my career. There's Shirley. There's Pastor Clarence the Bulldog. There's Bob's agency, which employs ten people and has to be saved. There's writer's block. There's the Woodside police department. There's Doctor Jim. There's Marie Laveau and my Voodoo dabbling. There are the deaths of my mother and grandmother, which haunt me still. There's my endless, often debilitating politeness, so ingrained in my psyche it swims deep in my bones, a contaminant, afloat in the marrow.

I remember leaving Vancouver for my university in Illinois, folding the top down on my car before hugging my gray-faced parents. "Be a good girl," my mother said, giving me the worst advice of all, not knowing herself that it's okay to be somewhat selfish and follow your own dreams, rather than live on the sidelines of someone else's.

My frail grandmother leaned forward to kiss me. "Do *yourself* proud," she said, giving me her final piece of advice. She died the day I moved into my new university's dorms.

I yearn for the satisfaction of my old defiance, the exhilaration of my lost wild streak, the joy I found during my brief fling with freedom. On my own, I drove 2,000 miles across America, blasted through my university years, and fired up my life's path in apartment 1313. I did myself proud. I fought for my freedom. It deserves to flourish.

I think: If I tie up my camels, I bet I get rid of writer's block.

I say, "Thank you for the wise words, Mohammed."

He hands me his card, which is purple with white lettering. "You call JC Cabbs whenever you need a cab. Right?"

"It would appear that there's none better."

"That's true."

When he opens the door of his taxi, Mohammed pauses to brush a speck of dust from the hood. Behind the wheel he makes a minuscule adjustment to the rear view mirror. All the while, he smiles and talks. I watch as he drives Jane away from the house, his cab lighting up the landscape with the color of royalty.

•

A forgotten Stefano's box remains on the counter. I lift its lid. Inside sits a tall wedge of lemon meringue pie, a gift from Jane. I remember my dream and the deserted cafeteria, see myself standing with my mother and grandmother. Goosebumps fly all over me. From now on, the choices are all mine to make. My eyes glance around the room and my taste buds tingle. I lift the pie onto a plate and grab a fork.

8

Sunbeams pierce the bedroom blinds, sending brilliant slivers of light across the sheets. Outside, the birds argue loudly. I hang on the edge of my side of the bed, gazing at the wall beneath the window, in much the same way that Bob did when he lay dead. I'm eight years old again. Mom's explaining why she's not replacing our old white fridge with the trendy green one that I like. "*Change* changes everything," she says. "If I buy the green refrigerator, it won't work with the white stove, so I'll have to change that too. With two green appliances, I'll have to consider new wallpaper. Then there's paint. And how will this flooring look? It'll look worn. Same with the cabinets and counters. My God, there'll be no end to it." She shakes her head. "Nope, I can't afford to do it. I have to stick with white."

I've decided to go for the green. And I'll endure whatever it takes to get there.

•

It's one o' clock, the thirteenth hour. Detective Jonathan Wilson from homicide stands on the doorstep holding a yellow notepad in one hand and a pair of sunglasses in the other. He hands me his business card. "I'm sorry to bother you at such a difficult time, Ms. Jamison, but I need to ask you a few questions. May I come in?" Dressed in a light gray suit he is immaculate. Even his short black hair looks starched.

I turn my back to him while I prepare coffee. Filling the pot with water, pouring ground coffee into the cone, switching on the coffee maker, taking mugs out of the cupboard, pouring cream into the creamer, and adding sugar to the sugar bowl gives me a minute or two to calm down and prepare myself.

Throughout all of my busy-work Detective Wilson watches me. I place the sugar and milk jug on the countertop and look straight at him. Bob always claimed that people like it when you face them directly and use their names. "It's disarming," he said, "it makes people feel less suspicious and more inclined to be trusting and friendly."

"Cream and sugar, Detective Wilson?"

He pours in enough cream to turn his coffee beige.

"Cookie?"

"No thank you, Ms. Jamison, I'm watching my figure."

My eyes drop to his stomach.

He smiles, "Not really."

I can't stop my mouth from turning up at the corners. I remind myself that he likely wants to disarm me, to cause me to relax and prattle on until I say something stupid. What's safe to discuss? A practical question comes to mind.

"When can I arrange my husband's funeral?"

"Just as soon as the medical examiner releases Mr. Jamison's body. Soon, I hope."

"How long do you think it'll be?"

He glances at his notepad. "Let me tell you exactly where we are right now, Ms. Jamison."

These quietly spoken words do not inspire confidence. In fact, I feel quite frightened and faint over what I might hear. Detective Wilson studies me. I suddenly realize I'm sitting rigid in my seat with my legs crossed and my arms folded, forgetting everything Bob told me about the importance of body language. He prided himself in always watching his own, as well as the body language of others. He said it helped him develop an advantage over them. For example, he knew that prospective male clients were finally won over when they would unfold their arms and lean back in their chairs, legs splayed. Judging from the way I'm sitting, I could not look guiltier.

Detective Wilson is giving me a serious stare. His notepad lies flat on the counter, facing him and sideways to me. My time spent opposite clients while negotiating projects and advertising budgets has taught me to read upside down writing. If he'd look away for a few seconds, it'll be a cinch to read his notes.

"What questions do you have for me?"

He watches me with steady eyes, using silence as a tool to make me squirm. I resist the urge to fill in the awkward gap in our conversation lest I say the wrong thing.

"Do you know your blood type, Ms. Jamison?"

"My blood type? Why do you need to know my blood type?" My heart's flopping about so much, I sound breathless.

"The hospital's new pathologist requested it. He's extremely thorough."

Bewilderment sends my brain into a muddle.

"It's just for the record, Ms. Jamison."

I nearly jump out of my seat when his cell phone rings.

"Sorry, I didn't expect that either. Let me turn this off." His hand goes into his inside pocket.

"Please, take the call. It might be something important."

He checks his caller ID, hesitates for a moment, and then taps in a text message. While he's occupied, I scan his notes. Under "Blood Types" are three bullet points.

> *Mr. Jamison: A+*
> *Ms. Jamison: A+*
> *Unknown: O- (rare, only 7% of population)*

Horror strikes. With all of the upset, I completely forgot about Bob's disappearing undies. What happened to them? Did Bob put them on before climbing into bed and dying? Had he worn them all night, under his pajamas, as he lay next to me?

The detective switches off his cell phone. "Thanks for your patience," he says, putting it back in his pocket.

Maybe he's thinking that a woman with O negative blood has deposited a red dot on my husband's underwear. My hands shake so hard I set down my coffee mug. There, written in blue ink on yellow paper is the humiliating truth, and everyone in the local police department, as well as Jim Burdick and god-knows-who-else at the local hospital, knows all about it.

"I can arrange a blood test for you, or get permission

from you to check with your doctor," says Detective Wilson. He's a bloodhound sniffing about for clues, his nose primed for the chase.

I think: How much trouble will there be when it's confirmed that neither my blood type nor Bob's matches the big O? But I say, "What does my blood type have to do with anything?"

"It's normal procedure, under the circumstances."

There's no way out. "I'm A positive, same as Bob."

I imagine stabbing Shirley's uplifted chest a few times with a big dagger. We're in a deserted area. She can't crawl her way to safety. She's bleeding herself dry, the way she bled me.

Bob never stopped wanting to make love to me, even though he was juggling who knows how many women. He could have given me AIDS, or syphilis, or some other dread disease. Of course, he'd try to convince me that I caught the disease through osmosis, or from a toilet seat in a major department store, or offer some other outrageous, stupid lie that falls under his truth-is-stranger-than-fiction ploys.

Once more, I realize that Detective Wilson is watching me. I don't care. He's known my blood type all along. He's been testing me. I was once admitted to Woodside Hospital and wonder if they were made to turn my blood information over to him. Just the thought of it siphons off the last of my fighting energy.

"Is there anything else to discuss?" My voice has no oomph.

"No. Not at the moment." He drains his cup and stands to take in a panoramic view of the kitchen and family room. "Thank you, Ms. Jamison. You make a fine cup of coffee."

Evidently, Detective Wilson knows all about using a person's name in order to disarm. He uses mine at every opportunity.

At the front door, he says, "I'm sorry to put you through this, Ms. Jamison. You have my card. Please call me any time, should you have further questions."

He looks about my age. His eyes are gray-blue flecked with gold.

"I'll keep in touch," he says, before walking over to his car.

I lie prone on the couch awash in guilt. What will the police do to me if they suspect I Voodoo'd my husband to death? Arrest me? Put my name down for the first available bed in a mental ward? Both?

Should I be a good girl and call Detective Wilson and say that Shirley's blood *might* match the O negative on Bob's clothing because she's busily bopped my husband for god-knows-how-long? Why should the police care anyway? Her bopping Bob didn't kill him.

Besides, if the police take on the idea that I found out about the two of them, they might view me as a murder suspect under the hell-hath-no-fury-like-a-woman-scorned theory.

No. It will not do to assist the police.

The pain of betrayal jabs through me. The last time Bob brought Shirley to our house for dinner, they sat together at the dining room table, drinking wine and laughing over office politics, while I fussed in the kitchen over baked salmon, steamed asparagus, parsley boiled potatoes, and warm, crusty, French bread. They watched with amused eyes as I served them food like a handmaid.

The second she left, I turned on him. "I'm sick and tired of having to watch the two of you act like lovers in front of me."

"I'm sick and tired of having you imagine such outlandish stuff every time Shirley's in the room. She's my company vice president for chrissakes! We *need* to socialize with her. It's good *business!*"

His responses always contained hints of truths, shadows of doubts; they were leaky escape hatches designed to release him and ensnare me.

"She's so unimpressive. Why is she your second-in-command? What were you thinking *with* when you decided to keep on promoting her all the way up to vice president?"

"Jesus Christ! You spoil everything with this paranoia of yours."

By the time we went to bed that night, he had me wondering if he was right.

"Never argue with an idiot," Grandmother says over my shoulder. "He will drag you down to his level, and then beat you with experience." I should have listened sooner.

9

All of those hours spent inert have produced in me a vengeance idea. All I need is a dynamite spell. Rolling out of bed, I yawn deeply, my gaping mouth stretched to its limits. An hour later, I'm lolling at the patio table, heat enfolding me in a lazy grip, absently opening up *Spells for all Occasions*, my Old Town's Spiritual Magic Shop free gift. A bee drones nearby. Fatigue creeps along my bones. I glance toward Mount Everest, which looms ugly at the edge of the flower garden. Maybe I should just bury Shirley Doll with Bob Doll. That pair of weasels can rot together.

Struggling to my feet, I collect Shirley Doll from the wastebasket and pull out her pins. Holding her at arm's length between my forefinger and thumb, I trudge across the lawn, pick up the garden fork, and give her the Sir Lancelot treatment. I hope I've poked her into the right spot, and picture Bob's surprise.

On the chaise longue, I stretch, yawn, and begin to idly flip through pages blinking hard to keep my eyes focused. *Spells for all Occasions* is about the size of a slender notebook. Wrapped in a fine black cover, its name scrolled across the top in shimmering silver ink, I feel charmed just holding it. Its pages look aged, a mottled ivory with darkened edges. Beneath scrolled silver headings its spells fall like poems written in delicate black lettering.

Weariness is getting the best of me. My eyes slowly close. Just then a loud, rolling boom belches out from somewhere very close. My head jerks upward, jarring my brain into action, launching me onto my feet in time to see Bob's volcanic compost heap falling in flaming bits and pieces back to earth like clouds of swarming fireflies. Gathering my scattered wits about me, I watch what remains of the spontaneous combustion process. Mount Everest has blown its top, its contents left strewn across the yard in hot clumps. Singed and smoking Bob and Shirley Doll lie in sight just a few feet away.

Compost heaps have been known to smolder, some have burst into flames, but I've never heard of one blowing up. "It's Bob!" I shriek. "He's haunting me!"

I'm agape, staring at the innocent looking mound that remains, my heart pounding in my ears, my brain boggled. The spell book lies face down on the patio where it fell. I open it up in one swift move and land on "A Spell for Satisfying the Soul." My eyes scan the details, which are written out like a recipe.

2 white candles (tapers)
2 candleholders

1 match
1 ruler (13 inches or longer)
1 non-flammable container (big enough for 2 dolls)
2 pins (preferably long ones)
Priestess robe (if desired)

Blocking out the idea that I'm acting like a nutball, I grab Shirley and Bob's worse-for-wear dolls from their hot glob of compost and head for the kitchen. I collect two white candles, find my red and white lasagna pan—to use for the symbolic burning—and retrieve my selected pins from the desk drawer. I check off my items against the spell page and rush upstairs for my black priestess robe. I need all the help I can get.

After thoroughly brushing off Bob and Shirley, I follow the spell's first instruction. Using my red plastic ruler as a measure, I place the candles thirteen inches apart on the kitchen island altar. The two dolls wait in front of them. Matches and pins are at the ready. The spell page lies open.

The phone jangles loudly. Since Bob's death, I've let almost every call go straight into voice mail, and listen to the collected condolence messages in one sitting. I rarely talk to anyone, not even Jim Burdick who's now phoned three times. I listen to his new message. "I'm worried about you, Molly. Please call so that I know you're all right."

My stomach tightens. Is his interest in me fuelled by a big heart or deep suspicion? Is he secretly wondering what really happened to his healthy friend, Bob, whose laid-open body must have died from something puzzling? Jim is a prize schmoozer, a man whose charm might lure a person to accidentally give up her darkest secret.

How much longer can I avoid him?

Brushing aside my irritation, I turn my attention back to the ceremony, making sure that everything's properly arranged before lighting both candles with one match. I produce the two pins with traces of my toe and knee blood on them. Since Bob and Shirley shared her blood with me, it's fair for me to respond in kind.

I pierce each doll through its heart with its own personalized blood pin. This is said to open up the most hard-hearted souls to the truth of their ways. I place both dolls in the ceramic dish and light a match under them. This is to burn my enemies to ash, to render them powerless over me. Feeling a little like a witch hovering over a cauldron, I watch them start to smolder. Satisfaction curls my lips.

But then, a sudden tongue of fire darts up from each doll, narrowly missing the tips of my hair. Now, flames and choking black smoke billow out of the lasagna pan and into my face. I stand stultified until my brain screams at me: This fire could spread through the house, and I'm still in it!

Grabbing my oven pads and the smoking, fiery mess, I cough my way to the open patio door just as the front door bell rings. In a blind panic, I toss the pan and its contents outside. I tear off my robe and swing it around and around from ceiling to floor in an attempt to wave fresh air into the room. Then, I scurry along the hallway to see who's here.

A quick glance through the peephole reveals Detective Wilson standing on the doorstep. Since I left my car out on the driveway, he'll know I'm home. The bell rings a second time setting my heart into a spin. I take a huge, shuddering breath before daring to open the door.

The detective's shocked face takes in the sight of me. "Ms. Jamison, are you all right?"

"As good as I can be under the circumstances." I stammer. "Please, come in."

I wonder if he's brought me any autopsy news. I walk in front of him down the hall taking care not to fall over my own feet.

After seating him and his sniffing nose in the kitchen with a soda, I excuse myself and disappear into the bathroom to check out my appearance. My uncombed hair springs out of my head like a collection of dark, clockwork coils. My upper lip is tinged in black, a soot stain from the smoke. Cursing myself over my stupidity, I scrub my hands and face. I now understand his shocked expression. I look like a flaming lunatic.

"Ms. Jamison!"

I rush down the hall.

"You have a burning bush on your patio."

"What!"

We run for the door. Grabbing the garden hose from the corner of the house, he pulls it across the yard and aims it at the dead, potted gorse bush that I intended to chuck out weeks ago. I turn on the water. By the time the first trickle presents itself, thick smoke is giving off puffs and clouds like Indian smoke signals.

"You haven't seen Moses around here, have you?" Detective Wilson stands before the former bush, pretending to warm his hands. His eyes scan the yard and the huge, messy area on the lawn around the flowerbeds. "What happened to the yard?"

"Just spreading a little compost and burning a bit of

debris … stuff like that." I emit an embarrassed giggle and fuss with the hose. "I'm not exactly myself, you know? And I'm trying to do things to keep myself going during all of this."

Shards of red and white pottery from the broken lasagna pan lie scattered across the patio and a chunk lies in the soil. He stares at what appears to be a fragment of scorched fabric, its rounded end shaped like a foot. Ashes lie all over the place. It's hard to see what they were. But then, I'm not a detective.

"What happened here?"

I panic and blurt, "Don't ask. Moses moves in mysterious ways."

"A burning mystery?"

"That sounds like a tawdry novel," I say. "I was just being a bigger klutz than usual with a plant pot or two."

When he smiles, I notice his lovely, pearly teeth. "Glad to know somebody's as clumsy as me."

On rubbery legs, I lead him back to the kitchen. "What brings you here today, Detective Wilson?"

"I was passing by and wanted to see how you're doing. These circumstances are difficult to endure, especially when you're alone."

I wonder if this is a ploy to disarm me, to catch me out, and note that his eyelashes are better than mine.

He bends over to pick something off the floor. "Here," he says, handing me one of Shirley Doll's pins. "These things are dangerous, especially when you're in bare feet."

I resist the urge to snatch it off him. "Thanks, that's true," I say, putting it next to the sink behind my dirty coffee cup.

When I turn to face him, he stares into my eyes for a few seconds before abruptly turning his attention onto his watch. "Well, Ms. Jamison, since the burning bush issue is resolved, I'll be on my way." He walks toward the patio doors and looks outside. Nerves joggling I stand behind him as he scans the yard.

I walk him to the front door feeling slightly off course, wondering how much I've said and done to make myself look unbalanced and guilty. When he drives off, I carefully sweep up all of the doll bits and drop them into the garbage can where they belong.

•

That night, I dream I'm in New Orleans. There's a sign above my head that reads, "Saint Louis Cemetery Number One." Voodoo Priestess Marie Laveau lies here.

In front of her crypt two women have their backs to me. One chalks three Xs on the tomb. The other knocks three times. Together, they turn in three circles. They want her to cross their paths and help them solve a dilemma.

A third woman materializes, an enormous snake, her conduit to the spirit world still coiled around her. She and the two Victoria Plants turn to look at me.

I awaken with a start. A great nervousness settles on me, drying my mouth and dampening my palms. Am I in the midst of a three-woman Voodoo intervention? It's written in the New Orleans tour books that even now people the world over come to Marie Laveau's crypt to perform these ceremonies and ask for favors. When the Voodoo Queen's sympathies are captured, sightings of her often follow.

I remember gazing at the Marie Laveau portrait I found online. She stared back at me from behind my computer screen, her mouth a Mona Lisa smile, her dark eyes tinged with an admirable defiance. Her skin was golden, her cheeks peach, her back straight, and her bearing regal. She wore a black dress, red shawl, and traditional *tignon* high like a crown, a shine of straight black hair showing at her temple.

I envision The Old Town's Spiritual Magic Shop, and mile high goose bumps scatter from head to toe.

I shouldn't read any more about this stuff; it's putting too many ideas into my head.

10

Friday, one week after Bob's death, Detective Wilson again stands on my doorstep, his expression serious, his left hand tapping out a nervous tattoo on his thigh. One look at him has me envisioning the inside of a prison cell and the bed-lined wards of mental institutions.

"May I come in, Ms. Jamison?"

I wobble ahead of him to the kitchen, wondering if this is my last day in this house.

He goes straight to his usual chair at the counter and sits down.

I am a robot hostess. "I'm having tea. Would you like a cup?"

"Yes, thank you."

I shakily pour tea, and notice his hands. Just like the rest of him, they look sturdy and strong. You can learn a lot from a man's hands, I think, picturing Bob's fragile, tapering fingers.

When I look up, the detective lowers his eyes. He's been watching me, watch him.

I take my usual seat and ask in a quaky voice. "So, what's on the agenda today?"

He speaks softly. "The autopsy results have been released."

The air floats dark splotches in front of my eyes. "Results?" I struggle to absorb the horror that the world is about to find out about stab-happy me, the woman no one in my life will recognize. I hear a cupboard door open and water flow. The detective gently hands me a full glass, and waits while I take a gulp.

I start searching for a way to delay hearing the news, as if pushing it off and wishing it away will help change the facts. Something niggles at me. "I thought autopsies took longer than a week to complete."

The detective hesitates for a few seconds, as if carefully choosing his words. "To be frank," he says, "in your husband's case the cause of death should have been noted immediately. There's been some sort of communications snafu between pathology and the rest of us. Why it happened is a complete mystery. Doctor Burdick said pathology is going round and round over it."

I imagine the young pathologist and Jim Burdick twirling in circles across a white-tiled autopsy lab. Bob lies dead center on a cold stone slab. I can't bear to look at his face. I think: Communications snafu, or *Voodoo* snafu? And then shock rattles through me enough to make the air turn foggy.

"Jim Burdick and I ran into each other in the hospital this morning. We soon realized he knew about the autopsy results and I didn't, so we started to investigate."

The detective stops talking, no doubt hoping for feedback, but I cannot speak.

"I want to apologize for the confusion, Ms. Jamison. You shouldn't have had to wait."

After once more telling me he'd be home on time Bob was deliberately making me wait. I sat for hours, holding onto my fury, imagining him acting the big man, buying rounds of drinks, and cavorting openly with Shirley. I could hardly stand Bob's gall. I thought: At least I didn't make dinner this time.

At midnight, a hand slid between my legs. Awaking with a heart pounding start, I was out of bed in a flash.

"Jezzuz Christ, Moll," slurred Bob, "you scared the fuckin' life out of me."

He stunk of booze and cigars and garlic and Shirley's Giorgio perfume.

In the dark, I rushed toward the door. I lay in the guest room bed like an entombed Egyptian mummy. Across the hall, Bob was already snoring loud as a freight train.

I thought: He must believe I have no limits. The shame of it almost crushed the life out of me.

Jonathan Wilson hands me my teacup. I dutifully take a sip and place it back on the saucer. "Mistakes like this aren't deliberate," I say, hoping people will be this kind to me when they learn about my mistakes. My heart is thudding like mad. I raise my eyes to meet his. "What happened to Bob?"

"Your husband suffered a subarachnoid hemorrhage."

I stammer, "What's a subarachnoid hemorrhage?"

"It's a cerebral aneurysm. A brain aneurysm."

I think: Oh my God, I jabbed so many pins into Bob Doll's head, he looked like he was wearing a frigging royal crown. I pinned Bob's brain to erupt like Mount Everest. And it did!

Guilt flings me backward. I see light brown bubble curls, hands on mine, and blue-bagged Bob lying on a gurney that takes flight down a corridor. I feel the stifling, humid, August heat, and picture the salivating, knife-wielding, brand new pathologist eagerly awaiting a fresh body to chop away at, grateful to cut a little boredom out of his Woodside life.

"Are you all right, Ms. Jamison?"

"What happens now?"

Detective Wilson speaks slowly, gently. "The medical examiner has released your husband's body. You're free to make funeral arrangements."

A dull ache crawls along my brow. I close my eyes and massage my temples with stiff fingers. "You're saying that Bob really was sick?" I want this to be true.

"Very sick."

"Why didn't he tell me?"

"Maybe he didn't know."

"He had no symptoms? Is that possible?"

"Perhaps your husband ignored them. Many men have been known to ignore their medical problems until it's too late."

We sit in silence while I struggle to absorb this new twist.

"Is there anything you'd like me to do for you?"

"Thanks, but no. I can manage now." It hasn't occurred to me that I should cry. I need to let the impossible news sink in. Bob suffered a cerebral aneurysm. My husband died from a cerebral aneurysm. I'm the widow of a man who died of a cerebral aneurysm.

The detective hovers over me. "Is there someone I can call? Someone who can stay with you? A family member perhaps?"

"No."

"You have no family here?"

"My father and his wife live in Vancouver. They're spending a few weeks in Australia with her family."

He looks at me kindly. "A friend then?"

"I'll be fine. Really."

He picks up the teapot. "What's left in here has cooled off quite a bit. Shall I boil water for refills?"

"That would be nice."

He busies himself, filling the kettle, plugging it in, rinsing out the teapot, and counting out spoonfuls of loose tea. "I love a good, hot cup of tea," he announces. "Never did manage to like that iced stuff. Cold tea seems wrong somehow."

"Yes, it does." I can tell that he's an expert tea maker.

He rinses out our cups, dries them with a paper towel, and sets them down again. He glances over at the kitchen desk, my idle laptop, and the stack of *City Gardener* magazines beside it. "You're the Molly Makepeace Jamison who writes for that magazine. That's impressive."

I blush with pleasure and then feel stupid. "Thanks," I croak.

"I especially enjoyed your 'Prepare to Get Potted on the Patio' piece. Very witty. Helpful too. This year, I grew the best tomatoes, ever."

Detective Wilson is a fan. I'm amazed. He stands with his back to me, pouring boiling water into the teapot and briskly stirring. He wears black shoes with thick soles that make his feet look big and round. I startle. A pin peeks out from beneath his heel.

"What is it?" His eyes have followed mine. They search the floor around his feet.

"Sorry. I was mesmerized by your big shoes."

"Did it ever occur to you that you are insulting my *big feet*?" His eyes crinkle when he smiles.

"The upside is that you'll always have good balance."

"I wish that were true."

"So, you like gardening?" I ask, forcing my eyes to keep away from the floor.

"I like growing things," he says, "and I like the fact that in your articles you don't pretend to be an expert gardener. It's refreshing."

"My mother Victoria Plant was the family expert. My grandmother Victoria Plant started off the gardening tradition. She believed in encouraging what she called 'plant power,' particularly when it comes to weeding."

"Give life to the plants that want to thrive by removing those who don't," he smiles. "Or words to that effect."

"You really have read my stuff."

"I enjoy the messages found in your work."

Messages?

"You sound like a wise woman."

Wise?

Ignoring my dumbstruck expression, he holds the teapot high and pours thin streams of steaming dark tea into our cups, ending with a flourish. "What are you working on now?"

What can I honestly say, except, "Not much?"

"Really?"

"Well, I mean … this is a difficult time." My excuse sounds pitiful, even to me.

"I understand. My own writing stalls or takes a back seat during times of stress. I've had to learn to get out of my own way if I want to see it flow."

"You write?"

"Not as well as you."

"What do you write?"

"Detective stories. What else?"

"I should have known. Published?"

"My first novel was accepted a while back. It might be another six months before it's on the shelves."

"Do you have family in the Chicago area, Detective? They must be so proud."

"My parents live in Oak Park. My sister and her family live in Lincoln Park. That's it."

"And you? Where do you live?"

"Last year I moved to downtown Chicago, the Near South Loop."

"In one of those tall buildings? But you must have a patio or terrace. Which is it?"

"I have a terrace. How do you know that?"

"You grow tomatoes."

"Of course, we just talked about 'Prepare to Get Potted on the Patio.' Detectives are supposed to remember details."

"*Women* tend to remember details."

"So do *writers*. We should each be doubly blessed."

I picture him in the dead of night, tippling exotic teas, pounding out prose on his computer, dazzling city views capturing his attention whenever he stops to mull over his story's twists and turns.

"Are you working on a new detective novel?"

"Yup. I have almost a year left to finish it," he says.

"I wish I was that far along."

"They say that great sorrow produces great writing. Do you think it's true?"

"I really don't know."

"I bet a new idea will soon flash into your mind and you'll be off and running," he says, softly. "Your talent is always there, waiting for the right time to spring into action." When he's not smiling, his full upper lip gives him an appealing, ever-so-slight, upside-down pout.

"I'll do my best to hold that thought." I bet his mother dotes on him. She probably has a large, sunny kitchen where they sit and drink tea and talk about family and detective stories.

He checks his watch. "I have to get back to the office, although I'd rather not."

Hiding my disappointment, I hold onto a benign expression.

"Are you sure I can't call anyone for you?"

"Quite sure, thanks."

He carries his cup and saucer to the sink and rinses them out. "I'll be on my way."

Pressure builds behind my eyes. "Thank you for bringing me the news."

He hesitates. "Please let me know if I can do anything at all for you. Call me anytime. I'd like to help."

"There's nothing. Really."

He looks around. "This is a beautiful home you've created, Ms. Jamison. Lots of books, interesting artworks—it really fits you."

With the place to myself, I sit like a lump, staring into my teacup until my tea turns cold. I lie for hours on the couch, ignoring the persistent jangling of the phone, which receives a total of thirteen calls. No matter what they say, I know what really happened.

11

Jane's voice sounds tight, urgent. I picture the phone pressed hard against her face, her fingers clamped around it. "You need to sit down, Molly. I have news about Shirley."

"What is it?" I imagine Shirley Doll's pinned head and fear that another Voodoo aneurysm might be on the agenda.

"Our client, your editor Alex Fox, phoned." Jane sounds nervous. "Shirley just left his office at the *City Gardener*. He said he doesn't want to worry you with this—with Bob's memorial service tomorrow you have enough to contend with. But I think this is something you need to know."

"What is it?" I repeat, louder this time.

She pauses. "Alex thinks that Shirley is pitching agency clients for herself."

"What?"

"He thinks she's trying to *steal* clients, trying to start her own business with our accounts."

My heart is hammering. "Why does he think that? What did she do?"

"She tried putting doubts into his head about our effectiveness. You know, saying stuff like, 'Now that Bob is gone, I'm concerned about Molly and the gang at the office pulling it together,' and crap like that. Seems she hinted about clients needing 'new beginnings' and 'fresh starts' and what have you."

When I manage to speak, my voice is barely audible. "Shirley tried to steal Bob from me. Now she's trying to steal the business from me. She's been stealing my life away forever."

"Too true," growls Jane, "and she's not slowing down. In two weeks we've lost Drake's Jewelers, Sarah's Steak House, and Murphy's Landscaping. Now she's edging up to bigger accounts like *City Gardener*. Apparently, she forgot that you did Alex's advertising for years, before moving the account over here."

"She can't do this legally, can she?" I blurt. "Everyone on the staff signed non-compete agreements, didn't they?" To convince myself further, I say, "Nobody on staff can compete against the agency. Nobody can compete against the agency." I'm like an old time record with the needle stuck. I press my hand against my mouth to keep it quiet.

"Let's hope Bob included her, Molly. She started as a receptionist years ago. He might have let it slide.'

This is the point where I'm supposed to come up with brilliant ideas with which to trounce Shirley. But all week my head has been deep into funeral plans: ideal caterers had to be found, a trusted florist was hired, and meetings with Blackstone's Funeral Services took place, Bob's favorite music from myriad CDs took me days to collect, and then record into his perfect memorial playlist, as I promised him. My business wits have dulled. All I can come up with for Jane is, "Where are the personnel files?"

"Bob kept them in his office. But until I locked his door, she had access to every file in there. Her non-compete could be a pile of ash by now."

"I think we need to find out," I say, sounding uncertain. "Don't you?"

Jane answers gently. "It makes sense to me, Molly."

I'm relieved to hear that and feel a tad strengthened. "When those clients left, what reasons did they give? Did they say they were taking their advertising in-house, or did they say they were hiring other agencies?"

"According to Shirley, they were nervous about our ability to continue without Bob. They phoned to say they wanted their advertising schedules pulled and their creative handed over. She got no feedback on where they were taking their business. She claims she tried to stop them, but we know she's a liar."

I said, "She's that all right." But I think: We've lost a top jewelry store and a classy restaurant along with Murphy's. Where was Shirley's jewelry purchased? Where did she and my husband go out to eat? Did Bob trade out advertising work for jewelry and meals? Was trade set up for personal use and not strictly for client gifts and business entertainment?

"I can ask Lucille, our rep at the buzz, to phone all three clients and see what's up," Jane says. "Lucille's boss will expect her to know who's buying their airtime now, so she'll be grateful to us for the clue-in. What do you think?"

"That's a great idea. Let's do it." I wonder how we can hang onto Shirley in order to appear stable, while getting rid of her at the same time. "She's not going to win this," I say.

It takes our mole, Lucille, twenty-five minutes to bring our lost clients' whereabouts back to Jane, who then relays the news straight to me.

"Lucille spoke to the jewelry store manager, the steakhouse owner, and Murphy's general manager. They all referred her to Bills Advertising. She then called Shirley to confirm."

"She called Shirley at *work?*"

"Imagine that," Jane hisses. "Five minutes ago, Shirley sat in the office next to mine telling Lucille to keep quiet and hinting that she'll be buying big WBUZ airtime schedules to seal the deal."

We each have a silent seethe, awed by Shirley's audacity.

"She must have started courting Bob's accounts the minute he died," I say.

"If not before."

"Has she found time to open up an actual agency?"

"She set up a home office, Molly, lickety-split."

"So, during the days she's working to grow her business by trying to steal even more of Bob's accounts."

"It's a fact."

"And she's getting paid for her thievery. By me."

"She's got more balls than a bowling alley."

Rage has revved me up. "Do you have time to get that file now, Jane? Let's see if there's a signed non-compete agreement in there. Let's see what we have for ammunition."

Soon, I hear the rustle of papers. I wait, my breathing shallow. At Bob's memorial, Shirley will put on a show of sympathy for me, and I'll have to get through it without giving her a hint of what I know. How will I manage that?

"I'm not finding anything," Jane mutters.

"There's still the spirit of the Law to consider," I say. "Surely an employee isn't allowed to sabotage a business in order to walk away with it herself?"

"I just don't know. We've never had this happen before."

I picture Shirley sitting behind a huge ornate desk (baby pink with lots of gilded scrollwork), her chair an oversized throne in faux gold, her feet (encased in white fur-trimmed boots) dangling high above a mottled pink carpet. "Imagine the big plans she has for herself."

"She told Lucille she expects to expand her agency fast," steams Jane. "Seems like she's predicting we'll fold before the end of the year. She's actually spreading that rumor."

I say, "She obviously underestimates us." But I think: I hope I haven't underestimated her.

"We need a plan, Molly."

"I need accounting advice. How would you feel if I bring in Bernie? I trust him. Do you think he can take on one more client?"

"Since he's my hubby I'm biased, of course, but it can't hurt to bring him onboard. He's not yet crazy-busy, although he has no regrets on leaving that huge firm. He's just hired an ace assistant, and he's building his client base bit-by-bit. He'll be delighted to work with us, Molly.

"Do you think he can do a fast audit?"

"If he can, he will."

"Do you mind asking him if it's possible to get started next week?"

"I'll call him now."

"We'll come up with something, Jane. For now, so that they'll receive them before the memorial, I'll write personal e-mail letters to each of our clients reminding them that I'm still here. I'll remind them of my own agency experience. I'll thank them for their loyalty through this difficult time, and assure them that their trust in Jamison Advertising continues to be well placed. I'll cc you on all of them. What do you think?"

"That's good," she says, "and it should slow her down a bit."

"It's a start. I'll be in next week."

I put down the phone, rest my head in my hands, and think about camels.

•

At Bob's office building, Eddie, the underground parking lot attendant, catches sight of me before I can get to the elevator. Waving for me to wait, he rambles over. His dark blue uniform hangs in folds from his shoulders and waist, giving his tall, narrow frame an emaciated look. He coughs a chest-rattling cough and covers his mouth with a big, light blue handkerchief. "I'm sorry to hear about Mr. Jamison," He rasps. "Your husband was a great guy, a real fun guy. Real fun." His eyes portray an empathy that makes me want to weep.

Shaking his head, his face as droopy as a hound dog's,

he holds my arm as I step into the elevator. "You gonna be all right up there? The building's deserted, except for the cleaning crew. You call down here if you need me, you hear?"

I wonder if he thinks I'm here because the office is empty. Of course, I am. Besides, since Bob's memorial is tomorrow and Labor Day Weekend follows, it won't reopen until Tuesday. After hearing about Shirley, I can't stand to wait that long. I have Jane's administrative password. I can get into the office IT system.

"I'll not be long, Eddie. Thanks."

His pale, gaunt face and unhappy eyes watch me as the doors close.

Nerves jittering, I punch the elevator button for the fourteenth floor and then stare at the wall panel. The floors are numbered one through twelve, and then fourteen through forty. Bob's fourteenth floor office is actually on the thirteenth floor—my lucky number—meaning the building has thirty-nine floors, a number divisible by thirteen. I take this as a good sign.

The frosted glass panel above the double-doors reads, "Robert Jamison Advertising Agency, Inc." I gaze at it in wonderment. For the past nine years, everything I accomplished, including my writing, gives credit to the Jamison family. Even though I funneled practically all of my business into Bob's company, it never occurred to me that my name deserved to be on the company logo alongside his own.

He persuaded me to move accounts over to him rather than expand my own company. "My agency is full service already," he nagged. "It's not like you're *losing* accounts.

We're married. You'll still reap the benefits. What's the problem? Don't you *trust* me?"

He chipped away at my agency non-stop, using my life's dreams against me. "You always wanted to stay home and write full time," he said, "Here's your chance to get established in your new career before we make our baby." He made everything sound logical and fair, as if his commitment to me was forever secure. Yet with every chip, he was taking away my independence.

After his memorial, I will take back my own name and never again give it up.

The office is silent, eerie. I imagine Bob's ghost hovering about the place. I unlock his door and stare at his desktop, which is neat and tidy. I sit in front of his computer, my throat on fire. The last time he was here, he couldn't have imagined that he would never sit here again. No matter what Bob has done, I still can't help melting at the idea that he was, in the end, so vulnerable.

I log in as the office IT administrator. Straight backed, I stare at Bob's monitor. His icons are arranged in the neatest of rows.

I need his password to get into his personal e-mail. He said he always wrote down passwords. Where did he put them? I unlock his desk and have a good rummage through. Nothing. I tap my pen against the chair arm and think. I look under his chair, beneath his pen set, and on the back of his computer. I'm starting to panic. I upturn his keyboard. A tiny strip of paper is taped alongside the logo. On it he's written, "Mollysmygirl." I punch it in, and it works.

I want to cry.

As always, Bob is nothing but efficient and tidy. His mailbox is almost empty, no doubt because he answered everything important, and deleted anything he didn't want found. But, on the day of his death, before anyone knew he died, there were at least a dozen new ones. It's the one from Mary Murphy that catches my eye.

> *Hi Bobbo,*
> *I can make it at the discussed time for another full round.* ☺
> *Same place? Let me know ASAP.*
> *Hugs,*
> *Round Bottom* ☺

My mother murmurs from the corner, "The quiet ones are the ones to watch."

Pictures from the past bombard my head: Scarlet Mary peeking out at me from behind her husband, Nervous Mary lying about her dental appointment and then rushing away from me in Old Town's Spiritual Magic Shop, Shy Mary always refusing to look at me, always attempting to hide a face crimsoned with *shame*.

Bob thwarted me with a classic ploy, a plan designed to confuse me about what was really going on between him and "here's my head my ass follows." They were having a big-ass affair, while I believed he didn't even *like* her. "She's one dull woman," he said after chatting with her during our Independence Day party. "Take away her stupid power walking and there's nothing there."

If he were not already dead, I would pin him all over again.

•

"No way!" cries Jane. "Well, now we know for sure why she whipped her account out of the agency as soon as Bob died. She has a guilty conscience."

I'm in bed, on the phone, covers pulled up to my chin. "I never even looked into Shirley's computer."

"I'll do it, if you like."

"I'm glad Bernie is free for the audit. I think we really need one."

"Oh my God," hollers Jane. "Mary moved Murphy's Landscaping into Shirley Bills' secret, brand new agency."

I can't help but brighten. "Obviously they don't know about each other."

"Well they damned well deserve each other," Jane sniffs. "They've got more balls than a driving range."

"I don't know if I can stand this."

"You have to Molly. Success is the best revenge."

12

It's Bob's memorial day. I lie in bed pondering my predicament and watching the day dawn bright and sunny. Two weeks have passed since I found him lying dead beside me. I feel a bit shell-shocked. Not only because of the sudden loss of my husband, and the current trauma-dramas that threaten to produce more highs and lows than Chicago's weather; mostly, I'm in a furor at myself for handing nine years of my life to Bob—over ten, if I include our time spent dating. Voodoo Woman Marie Laveau gave Jacques Paris one year to prove himself. Grandmother did the same with my grandfather. Not me. I was the goody two-shoes who *worked* on my marriage.

I gaze across the room at my black silk suit. It hangs on the closet door handle, my new black, sling-back pumps sitting side-by-side underneath. I'm playing this last role with a brave face. I'm the stoic wife, a good girl to the end.

In the bathroom, I flip on the radio, toss my pajamas down the laundry chute, and pick up my toothbrush. Turning to the mirror, I'm struck by my own appearance. I stand this way and that, admiring my slim figure and clear skin. When did I stop looking at myself? How was my life reduced to revolving around Bob? He always told me how he worked people. I knew his tricks, his charming, manipulative ways. Why didn't I realize he was using them on me?

In the shower, standing under a forceful spray of warm water, I work to crank up my spirits. When I burst forth with "Voodoo Woman's Anthem," it blasts out of the radio at exactly the same time. I stand frozen, shampoo flowing in frothy waves from my head to my feet.

Visions of Bob and Shirley's exploits fill my brain. Like the time I was in his office and she slapped him across the ass right in front of me before sauntering out of the door like some vacuous trollop. I always regretted letting her get by with that, but what does one do? Have a catfight? Besides, I believed Bob's incredulous response. "She needs reining in," he steamed, "and I'll damn well do it." Now I wonder what he promised her to make her behave. Those earrings?

I picture Mary Murphy, Woodside's blushing beauty at our Independence Day party. She must have handed Murphy's Landscaping to Bob shortly after that. No doubt he gave her a damned good landscaping himself just as soon as he managed to fit her in. Considering the amount of business he gave the O-K Hotel, he probably got reward points.

Shampoo lathers up as I work more of it into my hair. Anger snaps at my heels. My hips start swaying and my feet turn me around in a circle. At full throttle I sing along with Crazi-O's raspy-voiced vocalist.

> *"I'm a Voodoo Woman, and don't you forget it.*
> *I'm a Voodoo Woman, hurt me and you'll regret it.*
> *Cuz my magic will bring you down, will bring you down*
> *Yes, my magic will put you down, on the ground*
>
> *I stay true to myself and you ain't gonna change it*
> *Whatever you try to do, I'll have a spell to rearrange it*
> *Cuz, my magic will bring you down, will bring you down*
> *Yes, my magic will put you down, on the ground*
>
> *Yes, I'm a Vooooooooooooooodoo Woman*
> *I stay true, true, true to myseeeeeeeeeeeeeeeeeelf*
> *Before anyone else."*

"I love your *Spitfire*," Grandmother murmurs. "I love your *Triumph*. You must learn, Molly, that sometimes you have to do both."

The first thing discarded is my traditional black grieving outfit (a Voodoo Woman should not look demure when it's not in her best interest to do so). Giving myself a healthy spritz of Miracle perfume, I open the closet door and sit on the bed to consider the offerings inside.

Today, Bob's clients will be assessing me. I'll give them plenty to look at. My red silk dress—form fitting, knee length, sleeveless, scoop neck—fires up a row of little black dresses. Last summer, when Bob and I were in Hawaii on a business trip-slash-vacation, I wore it to a private party in an elegant country club. Admiring eyes watched us arrive.

Bob held my arm possessively; I was a woman too precious to lose, then.

I take the dress off the hanger and place it on the bed. Balanced on a stool, I root around the closet's top shelf to find my high-heeled, strappy "do me" sandals. Next to them lies my delicately spangled evening bag. Taking hold of them all, I toss them next to the dress.

It is 11:47 a.m. (thirteen minutes before noon). I'm dressed and ready to head out the door. Only now do I realize I'll be late for my husband's funeral.

Today, Bob is waiting for me.

13

The way to the crematorium lies along tree-lined streets and short stretches of country road. Here and there, between houses, over low shrubs and across blooming flowerbeds, eye-candy views of Lake Michigan surface, its deep turquoise seas sparkling under clear skies. Bob couldn't have wished for a better day.

The Blackstone grounds are expansive and manicured. A huge Romanesque style building surrounded by velvety lawns provides grandeur. Its crowded parking lot is landscaped into two neat rectangles separated by clipped shrubbery. Following the advice of Mr. Blackstone, I park the Triumph in the VIP spot nearest the entrance. This, he assured me, is always reserved for the most profoundly affected persons, like myself.

Standing in the central arched doorway of the Passages room, I survey the turnout. Over one hundred people sit quietly chatting at small round tables that are strategically arranged between three churchlike aisles, the widest cutting through the middle. The Beatles' *Ticket to Ride* plays in the background. At the front of the room under a bright stained glass window sits the brass urn containing Bob.

A sudden desire to race off swoops down on me, myriad excellent reasons supporting the idea, strengthening it, giving it a heady value. I want to lift up my dress, swing myself around, and start sprinting like a track star. Why should I suffer through this? The humiliation of this event alone has to be far worse than the loss of client confidence my running off would create. How many people here are involved in the cover up, faking innocence whenever they see me, lying through their smiles? How many of them have enjoyed a snicker here and a tee-hee there at my expense, grateful that they're not the recipients of such devastating disloyalty from their spouses, or at least praying they're not? How many times have they speculated about what's wrong with me for losing such a charming man?

The rotund, gray-haired Mr. Blackstone catches sight of me and hurries over, his smooth face a practiced picture of concern, his jowls wobbling. I've dithered at the door too long.

"Ms. Jamison. I've worried about you." He avoids looking at my dress. "I do wish that you would have let us pick you up."

"Thank you, Mr. Blackstone, I'm sorry to have worried you…but…you know how it is."

"Of course." He takes my arm and my black canvas carrier bag. "Let me escort you to the display so that you can arrange your chosen items as you prefer."

My ability to move smoothly into robot mode is uncanny. I suppose it's because I'm so practiced. Things in me feel broken, yet here I am acting like Jacqueline Kennedy Onassis at her husband's funeral, straight-backed, calm, a wan smile attached to my lips.

By now the buzz has flown around the room. All eyes rest on the red-dressed widow. I hold my head high and lay my hand lightly on the director's arm as we slowly walk down the center aisle toward Bob.

On either side of his urn stand two large crystal vases, each filled with thirteen blossoming red roses. Mr. Blackstone sets my bag on the edge of the table and waits to assist me. Unzipping the top, I open it up to reveal four personal items. Like a well-trained butler, he gives a solemn nod of approval.

First out is the wedding photo. Bob has me in a bear hug, his face suffused with love. Who could look at this picture and believe that this day was a subtle turning point? Yet it was the day he began his change from doting date to indifferent husband. I place it in front of one vase.

Then comes our ninth wedding anniversary photo taken in Stefano's restaurant just last month. Unbeknownst to onlookers, we were toasting ourselves for our umpteenth new start. Champagne glasses touch as he smiles lies into my eyes. This is propped up in front of the second vase.

Beside it, I place my anniversary card from Bob. Inside, he wrote in large print, *"My darling Molly. It's only been nine years. I will love you forever."* On the front, two adorable rabbits hold hands. The caption reads, *"Stay with me, the best is yet to be."*

Last, comes an eight-by-ten, silver-framed photograph

taken by a professional photographer on our fabulous night out in Hawaii. There we are on the dance floor in each other's arms, me in my red dress, him in his tuxedo. I face the camera, smiling, relaxed. Bob's lips brush my cheek, his eyes are half-closed, his expression adoring. No one seeing this picture will imagine that Bob was playing his cat-and-mouse game. He wanted me happy that night, so he behaved like a doting lover. It was convenient. That's all. I set the photo down hard in front of his urn.

Stepping back to gauge the effect, I'm satisfied that the display effectively attests to Bob's great and abiding love for me, which glows for all to witness.

Mr. Blackstone speaks with just a hint of the dramatic. "That's lovely, Ms. Jamison, just lovely." He folds my empty bag for me. "Would you like me to seat you at your table now? It's this one right in front."

"If you don't mind, I think I'll just stand here for a moment and reflect."

He pulls out a sheet of paper from his inside jacket pocket. "I'll make the memorial announcement and ensure that everyone is comfortable and has whatever they need."

Clearing his throat and lifting his arms high in the air to catch everyone's attention, Mr. Blackstone begins his speech in a booming, theatrical voice.

"Ms. Molly Jamison thanks you all for coming to pay your respects to her dear husband Bob." He pauses to look around, his face mournful. "Many of you know that Bob was not a religious man. Today we're abiding by his wishes by holding no religious service. Instead, his friends and colleagues are invited to speak. Jane and Bernie Silverberg and Dr. Jim Burdick will bring their reminiscences to us at two o' clock. Please feel free to add your own thoughts." He perks up. "Meanwhile, Ms. Jamison wants you know that her husband's favorite wines and hors d'oeuvres are now being set out on the buffet tables at the back of the room. Please enjoy Mr. Bob Jamison's favorite music, the refreshments, and each other's company per his request. Thank you."

With that, he walks with a grand air toward the side door leading to the kitchen, where he'll keep an eye on the food and drink and see that it's replenished when necessary. Stationing himself there, he stands at attention, his head nodding to the sounds of Mick Jagger and the Rolling Stones singing "It's All Over Now," Bob's best loved sing-along song.

Shirley beats everyone in her mad dash to stand next to me. Hanky at the ready, she gasps, "Molly, you scared us. Where were you?"

"I just couldn't decide on which cards or photos to bring. There were so many, you know. In the end, I chose the most significant." I motion for her to check them out, and point to the anniversary card I received from Bob just last month.

She stands still as a stump. It is, after all, a lot to take in. Bob will have told her the kind of thing married men tell other women in order to get what they want from them. I imagine her head bobbing in agreement as he said things like: Molly is such a bitch; Molly and I never have sex; I stay with Molly because she'll take my business right out from under me if I try to leave, and other lies designed to camouflage. She isn't acting triumphant today. Looking at contrary evidence to her perceived position in Bob's life, she appears quite pale and shaky.

"Why, Shirley." I simper, "Are you all right?"

Behind her, a low moan erupts. A growing wail is rising from Mary Murphy who has the nerve to be here, despite bopping my husband and dumping his agency now that she knows it's mine. She's holding the anniversary card, reading the cover and then the inscription over and over, her mouth twisted by tears like a child's.

My stomach curls into a toxic knot. "Excuse me, I need some air," I say, just like my mother. But when I turn to walk away, my grandmother-like mouth whispers into Shirley's ear, "She was having an affair with Bob."

Shirley's eyes and mouth are a trio of Os. She fixates on her stolen client, as she works to compute the size of Bob's betrayal.

Arranging my face into a calm expression, I turn away from Shirley Bills, Mary Murphy, and the people standing in line waiting to tout Bob's goodness to me. Anger peppers my gut as I set off down the aisle. How many more women are there? How many of them are here today?

"All anyone wants is for people to act decent," Bob used to say. "I mean, how hard can it be to act decent?" He hid his indecent agenda from me with nothing more than a bit of decent talk and a very clever act.

Suddenly, my eyes land on Pastor Clarence the Bulldog as he rises up from the corner, a pale specter dressed in black. "*One moment please*," he shouts. The Grim Reaper squeezes past a table, his Bible held high above his head, he shouts, *"Everyone take your seats! Please take your seats!"* He's heading for the front of the room, his preaching voice warmed up.

I wonder if fury has turned me the same color as my dress. Eyes on the urn, adrenalin pumping through me by the gallon, I fly back toward Bob. At the sight of the black-suited, Bible-waving man tearing up one aisle, and the widow in her red dress striding up the other, the mourners remain where they are, shocked into silence.

Clarence and I meet in front of the display table. I grab the urn and hold Bob tight to my chest like a long lost lover, my heart doing leapfrogs.

"Put that back."

"No." Once more, I make for the door.

At the end of the aisle, a hand touches my shoulder and a soft voice says, "Ms. Jamison." I look into Detective Wilson's kind face, and blink back tears. "May I accompany you? I think that man is likely to head your way."

I look behind me. People watch the show as if at a tennis match, their heads turning back and forth between Clarence and me. Mary Murphy stands with her buttocks to the room, still sniveling. Shirley's disappeared. But the man who once told me, "Men are designed to lead, woman are designed to follow," has proven far too proud to trail behind such an ungodly woman—and up the aisle no less—not even for the sake of his baby brother's sorry soul. Pastor Clarence's feet remain fixed in front of the display table, thwarted by a plan gone awry.

I whisper, "Let's go."

The detective is holding a small package and uses it to point the way. "There's a patio out back." Taking my arm, he ushers me away with remarkable efficiency.

Halfway to freedom, I almost fall over Jane as she walks out of the ladies' room.

"What is it, Molly? What's happened?"

"Clarence is here."

"Oh no!" Her eyes take in the clasped urn.

Detective Wilson gently moves me forward. "Please, excuse us. We're taking cover on the patio." He maneuvers me past Jane's astonished stare.

Two comfortable chairs and a small table on the far end of the patio feel secluded. At my request, Detective Wilson goes in search of red wine.

Warm breezes offer a comforting caress. Roses from the patio's planters scent the air. Breathing deeply, I lay my head back, close my eyes, and try to calm down. Seconds tick into minutes.

"Molly, I must insist." My heart wallops against my ribs as Clarence reaches for the urn.

"No!" I push his hands away.

"Give me that!"

"No! Stop it!"

We struggle for control of Bob's urn, each of us hanging onto it, pulling and tugging. I imagine Bob cascading out of the urn onto the potted roses, and remember being told that roses like to have ashes spaded into the soil around them. It makes the earth more alkaline. Or is it lime that does that? I should know the answer, but I just can't think any more.

Clarence and I huff and puff. "Let *go!* Stop it Molly!" He yanks at the urn.

My hands are beginning to cramp. "No, *you* stop it, Clarence!" I yank back harder, and win the prize.

"*Hey!*" Clarence and I jump in unison. Detective Wilson strides toward us, a wine glass in each hand. He puts them on the table and turns on Clarence, his face set hard as steel.

"What do you think you're doing?"

Jane and Bernie are racing toward us. Bernie looks fierce and is rolling up his sleeves. I turn to see Mr. Blackstone and dozens of astonished mourners staring out at us from the Passages room's floor to ceiling windows. I think my heart might burst.

"I am *Pastor* Clarence Jamison, Bob Jamison's brother. I'm here because there's work to be done on behalf of the Lord."

"Well, I'm *Detective* Jonathan Wilson. I understand that this is an extremely emotional time for everyone, but if you don't stop harassing Ms. Jamison, I'll be forced to act on behalf of the Law."

Clarence's mouth slackens, each corner drooping like an empty pouch. His Bob-eyes, at first shocked, turn thunderous. "Don't you dare threaten me."

I envision him naked in his office shed, bopping blond Mrs. Schultz and see him swinging the punch that knocked his terrified little brother out cold. I hug Bob's ashes tighter.

Detective Wilson leans in closer. "Pastor Jamison, my position requires me to stop anyone from harassing a widow at her husband's funeral."

Clarence's face is whiter than alabaster. He's shaking so hard I wonder if Bob is going to have to move over in his urn to make room for him. He stabs his finger toward me. "You haven't heard the last of this."

"For your sake, *Pastor*, I hope Ms. Jamison has indeed heard the last of this."

Clarence stomps off, his Bible clutched to his chest like a piece of armor. Detective Wilson waits until the patio door slams behind him before sitting me down. "Are you all right, Ms. Jamison?"

"I think so, thanks to you guys." No man ever defended me the way Jonathan Wilson just did.

He smiles, "You have strong arms."

"It's a good thing with Clarence around."

"I hope your other relatives aren't quite so interesting."

"Don't get me started."

Jane stands, her hands resting on my shoulders. She's trembling. "Can we get you anything, Molly?"

"I just need a minute to recover. Although, I wish I didn't have that audience." I give a discreet nod toward the windows.

Bernie says, "You did yourself proud, Molly," which makes me choke up.

"Damned right you did!" Jane says. "Sit here with Detective Wilson, Molly. Bernie and I will go inside and get people back in their seats."

"I'll let you know if the Bulldog is still around," Bernie says to Detective Wilson. Then he puts his arm around Jane as they hurry away.

Next time I glance toward the windows, I see them with Brian Blackstone and Jim Burdick, trays in hand, luring the advertising community away from the windows with Bob's favorite wines.

The wine in my glass is Bob's well-loved California Pinot Noir. I take a big slug, and then realize I'm being studied. "What is it?"

"Is he really a Pastor?"

"He has the training, the qualifications, but not the heart if you know what I mean."

"I think I do."

We sit quiet. I wonder what's in the small package he's placed next to his seat. I say, "I'll bet this memorial is a bit different than the norm."

He shrugs.

"Do you always go to memorials for people you've never met?"

His eyes inspect the trees. "Not often."

"Why are you here?"

His cheeks flush. "Memorials are for the living. You've been put through a lot."

I feel a rush of affection for this unusual man. I see him sitting at his computer in a room lit by one desk lamp, typing up a slew of clever stories, his tomato plants growing tall and strong outside on the terrace.

"Why do you think husbands betray their wives?" I blurt, tears hot in my eyes.

Detective Wilson hands me a handkerchief that's so clean and white I hate to use it. He thinks for a moment, before saying, "I think some men are so frightened and insecure they can't bear the idea of being left alone. So…they protect themselves in case their wives leave them."

"Bob paraded the two that I know of in front of me."

"Nothing that's wrong can ever turn out right. Sometimes people don't know that."

Mr. Blackstone is walking toward us. It's two o'clock. Time to go inside.

When we step into the building, I catch sight of Shirley Bills and Mary Murphy nose to nose at the end of the hallway. Shirley looks on fire, words flying, arms flapping. Mary Murphy stands like a defiant teenager—hands on hips, face hard and insolent.

People turn and smile kindly as I walk back into the Passages room. Brian Blackstone places Bob back where he was, alone in a crowd amongst the roses. Jane starts speaking from the podium about her great boss. I know her well enough to recognize that her heart is no longer quite in it.

Bernie is next, making everyone laugh with his story about the time he and Bob decided to barbeque a whole turkey outside on the grill in the dead of winter, and couldn't get the grill to heat up properly. "In the end," he said, "Bob persuaded me to help him drag the grill into the garage where the smoke almost asphyxiated us all. The sad thing is, I *knew* that would happen. Such were the persuasive powers of Bob. He was one of a kind."

I place an interested look on my face as Jim Burdick, David and Rebecca Rose, Cameron from the office, and a variety of others state their views on good guy Bob and describe fond memories. I can't listen.

•

It's almost five o'clock. I sit with Jane and Bernie and Jonathan at my table in front of Bob's display. (Jonathan and I are now on a first name basis). Jim Burdick sits at the table next to us, occasionally adding to our conversation. People are stopping by to reiterate their condolences before leaving. A subdued Shirley and the staff follow. I'm not sure where I am, but I'm not quite here. I try to stifle a yawn.

"I think it's all right if you leave too, Molly," says Jane. "Bernie and I will host until these last few diehards get out of here."

"I'll be happy to drive you home," Jim Burdick says quickly.

I stare over his shoulder. Mr. Blackstone is rushing toward us, wiping his face on a dark paisley handkerchief. "I'm so sorry to intrude. There's been a terrible accident right outside the gates. It's Ms. Mary Murphy," he babbles. "She was alone and inconsolable and tore out of here sobbing. A city bus rammed her. She's pinned inside of her car."

I think: *Pinned!*

Jonathan is on his feet. He thrusts the small package at me. "This is for you, Molly."

Jonathan, Jim and Mr. Blackstone rush away.

Jane says, "Jesus! I thought Mary left ages ago."

"Me too." It occurs to me that Bob's extra curricular women are both blonds. I wonder if they look anything like the treacherous Mrs. Schultz that Clarence bopped for years.

The room has emptied, the diehards making a beeline for the crash scene.

"I can't face this." I say. "I'm going home."

"Let us drive you," says Bernie. But I can tell that he's dying to see what's going on outside.

"No need, I have my car. You guys have been great. Maybe you can do something out there."

Bernie brightens. Jane gives him a don't-you-dare look that he blithely ignores. "I wouldn't mind seeing what's going on," he admits. "Maybe I can help."

"Accounting is so dull it does this to people," says Jane, giving him a dig.

I hug them both and smile. "Get rolling. We can talk tomorrow."

I sit for a few minutes on the Passages room patio, giving the emergency services ballyhoo a chance to slow down before driving past the gates. I've failed to conjure up much sympathy for Mary, the latest woman to lance my heart. I imagine Jim Burdick telling her to stay calm while emergency crews look for ways to get her unpinned. Jonathan stands beside him, notepad in hand. He's licking the end of his pencil before committing words to paper. He is reassuring Mary that she's doing fine. Even though it's mean, I can't help thinking that so long as she landed on her ass, she'll be okay. I take another taste of wine and a final scope of the gardens before groaning to my feet.

My mother whispers, "This too shall pass."

I trail indoors, my purse slung over my shoulder and Jonathan's parcel under one arm. In the Passages room I stand before the display table. Silence testifies to my husband's abandonment. Bob is in his urn, forlorn and alone, nobody pandering to his ego, the worst of his fears come true.

Alone myself, I drive past the crowd around the crash site. I wonder if Mary is my second victim. I think: Why did I start this? Where is it leading? When will it end?

14

Our driveway winds a graceful path through the stretch of woods that is our front yard. I drive slowly, watching for birds, rabbits, squirrels and chipmunks. The house still surprises me. It looms large and appears without warning after a sharp curve. Wrapped in silvery-green cedar siding, topped with an elegant slate roof, it looks comfortable on its three-acre lot. This is the dream home Bob wanted. Now it's my haven.

I press the garage door opener and sit mesmerized as the door rolls smoothly upward. Once inside the garage, my two-seater with its shiny wire wheels feels like a matchbox car. Lying back against the headrest, I give an enormous moan. My anger simmers, but there's something else at work—something I can't quite put my finger on. It feels like a living thing snaking around in my stomach, tightening up my chest, making my throat hurt and my bones burn.

A stiff drink is needed. At the bar, I take out a bottle of chilled vodka and take a swig, and then another. I open the doors and sit at the kitchen table. Bird squawks and earth smells drift into the room, refreshing it with bit of life.

I wonder what Voodoo Priestess Marie Laveau's funeral was like. A colorful affair, I imagine, filled with Voodoo and Roman Catholic rituals. Priests and practitioners no doubt called upon their shared saints and ancestral spirits in front of thousands of her followers.

Pastor Clarence wouldn't have dared mess with her choices. If he had told her, "You haven't heard the last of this," he would soon find out that indeed, she had.

Lucky for Pastor Clarence there will be no more Voodoo dolls in my life.

After making myself a large tuna salad sandwich, I fill a tall glass with iced water and settle myself at the island. It's the first food I've had since breakfast. I eat as if starved.

Jonathan's package remains where it was dropped—right in front of me. Just looking at it makes me feel nervous. What is in there? At first, I wondered if he'd given me a copy of his book, but then remembered what he said about the publishing date being months away. This is definitely not his novel. Finally, I hold it next to my ear, shake it, sniff it, and then tell myself to stop acting stupid and just get it opened. I rip the paper wide apart.

A black cardboard box sporting an Old Town's Spiritual Magic Shop seal lies unveiled. I hear my shocked gasp, feel a rush of adrenalin, and say out loud in a choked voice, *"What the…what is…oh, my God?"* I run fearful fingers across the seal a few times before daring to break it open.

Beneath black tissue paper smiles a Voodoo doll, a

beautiful female with wild black hair and round green eyes. Her face looks familiar. Pinned to the front of her blood-red silk robe is a hand written note in blue ink on yellow, lined paper.

Dear Ms. Jamison,

I hope you like this doll. She reminds me of you. I've been on this street and never noticed this store before. She was in the window. You said you've been struggling with writing. Perhaps she will bring you good fortune.

Best wishes,
Jonathan Wilson

When I lift out the doll, I'm shaking like mad. Is this a game? Is he doing this to unnerve me? Does he know what I did to Bob?

At Bob's memorial, did I get him wrong?

15

I stand in white cotton pajamas stretching my arms toward overcast skies. A filmy cloud of mist appears suspended in front of the trees, wrapping the world beyond in a silvery haze. Bob's memorial was a bit of a fiasco, I think, not sure that I actually believe it. I wonder what happened to Mary. For all I know she's dead too, a second pinning come to fruition. I shudder and step back into the kitchen. The house is colorful and uncluttered. Jonathan Wilson said that it fits me. It probably does. Bob left the decorating up to me. "Do your magic," he said, never imagining that one day I would. My eyes avoid my neat desk and the laptop that waits to receive brilliant prose spilling from lazy fingertips. I pour fresh coffee and pad back toward the chaise longue.

I am about to call Jane when the phone rings. "How are you doing?" she asks.

"Considering yesterday's craziness, not too bad. Is Mary all right? Have you heard?"

She sighs, "Well, it appears that despite being a cow, Mary's got the constitution of an ox."

"She's okay then?" I say dully, trying not to feel ungenerous.

"Yes, but she was injured. Pinned so tight she had to be cut out of her car. Blood everywhere. She needed a transfusion.

"That sounds really awful," I say, feeling a sudden smidgen of shame.

"Apparently, her leg injury looked a lot worse than it was."

"So all she needed was a transfusion to put things right?"

"More or less. By the way, that lovely detective was a godsend. You never told me how attractive that man is."

"I hadn't really noticed," I stammer.

"He likes you, Molly," she says, gently.

"Can we *please* get back to Round Bottom's predicament?" I ask primly.

She laughs, and then turns serious. "Well, I think you'll appreciate that it got pretty interesting out there. It turns out, Mary has O negative blood, which is quite rare."

My heart leaps so hard, my eyes lose focus. It was *Mary's* blood on Bob's jockey shorts? *Not* Shirley's? My brain labors to grasp what I just heard. "Really?"

"I overheard Mary telling Jim Burdick and the paramedics to alert the local hospital's ER doctors. Imagine the problems a lack of O negative blood presents. It's the only blood her body accepts."

I'm too dazed to say much. "Riiiiiight."

Jane pauses for dramatic effect, "Of course, I told the paramedics that Shirley Bills has O negative blood too, and that if they needed any extra for Mary, I was sure that Shirley would be happy to donate a pint or two."

"They both have O negative blood!" My pulse pumps like it belongs on the Hoover Dam.

"You know, it's a good thing I came up with that suggestion, Molly. Shirley got the hospital's call for blood while driving home."

"Oh-my-God! What did she say?"

"What *could* she say, Molly?" Jane pauses, and we both burst out laughing, her hoots practically deafening me. "She said *yes!*"

I conjure up the picture of Shirley receiving the O-negative-blood call, her face frozen into a dopey stare.

Jane carries on. "So, Mary will be in the hospital for a few days; whereas, Shirley will be coming back to the office a couple of pounds lighter."

"This is unbelievable," I whisper, imagining them pinned together like two-for-the-price-of-one sale items.

"Yet, it's *true,*" says Jane, with relish.

My mouth blurts, "I have a confession to make."

There's a short silence. "You didn't…um…*persuade* a certain bus driver to shoot his empty bus toward a certain car, did you?" She sounds like she actually wants to be horrified.

I hesitate, picturing my fateful pinnings. "Of course not."

"What then?"

"After your imaginings it doesn't sound like much. I just happened to let drop into Shirley's ear that Mary was having an affair with Bob."

"Oh-my-God!"

"And then I saw the two of them having some kind of confrontation in the hall."

"Oh-my-God!"

"So I suspect they found out about each other right then and there."

I can almost hear Jane's brain ticking through the phone. Finally, she says, "She and Mary won't want to work together on Murphy's Landscaping, not after discovering they've been taken for fools waiting for Bob to leave you. Then there's the additional humiliation of the O negative blood give and take. It's negative all the way with those two."

"That's true."

"AND, Shirley isn't likely to talk about this again in case she opens up her own can of worms with you. She needs time to steal more accounts."

"It's worked out okay, all things considered," I murmur.

"This is better than a goddamn movie."

We sit for a while in companionable silence. We've known each other for years. After all of this time, I know when she's smiling.

"It's Labor Day Weekend, three days of R & R. Come stay with us, Molly."

"Thanks, Jane, but I really need time alone to think."

She sighs. "You know what to do if you change your mind."

For the rest of the day, I lie in a hammock beneath the trees, admiring flashes of sky glimpsed through trembling leaves, breathing in the last sweet smells of summer. I like what I did at Bob's memorial, and want to feel like this more often. It took courage to tackle Clarence.

I want a steady stream of courage journeying through my system, stirring blood, improving circulation, strengthening organs and muscle, chipping pieces off my own brittle cinder and ridding me of them. I want courage to fill all newly opened areas with a warm, not too rigid metal, like old silver, its rich patina aglow with a beauty that shines from within.

Grandmother comes up behind me. "One day, Molly, you'll have a metamorphosis," she whispers, "and you'll become a magical woman."

My Magic Molly doll poses on the windowsill, her red robe flaring out around her feet. Our eyes meet and hold. "Get me through this difficult time," I tell her, "and make sure I never have to go through anything like it again."

16

M onday, a week and a half after Bob's memorial, Bernie is sitting across from me in what was once Bob's office. Above his head hangs Bob's framed "Land is for the Living" poster that consists of a large red circle with a red line angled across it, behind which lies an ocean view cemetery filled with huge headstones and elaborate monuments. After suffering a few jabs of guilt while clearing out his stuff, I felt it necessary to keep this one thing on view. The rest of Bob's personal belongings—a large, silver framed photo of me sitting at the patio table (no doubt, so that his clients could see his fine house), a black-framed photo of him and Clarence glaring into the camera, and a heavy glass paperweight shaped like the John Hancock Building—are packed up in a box in our garage at home.

"Due to our time constraints, it's not as complete as it could be, but it's still a pretty good overview considering what we're looking for." Bernie lovingly pats his audit report, as only an accountant would.

"So the books look okay, except for a couple of odd trade-outs?"

"Yup. As suspected, Drake's Jewelers is the biggest puzzle. The jeweler gave Bob thousands of dollars of merchandise for an equal amount of free advertising—no problem there. But, there are a few high-priced pieces of jewelry that show up on the store's receipts. It appears odd that an agency would hand any client diamonds, no matter how much business they bring to the agency."

"We know who's wearing them," I mutter.

Bernie nods. "You can make a case for their return, Molly. Technically, Shirley doesn't legally own them."

I picture ripping the diamond earrings out of her ears. I envision myself wielding a machete, chopping off the third finger of her right hand and watching it land on the floor. It lies in its circle of O negative blood, and floats around like a diamond-studded log.

"Pick your battles." My grandmother speaks so loudly into my left ear I think Bernie must have surely heard her. Instead, he keeps on talking like nothing happened.

"So far as Sarah's Steak House goes, there's been a steady stream of trading services. Restaurant receipts show a lot of agency/client meals, but it's easy to insert any client's name on any receipt, whether or not they were present. Even if he took Shirley, which he often did, it can be argued that they were having executive meetings off site and away from staff."

"True."

He leans closer, his round face sweetly earnest. "Bob was

a savvy businessman, Molly. He made very few missteps. This is good for you. In fact, that condo in the Hancock Building he bought a few years ago is worth a small fortune, and it's paid for." He's staring at my gaping mouth. "Molly, what's wrong?" He stands up and leans over the desk. "You're white as a ghost." He's pouring water. "You didn't know the agency owns a condo?"

"Shirley lives in the Hancock Building."

Bernie has called Jane in. Now two worried faces stare at me from across the desk. I'm holding up Bob's key chain and hearing it jangle. "Well, now we know where this odd key goes. He gave that heifer my dream, and had me slide my accounts into his agency so that he could pay for it." I picture my internal cinder on fire and blazing. I'm shaking with fury.

"At least she doesn't have a balcony," mutters Bernie. "There are none in that building."

"And she probably lives next door to Jerry Springer," adds Jane.

"But she's at least forty-four floors up, because that's where the condo level starts," I say in a choked voice. "Imagine the views."

We stew in silence for a while. I make a note to take down Bob's "Land is for the Living" poster.

"Does she pay rent?" I ask.

Bernie looks stricken. "I thought you guys probably used it after a night on the town, or for out of town clients."

"In other words," I say in a voice that scares me, "she pays *nothing.*"

Jane says, "Prize fighters are always told to stay calm, Molly, or they'll lose focus. Make mistakes and lose the fight. You once said we're not going to lose this one, and we're not."

"Where is she right now?" I growl.

"She's still avoiding you."

"How does she manage that?" asks Bernie.

"Since Molly first sat behind that desk, Shirley's used every excuse imaginable to stay out of the office, even though we're swamped. While waiting for the audit results, we've had days of doctor and dental appointments, a dead uncle's funeral, and her caring for an elderly sick aunt, as if she would. More likely, she's been frantically setting up her new business, working on her stolen accounts, and wondering when she'll be found out."

"She's scared, so she's playing the 'how can I be fired if I'm never there' game," Bernie says. "If she's pressed for cash, she needs to keep her salary coming in until she's financially prepared to make her move."

"God knows what she's plotting while she waits." I pick up the phone. "But I bet she'll stop whatever she's doing to run over for a meeting with Alex Fox if he asks her to."

Bernie has his fingers in his ears. "I'm not hearing this," he sings.

•

Jane and I stand outside of Shirley's forty-fourth floor condo. Bob's key chain rattles as I try to fit the key in the lock.

"I can't believe we're doing this," hisses Jane in a

dramatic voice, looking up and down the corridor like a well-dressed thief.

"Alex said he'll keep her busy for about an hour."

"You could just give her the legal twenty-four hours notice on getting in. You're her landlady for God's sake."

"We have no lease, so she's an unwanted guest. Besides, a twenty-four hour warning would give her time to hide stuff."

The door swings open and there it is. "A bachelorette pad in pink," Jane snorts.

The condo is smaller than I expected, but neat as a pin. She would have had to keep it immaculate to please Bob. Evidently, the habit stuck. There's a living room/dining room, two bathrooms, a galley kitchen, and two bedrooms. We're standing in the doorway of her fancy-schmancy boudoir. I now suspect that there were no O-K Hotel nooners for her. Princess Shirley entertained my husband right here in this powder-pink apartment, in this flounced, king size bed.

"Don't look at it," says Jane, reading my mind.

I raise my eyes to the windows that frame wonderful city views. "At least she doesn't have full on views of the lake," I say, weakly.

Her home office in the second bedroom looks surprisingly professional, albeit painted shocking pink and containing pastel-pink ornate furniture with gold scrollwork, just as I imagined. Her white filing cabinets are two drawers tall and run along a short wall. Above them hangs a poster-size photograph of Shirley and Bob, arms around each other grinning like clowns.

"I'll start here." Jane whips open the bottom drawer and

starts flipping through the files.

I force myself to tackle the desk.

Jane says, "No Murphy's Landscaping file. But, here's Drake's Jewelers and Sarah's Steak House." She shoves their folders back down. "She's got more balls than a pool hall."

I gasp. "Here's *City Gardener's* folder.*"

We both start pulling out desk drawers, making sure to leave them as tidy as we found them.

"Here's the agency's client list."

We stare in amazement at the check marks Shirley has placed against a dozen or so of our accounts.

"She's still targeting smaller clients," Jane says.

"She has to. She's not yet set up to handle big ones."

My cell phone rings. It's Alex. "Hi Molly. All hell has broken loose over here. It's a deadline crunch. Shirley just left."

"Thanks Alex. I owe you one."

Jane stands wide-eyed. "Jesus. She'll be here in no time at all."

"We should have about ten minutes."

"Look at this." Jane pulls out a short stack of folders hidden beneath the desk. On top is Rose Manufacturing. "This one's not so small."

I snatch the folder away from her and stare at it in disbelief. "David and Rebecca would have told me if she tried to pitch them. I like to think they all would. She's still just strategizing, looking for inroads, preparing proposals, or whatever."

I want Shirley to suffer a pin death like her partner in crime Bob did. I envision her Voodoo doll's pinnings and transfer them to her head. I picture her shocked face as blood spurts up and out of her scalp like water through a pulsating showerhead.

"There's half-a-dozen more, Molly."

"Let me see."

Jane checks her watch. "We gotta get out of here."

Into my large black carrier bag go *City Gardener's* folder and the stack of files from under Shirley's desk. We straighten up her desktop before rushing for the door. We run along the corridor in our high heels and suit skirts like we're losing our minds, and land in front of the elevators in seconds. After an excruciating wait, we grab the residents' private elevator and shoot toward the ground floor.

In the lobby, we catch sight of Shirley scurrying toward the building's entrance. "Don't watch her," whispers Jane, "If she sees us we'll act surprised and say we've been up to the 95th floor for lunch." We manage to slink along the walls unseen as she flies past us.

Outside, we stop in an outdoor café for a glass of wine to calm our nerves. Jane says, 'Picture her face when she realizes she's lost the agency's files.'

And we laugh so hard people around us smile.

17

Jim Burdick has been turning my avoidance of him into a game, leaving a friendly message each time he phones, no doubt expecting that his cheerful persistence will eventually get through to me. Last week's appeal was: "Hey Moll, it's Jim. Don't make me send you a questionnaire and a SASE to find out how you're doing. Talk to me!"

Yet, I don't really want Jim in my life, especially after all that's happened. Even though I've known him for years, he was Bob's friend, and he always acted warmly toward Mary Murphy and Shirley Bills at our house parties. This thought alone is enough to make me want to take up residence under the carpet. Whenever I imagine his heroics at Mary's pinning, I feel doubly mortified. I picture him helping the paramedics edge her out of her crunched car and into the ambulance, sitting next to her all the way to the hospital, holding her hand, stroking her forehead, and whispering treacherous words, such as, "I'll have you fixed up in no time at all."

I bet he even greeted Shirley Bills in the ER to soothe away her fear of needles while he sprinted her toward Mary's room for the blood letting. I imagine him hooking the two women together with a long clear tube, and then watching the transference of O negative blood while sitting between them like a referee.

Granted, Jim had no choice but to offer aid and comfort to the enemy; he's a doctor after all. Even so, I don't want him ingratiating himself onto me. I just wish his gentle ribbing didn't make me feel quite so mean-spirited and guilty.

I think about this now as I step out of the shower and once more see his name displayed on my caller ID. I sigh and pick up the receiver. I do this even as the clock ticks away vital minutes, and despite developing a sudden light-headedness after my innards slide about for no apparent reason.

"Hey Moll, I'm so glad you answered," he says. "How are you? I hope you're not still hibernating."

"I've been working for almost two weeks." I'm impatient, wondering what he really wants.

"I'd like to help out if I can. You've been through so much, Moll."

I think: You probably know exactly how much. But I say, "I'm really sorry, Jim, this isn't a good time to talk. I have to be downtown Chicago by nine and I still have to get ready."

"My fault, Molly, I should have asked if you have time to catch up." His voice smiles his apology, wanting to put me at ease. "What if I call you back in a couple of days? Will that work?"

Instead of telling him that I'm too busy, or whatever, I freeze, struck for the first time about how much Jim cares about me. In the midst of this confusion, I turn polite. "That would be great, Jim. Thanks."

After I put the phone down, I groan.

•

Dressed in my black silk suit, new black pumps and white silk tee, I settle behind the wheel for the drive to the office. Bob's BMW's engine growls as I maneuver the driveway's sensuous curves. Rain patters on the windshield. Tree branches and ferns with leaves brightened by the shower toss and sway in the wind. Turning onto the street, I set off for the expressway, my nerves hopping.

Crossing the bridge over I-94, I see that the expressway houses bumper-to-bumper traffic. At the bottom of the on-ramp, I squeeze in behind an enormous, brown SUV, inch the car forward, and turn up the radio as Mick Jagger launches into "Ruby Tuesday," my favorite Rolling Stones song. Tapping out the beat with my left foot, wishing that I were bombing along in my stick-shift Spitfire instead of Bob's big boat of a car, I inhale like an opera diva and power up my voice for a loud and liberating sing-along.

Together, Mick and I fire out the warning, *"Don't question why …"* "Yeah!" I shout, my head waving back and forth to the music. Ruby's freedom is *never* negotiable. "Damn right!" I yell, my fist raised up to pound the air.

Getting ready for the high notes in the chorus, I take in another huge breath, at the same time turning see when it might be safe to switch lanes. With over-the–top enthusiasm, Mick and I holler out our passionate homage to Ruby, a Voodoo Woman who is completely unstoppable. *"Goodbye…"*

Still checking out the best time to move into the center lane, I glance into the car edging along next to me, and meet Jonathan Wilson's amused stare. He waves.

Agape in horror, I realize that he must have been watching me singing my head off, acting more like a merry widow than a grieving one. Cheeks burning, I turn off the music before giving him a stiff, regal wave back.

There are over nine million people in the Chicago metropolitan area. How have I managed to get stuck in traffic next to *him*? He beeps his horn and motions for me to ease my car in front of his. Then he drives behind me until I turn off at Ohio Street, still groaning in mortification over my own bad luck.

•

At the office entrance, the door swings open before my hand makes contact. On the other side, dressed in a tight suit and white frilly blouse, Shirley greets me with a nervous, "How are you this morning?"

"Surprisingly well."

I smile at our receptionist, Keisha, who gives me a sly thumbs-up sign.

"All of the files for the clients I'm currently working with are now here," Shirley says as we walk through to the conference room. "They're completely up-to-date. A couple of clients have promotions in the works, but I'm on top of them."

My eyes rest on the long black credenza. Arranged on the end of it, two mugs of fresh coffee steaming on a stainless steel tray indicate that she trusted me to walk in on time. She wants to impress me.

Parking myself at the head of Bob's enormous teak conference table, I gaze out of floor-to-ceiling windows at sheeting rain. In the midst of the downpour, Chicago's skyscrapers, filled with florescent light, give off a dull, watery glow. Beyond them, Lake Michigan's stormy gray waters meld perfectly with the sky. I picture Vancouver's wet weather and coastal beauty, and a pang of sadness catches me. After spending virtually half of my life in each city, neither place feels like home.

I say, "Let's start with those promotions."

Shirley places a coffee in front of me and settles herself in the chair to my right, her breasts resting on the table like a pair of snow cones. She begins to arrange her folders and papers. Staring down the length of the table, I picture the two of them going at it like rabbits, right on the spot where the polish looks a bit rubbed off. Glancing over at her, I marvel at her seasoned brazenness, her complete lack of shame. She's become smarmy and solicitous around me. Perhaps she imagines that I need her so much I'll dismiss all memory of those sly, pale eyes and triumphant smiles. I wouldn't put it past her to insist that her no-rent condo arrangement was merely a company vice president perk, an agreed to part of her salary.

She takes in air and begins her recital, reading from a bound presentation with her name on it. It's been put together by her account executive, Cameron. "When I left at eight last night, he was still sorting through files and adding details," Jane reported. "He did it all, Molly. Shirley closed her office door and told him to get on with it. She told him he must have lost the missing files. You can imagine how relieved he was when I handed them to him. So, everything is there now. Shirley must be scratching her head over that."

Cameron joined the company right out of college two years ago and was assigned to Shirley's team by Bob. He's exactly the kind of person we need to keep, an upright man who wouldn't have known a thing about her secret sabotaging when he worked hours of overtime to save her ass. I doubt he thinks much of her. I make a mental note to give him a bonus.

Shirley starts off with her authority-laden voice that carries a satisfying, nervous shake. "The Lakeview Heart Center is sponsoring the Chicago Heart Run next year. They want to give away a few free heart scans and other stuff. They also want to set up a large tent and a big screen so that they can show everyone how their brand new, state-of-the-art equipment works, and to remind people that heart scans are painless procedures."

A dark, half moon sweat stain is growing under her left arm. "We're working on their media buy—radio and TV ads leading in, and print ads right before the event," she says, holding up a folder and inhaling like a heavy smoker. "Then we have the Dixon Auto Group. They're doing a major tie in with Children's Hospital and WGN to promote childhood cancer awareness. They're considering raffling off one of their small cars—a mini, or a VW or something like that—to raise money. We're still figuring out all of the angles with the station rep on that one."

"Do you have media proposals pending on other accounts?"

"A few. I've put them in a separate pile."

"Are you up to date with everything?" I ask, picturing her sitting behind her closed office door last night, planning her strategies, plotting for a big win over our ruination.

"All except the Dixon promotion. Cameron's a tiny bit behind on that."

"Is there anything at all that needs our immediate, close attention?" I snap, annoyed that she's taken a swipe at young Cameron.

She stares straight ahead, her face contorted with the effort of studying. I imagine her brain heating up and giving off the odor of burning wood. I check for smoke rings in the vicinity of her ears.

I pick up the phone and ring Keisha in reception. "Are we all set out there?"

"They're here," she says.

"I'm doing well keeping up on my accounts," Shirley brags, taking all of the credit for Cameron's work. She glances at me from the sides of her eyes. "I'm not sure about how Jane is doing." She pokes through the last couple of files. "She's so tight-lipped about her comings and goings; it makes me wonder if she's in a little bit over her head and has something to hide."

I reach across the table and slide the papers out from under her fingers. "Do you think Jane is working the accounts that left the agency over the past month?" I say. "Are you suggesting that Jane is guilty of doing things that are, in fact, illegal? Should I not be making Jane my new vice president?"

"Huh?" Her mouth opens and closes.

"From this point on, Shirley, your services are no longer needed."

"What?" Her eyes dart to the door, as if she expects Bob to rush in like the cavalry and save her. "You're upset," she sputters. "You can't just fire me. You need me right now. You need me to keep this place open."

"I don't think so."

"I won't stand for this."

"What is it you do stand for, Shirley?"

Her eyes flash a flicker of fear. Then she leans closer, her expression hard. Paid for in lines and wrinkles, the heavy cost of her year-round tan shows all over her face. "I'm warning you now," she hisses. "Don't do this."

It's all I can do to keep my hands off her. "You will receive a generous—under the circumstances—one month severance package. Unless, of course, you choose not to accept it."

"One month," she echoes, sounding aghast, her eyebrows arching high. "You can't do this."

"You are advised to avoid any further pilfering of my agency's accounts," I say, like an attorney. "Further, you have one month to get out of the John Hancock Building condo, unless you're prepared to buy it from the agency immediately, at market price." I get to my feet. "Either way, my real estate representatives will inspect it at this time tomorrow, which gives you twenty-four hours notice to make it look like new."

"No way!" she rasps, loudly.

"You are advised to do this without issue," I shoot back. Then I walk over to the door and open it up to reveal two uniformed men from the building's security department.

"Before you're escorted out, Shirley, please leave your office keys, company credit card, and electronic garage key with Keisha. Your company car keys must also be handed over. Aside from your purse and coat, all other personal belongings will be packaged up and mailed out to you this afternoon. The company's lawyers will contact you later today about the necessary legal paperwork."

She stands facing me, sweat shining on her brow. I think that this too is part of her pinning.

"You can bill the company for your cab fare home, should you prefer to not walk a couple of blocks." I fail to conceal a tiny smile, just as I did the day Bernie told me that my company owns the lease on her car.

"You haven't heard the end of this!" she squeaks, so that nobody but me can hear.

"By the way," I purr, just as quietly, "aside from the stolen accounts, I don't suppose you want to reimburse me for that diamond ring and the earrings you like to show off to me, since it appears I own them too. And let's not forget the glorious sympathy bouquet you sent me, by express delivery no less. My accountant says there's probably a lot more. I just have to say the word and he'll dig for it."

"I'll sue you to death if you try and mess with me."

"You'll lose." I lift up her signed non-compete form, found stuffed in a file under her home office desk.

Her eyes pop. "Where did you find that?"

"That's an odd question, since we have personnel files."

She storms past me in the manner of Pastor Clarence. The security guards hold her purse and coat, which they hand to her as they walk her out. At the front desk, she throws down her credit card and keys. Within seconds, she's gone.

18

ate September sunshine skips across the lawn and through the patio doors, landing in a pool at my feet. A thick slice of hot toast oozes butter as I spread a heavy coat of marmalade on top. Two perfect days to write lie ahead, an entire weekend unmarred by the need to catch up on agency work, or do housework, or grocery ordering, or anything at all. Yet, I want to go back to bed and pull the covers over my head.

My laptop computer lies idle on the desk, its very presence a depressing testament to my laziness. Mostly, I use it to check on e-mails, or to work on company business, or to see if a new movie or play can tempt me away from the house, even though I don't want to go anywhere, in fact, won't go, which also seems lazy.

I work like a fiend at the agency, yet worry that wanting to be alone at home staying somewhat idle can become an addiction. Will I end up wild haired and woolly, asking myself pointless questions and then answering them? I imagine myself as a hermit shuffling and muttering my way through my derelict house, wearing grubby clothes that float in tatters about me. Surely, people who end up like that start out with a day of laziness here, a day of pointlessness there, until their days run together all the same.

I stick the last crust of toast in my mouth, swig down the last inch of orange juice, and rise to my feet. I can use my desire for solitude in better ways than this. Having placed the last of my old business in the hands of the agency's creative department, I no longer write for advertisers. The days of mulling over ways to get large marketing messages compressed into sixty-second time slots are over. Wide-open weekends like this one give me the opportunity to focus on a streamlined writing career. I need to force myself to stop being lazy, and get busy.

I'm sitting at the computer when the phone rings. It's Brian Blackstone. Surely I paid for everything?

"I'm afraid I've just discovered some distressing news," he says.

"Distressing news?" I echo, in a voice tinged with dread.

"Our new temp made a terrible mistake, which of course I take full responsibility for since I hired—"

"What's wrong?" A fit of panic overtakes me. Bob is back, his energy refusing to die.

"Your husband's ashes were left behind after his memorial. Unfortunately, our new temp mistakenly packaged them up with your CDs and photographs and mailed them to you. It's outrageous, I know. I'm so sorry. So very sorry."

My eyes scan the kitchen and family room as if expecting to find Bob's ashes resting on the mantelpiece, or the kitchen table, or the stovetop, or the desk. I say, "I don't have them. Where are they?" But I think: How have I forgotten to bring Bob home? I'm supposed to have scattered him all around our trees by now. What is the matter with me? I shake my head wondering if I forgot him on purpose.

"It's been brought to my attention that we never received a receipt for your husband's delivery, so I can only imagine they're, um…" He inhales loudly. "What I'm saying is that I don't have them here, and you don't have them there, sooooo…" He tapers off slowly and deliberately, as though he cannot bear to utter the words needed for my enlightenment.

The horror of what he means sweeps over me. "Are you saying that my husband has been lost in the *mail* for the last month?" I picture Bob sitting in his urn, his arms braced against the sides as postal workers toss him about willy-nilly.

"Well, I wouldn't put it quite like that," he huffs.

"How would you put it?" I demand, looking for ways to put him at fault. I envision him sitting comfortably in his grand office, elegantly suited up in his expensive funeral attire, his long feet propped up on the edge of his rosewood desk, his bleak eyes following the intricate design on his red Persian carpet seeking out the mistake that's been deliberately woven into it. Mr. Blackstone is like the grim weaver, a mere human, a man who never insults God by presuming to be perfect.

"Well, we've already placed a tracer on the package. Of course, we told the post office representative that it contains your husband's personal effects." Clearing his throat, he adds nervously, "We didn't mention his ashes."

Preferring to remain ignorant of the law, I stop myself from asking if it's legal to send a dead person through the U.S. mail—whether or not he was mailed out by mistake. Brian Blackstone's ashes catastrophe must remain his business. He'll have to accept the consequences. After all, he lost the damn things. I just forgot about them.

"What does the post office representative think happened to the package?" I say in my mother's sternest voice.

"He said that it could have been addressed incorrectly. You know how people like to blame others for their own mistakes."

Like I just did, I think with a splash of guilt. But I say, "What about the return address? Why didn't they just return it to you if it was undeliverable?"

"Well," he laments, "The temp swears he used a Blackstone's label, but if he didn't there would have been no return address on the package."

"Oh my God!" I clutch my throat. "What happens then? They wouldn't just chuck the package out, would they?"

I picture myself throwing Bob Doll's ashy remains into the garbage can under the kitchen sink after the Mount Everest incident and my fiery "Spell for Satisfying the Soul" performance. I see a post office truck rocking and rolling down pot-holed streets. Bob stands inside his urn like a hamster in a cage, running every which way just to stay upright. I put my hand over my eyes, hoping to block out the picture of him lying on his back in a post office dumpster, awaiting delivery to his final resting place—the local garbage dump in Bumblefuck, USA.

It occurs to me that Mr. Blackstone has avoided

answering my question. Pressing the phone hard against my head so as to hear any peep that comes out of him, I say, "Are you still there?" A long, reluctant sigh sounding light years away sneaks into my ear. "What will happen to the package if it has no return address, Mr. Blackstone?"

He inhales and exhales as if he's taking his last few gasps of air in this world. "It will probably go to the dead letter office," he mumbles.

Silence hangs in the air as we ponder this possibility. A titter lurks in my chest, and rises to my throat. I have to wait until I can safely speak.

"What are the chances of us finding him there?"

"The representative said that it *can* happen."

"It *can* happen?" I pray that Pastor Clarence never finds out about this. "It sounds like he was suggesting that Bob is buried somewhere in the dead letter office and might never be found."

"I prefer to think that Mr. Jamison *will indeed* be found."

I picture him wiping sweat from his brow with his silk paisley handkerchief, and feel ashamed at my impatience. I gentle my tone. "Is there anything at all that we can do now?"

"I'm afraid not, Ms. Jamison. All that can be done is being done. I'm so terribly sorry." He sounds close to tears.

"I'm sorry too, Mr. Blackstone. I didn't mean to sound so unkind. After all, I should have remembered to bring him home in the first place."

"Funerals are stressful times, Ms. Jamison."

"I suppose we just have to hope for the best," I say. And then, because I'm not thinking fast enough to stop myself, I add, "Please keep me posted."

•

"Oh my God!" gasps Jane. "Tell me you didn't."

"I did. I left him right there in his urn on that altar table with the rest of our stuff."

She groans. "Bernie and I were the last to leave the Passages room. Neither one of us thought of Bob's ashes. If we'd even remembered to ask you about The Scattering, it would have jogged your memory."

"It's not your fault. It's mine."

"You were stressed out. Bob's memorial was crazy enough, but then there was the crash. It was all too much for you."

"I have to wonder if it was one of those Freudian slips. If Brian Blackstone hadn't phoned, I might never have remembered. Ever! Think of it! It's ridiculous."

"It's an understandable mistake," she says emphatically.

"Can you imagine what Pastor Bulldog will do if he finds out?"

She snorts. "There's nothing he can do. If the ashes are gone, they're gone."

"Too true," says Grandmother from overhead.

"Just get on with your life," Jane urges. "Don't worry about this. You've done your best. It will have to be enough."

I put down the phone and sit still in the quiet. Mr. Suave and Debonair is lost in the mail. I rest my head on my arms to hide the wickedest of smiles.

•

Tonight I have another dream. Wearing my black robe,

I fly above a winding road keeping pace with the deep purple taxi speeding along below. Mohammed grasps the steering wheel, his expression stern. Behind him, dressed in blood-red silk, sits Voodoo Priestess Marie from the Old Town's Spiritual Magic Shop. Mom and Grandmother are with her.

When the road dead-ends against the beach, Mohammed carefully parks the car. His three passengers climb out and step in unison onto white sands. It is high tide. At the water's edge they examine Bob's open, empty urn. They look out to sea as he unwittingly body surfs toward them atop crashing waves. A wisp of a woman in a red polka dot bikini swims beside him. It's Shirley.

At the sight of the grim trio waiting at the shore, she manages to paddle away. But the ocean's contrary current conveniently launches him into the shallows to land in a heap at their feet. Mom and Grandmother stand like sentinels on either side of the fierce Voodoo Priestess, who holds his open urn out to him. Like a genie returning to a bottle, he dissolves into a river of ash and spins in circles back to his urn.

I think he's in Australia.

19

After arriving at seven o' clock on the dot, I've waited in the middle booth at Woodside's elegant Zeno's restaurant for twelve minutes. The tuxedoed maitre d' glows with pleasure at the sight of me, the good doctor's new guest is deemed most welcome—which makes me wonder if Jim has a habit of parading women past him. A selection of arias from *La Boheme* plays softly through the restaurant's artfully camouflaged speakers, Luciano Pavarotti's voice raising an ache under my ribs. All around me, couples sit under dimmed Italian sconces, holding designer martinis, red wines, or other colorful drinks in beautiful glasses, candlelight flickering romance across their smitten faces, defining my aloneness sharp as a pinprick. Warm currents of air waft away from trays of food carried on the shoulders of hustling waiters, sending the aromas of garlic and warm bread to torment my nose, making me ravenous. I sit like an angry, shrinking, sad sack in the middle of it all, my foot tapping at high speed.

I inhale a long, slow breath, expanding my lungs as far as I can, wanting to untangle the painful knot surrounding them. My gut feels raw. I sense the nameless, slippery thing that hides amongst interior shadows, daring me to catch it. Straightening my little black dress, I wish I'd worn something vivid and flowing, like my new red skirt with the handkerchief hemline, and a purple, off the shoulder blouse. Then I could swoosh out in regal fashion.

I never should have agreed to meet Jim in the first place, especially since Zeno's is such a romantic and expensive restaurant. But Wednesday afternoon, after dropping in at the house with his arms full of pale, yellow roses, he finally won me over. "Hi, Molly." He smiled, his puppy dog eyes melting away the niggling spot of worry that hit me when I first opened the door to him. "These are for the most beautiful woman I know."

My teeth clamp down on themselves. Part of me always springs a sliver of fear whenever I find another of Jim's friendly e-mails or receive one of his funny, chatty phone calls that used to end with, "I care about you, Molly. Please let me know what I can do to help." More recently, he's pressured me to get out of the house, "I'm just talking about two old friends having a pleasant night out, Molly. That's all. It's time for you to get out and live a little." Looking into his handsome, happy face over the glow of yellow roses, I finally dismissed my reluctance as unfair. Jim is a doting family friend; why shouldn't I have dinner with him?

"You have beautiful hair." The waiter pours water, smiling as he flirts.

"Thanks."

"How about a Zeno's martini? We make the best in town."

"Thanks, but I may soon be leaving." I finger my purse and consider sliding along the booth's elegant, tapestry seat.

"Doctor Burdick should be here soon. He's sometimes late. His job, I guess." The waiter shakes his head. "Any man who leaves a gorgeous woman like you sitting alone needs his head examined."

"I agree," I banter, embarrassment peppering me from top to bottom.

"Can I give you my number? You can call me anytime, day or night," he blurts, not realizing that Jim just rushed across the room and is about to lean over and kiss my cheek.

"So sorry I'm late, Molly. A bit of an emergency at the hospital." He plunks down across from me as the waiter disappears.

Concealing relief that almost collapses me, I chide, "You're fifteen minutes late. You don't have a cell phone?"

Lifting a Blackberry out of his suit coat's inside pocket, he grins. "Of course, but I can't always use it whenever I need to." He sets it down on the table beside his water glass. "Sorry I have to keep this out, but I'm on call and want to make sure I hear it ring. One of my patients is having a rough time of it."

"You could have phoned me from your car." I press on, feeling stung that he expects me to believe his flimsy excuse.

His eyebrows shoot up and he stares at me, his movie star face expressing the gravest of hurts. "Molly, I was talking to the hospital all of the way here. I made getting here my priority."

Guilt worms its way through me. "Well, okay then." I try to smile, and feel a chill scuttle between my shoulders.

"You didn't order a drink?"

"I wasn't sure how long I'd wait."

One sleek dark eyebrow arches its surprise. "You weren't going to leave me in the lurch were you?"

Guilt gives me another good wash down. "Well," I stammer, feeling like a big jerk, "I wasn't sure."

He stretches over the table to seek out my hands, both of which lie hidden on my lap. Operating on Jackie O politeness, one hand puts itself on the table. He clasps it slowly, as if protecting a precious thing, bringing it across the table toward him, pressing his full, soft lips against my fingers, his dark lashes curved skyward above high-planed cheeks, his eyes holding the promise of heaven. In the background, Luciano Pavarotti's voice soars to a spine-tingling high C. Jim gently kisses my palm. My heart flies about in excitement, setting off pangs of desire in my lower extremities. I gulp and reclaim my hand, telling myself that no true Voodoo Woman would fall for this. Jim's eyes rest for a moment on my breasts.

"Jim! Stop it!"

"Stop what?" he murmurs, liquid brown eyes beaming desire into mine, turning my legs all doddery. "Stop caring about you? It's too late for that."

"Can I get you anything from the bar?" The waiter grins at me.

My face burns a Mary Murphy scarlet. "Uhm…well."

"Molly?" Jim's voice adores me. "Do you still like Pinot Grigio?"

"That's fine."

"Make that two." Jim sighs sensuously, and seeks to take up where we left off, his arm stretching back across the table on a search for my hands. I scan the restaurant and pretend not to notice. He's charming me with his loving attention, waking something up in me, making my brain swoon. A camel tells me it has to stop.

"Molly, you must know how I feel about you. Surely it's obvious."

Believing it to be true, I shrug, speechless.

"I've been crazy about you since that day we met."

Pleasure plays on my mouth. I tell myself to stop paying attention to flattery, but I sit up straight so as to show off my figure to its best advantage.

"We were on your patio. You wore a white dress with those long, long legs, and bare feet. Ever since then, I've hardly been able to take my eyes off you. I imagine how soft your mouth must feel, and what you taste like, and … well," he smiles sheepishly, "I worried that Bob could see me lusting after you like that."

I grab my iced water and guzzle. "Jim, Bob has just died, I mean, he *just* died. This doesn't seem right."

He wraps my right hand in his. "It's been over two months, Molly. Ten weeks, in fact. I don't think Bob would mind me seeing you. There are worse men than me out there." His eyes burn passion; his forefinger rests on the center of his perfectly curved upper lip.

Things in me begin heating up like Bob's Mount Everest. I can feel Jim's strong arms fastening tight around me, keeping me safe, his smooth, clean hands searching for my dress zipper, wanting to unfasten my bra and tease off all my lacy underwear. I gulp more water. My temperature heads toward spontaneous combustion.

"Have you had a chance to look at the menu?" The waiter gives me the eye as he sets down our wine glasses.

Jim makes a smooth transition. "Do you like scallops, Molly? Zeno's are the best."

"I love scallops," I twitter, high fluster levels on public display, wondering what the hell is happening to me.

"Make that two with all of the trimmings." Jim rivets his attention back on me before the waiter has a chance to talk, ogle, or interrupt us further.

"Let's just keep getting together like this and see what happens," Jim croons. "No pressure, Molly. I want you, and I'm going to take my chance at getting you. But I won't ever push you into anything you don't want."

I know what I want all right, and it confuses me witless. "I need time to think," I stutter, trying not to imagine him with no clothes on, thinking that no man deserves to be this gorgeous, danger signs flashing like a set of strobe lights.

"Did you cab it over here?" he murmurs, his voice like satin on skin.

"I brought my car," I say, glad for a change in subject.

He tilts his head to one side and gives me a melting smile. "Hmm! I was hoping to drive you home."

My head takes flight again. We're parked on my secluded driveway in his long, low Jaguar. We're in the back seat, my dress flung somewhere in front, my lacy bra hanging over the steering wheel where it landed, my lacy bikini underpants lost after Jim tore them off and tossed them away. He is gently prying my knees apart when the food arrives.

"Italian salads for two coming up."

My heart almost stops at the sight of Jim's bemused smile. What has my face been doing? Desperate to connect with my sensible, dignified self, I pick up my fork and shoot him a confident smile, attempting to appear as if I have not just been happily ravaged on the back seat of his car. "This looks delicious," I gush.

"You look delicious," he gushes back, his knee brushing against mine.

To stop my disgraceful imaginings, I chew on a garlicky lettuce leaf and shake my head at him good-naturedly. But my brain is scattered all over the place. How have I managed to go from wanting to stomp out of the restaurant, to wanting to roll around naked with him in his car? All within a one-hour time span? I push a wedge of tomato into my mouth and look over at Jim's mischievous grin. I haven't felt this way since I first met Bob.

Over the excellent scallops, which are sautéed in garlic and lemon butter and served over al dente angel hair pasta, Jim broaches the topic we tacitly decided to treat as taboo.

"You've been hurt badly, Molly. It's hard to trust again after that. I know how that is," he begins, his mellifluous voice a lullaby.

My fork suspends the last tender scallop in front of my mouth. I drop it back on my plate. What exactly is he talking about? Bob? Shirley? Mary? All three of them? Is he about to spill the beans on even more women, thinking that I already know?

"It's true, isn't it?" he nudges. "We've avoided talking about lots of stuff that needs to be aired out."

"What stuff exactly?"

The tips of his square, white teeth reach over his lower

lip as he judges the wisdom of his timing. "All of that Bob stuff. You know what I mean."

"Oh?"

His hand once more catches mine. "Bob was a fool in some ways, Molly. That doesn't mean I am."

"You were his friend, weren't you?" I quaver. "Doesn't that say something about you? You know, birds of a feather and all that?"

"You were his wife. Are you like him? Do you have his belief system?"

I cannot come up with an answer. Reincarnated scallops swim around my stomach in circles searching for a way out.

"Molly, give me a chance. I'm single again. You're single again. It's allowed."

I shake my head and lament, "You know too much about my marriage. You've known two of his concubines for years. It's too much for me to deal with."

Solemn faced, he sips iced water before making a comeback. "Molly, are you going to let *them* dictate what *you* do?"

That was a clever move, I think. But I say, "You must have seen him out with one or the other. Perhaps even joined them yourself sometimes."

His eyes never waver. "Molly, whatever they did was nothing I could control. I wish I could have."

"So you went along with it, conspiring with them to deceive me. Doesn't that make you guilty too? How ethical is that?"

"I'm asking you to give me a chance," he whispers, his fingers tight on mine. "That's only fair."

"Are you all finished here?" The waiter checks on my

remaining scallop. "Did you enjoy your meal?"

"Everything was fine," smiles Jim, rescuing me from having to answer.

"Dessert and coffee?" asks the waiter.

"Decaf, Molly?"

I nod.

"Make it two, please."

We watch the bus boy as our table is cleared of every crumb. After the coffee's placed in front of us, I become the first one to speak.

"I'm taken by surprise."

"I don't think so, Molly," he soothes. "You've seen me drool over you for years."

We stare across the table, his knee pushing against mine, my heart trembling in my chest, common sense sifting out of me like sand through a sieve. With a desire that defies all logic, I yearn to be loved inside and out by Jim.

When I begin to mirror his adoring looks back at him, his forgotten cell phone rings out with Beethoven's *Ode to Joy* played at five times its normal speed. Jim makes a grab for it, but my talent for reading upside down words gets there first, rocketing me out of my deepening hypnosis. A woman's name shines out of his Blackberry's gray caller ID display. Shirley Bills is calling.

"Sorry, Molly, this is the call from the hospital I've been expecting."

My face freezes into a stricken stare. I nod, "Okay."

He presses the talk button and pronounces in his best doctor voice, "Please hold and I'll be right with you." Sliding along his seat to escape, he adds, "It's the ward nurse, I'll take it outside." He makes a beeline for the door.

I push my barely-touched coffee away. My hands pick up my white linen napkin and drop it on the table next to it. I lift my purse off the seat and search for a couple of dollars to give to the coat-check woman. Cash in hand, I move along the seat.

I run into Jim at the door, his face still grinning from the titillating phone conversation he has just enjoyed. His smile drops when he sees me.

"Molly, where are you going?"

Shall I tell him that his "ward nurse" should come and take her latest trophy off my hands and never bring it back, or say that I do not want to make the headlines in tomorrow's *Woodside Times* as the town's first murderess?

"Sorry Jim, I've just received an important message myself and have to fly."

He catches my arm. "Moll—"

I jerk it away. "Sorry. Gotta go."

"Moll, we were talking about us—"

"I know" I sigh. "But I just don't think we're compatible, Jim."

"Not compatible?"

"Nope. Sorry."

His eyebrows arch, his brow furrows, he shakes his head. "Wow! You don't have very high self-esteem, Moll."

A laugh bursts out of me. "Don't flatter yourself, Jim," I sing over my shoulder.

But I am devastated. Walking across the parking lot, I pull my soft wool coat around me and breathe in the late October air, its sharpness pricking my lungs. Opening the Triumph's door, I hike up my dress and lower myself onto the seat. With both legs stuck straight out in front of me and feet laid squarely on the pedals, I hold onto the leather-bound steering wheel and stare at the restaurant's door. By now Jim will be sitting at the bar, joking with the maitre d' about fickle, bitchy women like me.

It could have been worse, I think, desperately wanting to console myself. I walked away in time, left without giving him the chance to walk all over me. It could have been *a lot* worse.

But I stood on the brink of catastrophe, still not trusting my own alarm system above all else, still wanting to earn the wrong man's love and approval. I lay furious rubber on the way out of the parking lot. There will be no more nights like this. I'll live the rest of my life alone before I'll squander another minute of it on another man like Bob.

20

Waiting for brilliant ideas to strike, I play out an impatient drumbeat with my pen on the desktop and stare at the blank page on the computer screen. I've taken the day off thinking that a three-day weekend might help me relax, and still I can't *think*.

A heaviness of spirit plagues me, robbing me of peace. I wonder if this is how survivors feel when a lengthy war is declared over, their years of fear and turmoil gone in a second, their enemies defeated. Have years of endurance and stoicism produced in them an internal rewiring, their lips stiffened to project poise when under attack, their bodies turned strangely mechanical? When they begin to prepare for their new paths, do they manage to quickly unwire themselves, or is it safer to leave things alone lest an ambush occur?

I have battles left to win, but still, I expected to feel a bit better by now. Some days bring glimmers of joy; other days reissue old angers. Sights and sounds trigger memories that make me ache. Like when I walked into the office yesterday morning. My heart twisted when I found Jane sitting at her desk, her CD player quietly spinning one of Bob's favorite tunes, the Rolling Stones' "Sympathy for the Devil." Grief fluttered through me, surprising me with its intensity. I don't understand where it's coming from.

The months before our marriage haunt me. During those early days, Bob would call and say, "Come on over, you gorgeous woman. We'll go for lunch wherever you like." Even though we saw each other every night, and even though the timing might not be ideal, I would stop whatever I was doing to get there.

Standing up, I groan. It doesn't matter that a carefully chosen list of music is set up to play for hours, or that my hopeful hands are primed on the keyboard ready to connect with any outstanding concept that might fall out of my head. Why Bob chose to systematically ruin what should have been a wonderful pairing between us is what I want to know.

Whenever I put on makeup I think of him scrunched up in his address-less brass urn like the face powder in my compact. Where is he? Did a disgruntled postal worker toss him off an expressway bridge onto I-94, or drop him into the Chicago River, or fling him out into Lake Michigan from the end of Navy Pier? Did that same postal worker open up the package before dumping him in one of the aforementioned spots, keeping his brass urn, our CDs and our picture frames? Were our photos torn into little pieces that floated and bobbed in the wake of cruise boats, confusing hordes of hungry gulls that swooped down to peck at them?

The entire fiasco has sparked in me a touch of much-begrudged guilt. After all, if I had remembered to bring Bob's urn home, nobody could have posted him out in that afternoon's mail. Not that Bob didn't create that kind of unfortunate karma for himself, he did, but I feel twinges of discomfort over my own carelessness, and it irritates me to no end. "Why should I feel guilty about anything at all?" I grumble. "Especially after what he's done to me."

Magic Molly stands on her perch at the window, her eyes sympathetic on mine. Since giving her to me, Jonathan has neither stopped in nor phoned. He didn't respond to my thank you note, although, according to Jane, if people start responding to thank you notes, we'll go back and forth without end, thanking each other forever. She thinks Jonathan is shy. I think he's probably concluded that I either got away with murder, or that I'm just too dotty for words—especially after witnessing that ridiculous singing episode on the expressway. I sigh. Such a pity.

Stymied about what I might do to fill my day and avoid the computer, I stand at the patio doors and gaze at the sky, my spirits sagging. When the phone goes off, I moan in agony, afraid that it's Brian Blackstone with a continuation of the ashes epic, or Jim trying to find out why I ignored his "let's talk" e-mail (as if he didn't know).

But the caller ID displays *City Gardener*, setting me off into a heart-slamming panic. Alex Fox is about to ask me what I'm writing, and I'll be forced to admit that I haven't a creative thought left in my head. Before picking up the receiver, I have to sit down.

"How are you doing these days? I just left a planning meeting with Jane and you weren't there."

"I took the day off, and I'm fine, really," I say brightly. But, my mouth is as dry as the Sahara. Soon my tongue will stick to my teeth and refuse to budge. I mute the phone and keep listening while I dash to the refrigerator for a bottle of water.

"Are you ready to get back into writing?"

"Well, I—"

"Because I have an assignment for you."

Hoping to free my lips from each other, I guzzle more water. "What is it?"

"Let's have lunch today and discuss it."

"Today? Lunch?" Even during our most pressing projects, we often didn't see each other. At most, we hunkered down for breakfast at the diner across the street from his office to hammer out a few extra words, or to talk over one of his recommended edits.

"I'm guessing it will be good for you to be around old friends like me."

"It might just be what I need." I blurt, knowing at once that it's true.

"Is Tony's Pizza at one okay with you?"

"Tony's Pizza? Not the diner? Pretty extravagant," I tease, feeling better already.

He laughs. "You're worth it. But don't get used to it."

"I promise not to."

"I look forward to seeing you, Molly."

"Thanks, Alex." My throat is so tight, I sound strangled. Alex is trying to ease me back into the writing world. He's acting like a loving friend.

•

When I was eighteen, it took a few hair-raising donuts on a slick road in West Vancouver to convince me that my little British sports car is not designed for driving in slippery weather. But on dry days like today, it's pure magic. I stoke it up and barrel out to the street, the motor doing a delicious tiger growl, tires hugging the driveway, and the suspension holding flat around the curves. Wearing black wool pants, a red sweater, my surprisingly comfortable black, high-heeled, pointy-toed ankle boots, and my short, black leather jacket, I'm feeling quite the Voodoo Woman. I turn up the radio and tell myself not to sing.

Traffic is light all the way, no stops and starts, even on city streets. In front of Tony's Pizza, I'm amazed to find rock-star parking. The parking meter gives me a kiss; almost two hours worth of quarters are already in it.

Settled on a green vinyl bench seat in a window booth, I watch Alex's gangly legs carry him across the street toward me. My affection for him grows. Without any prompting, he's giving my professional writing life a kick-start. I'd better rise to the occasion.

The restaurant door opens and he strides in, his head turning this way and that as he scans the room. I call his name and he rushes over.

"I'm sorry to keep you waiting." He gives me a hug, his sandy brown hair falling over his eyes as he leans over.

"You're on time, Alex," I say. "I'm actually early. Not much traffic out there today."

He slides into the seat across from me and, as usual, we each carefully arrange our long legs so that we don't constantly bump knees beneath the short width of table. Once that's done, we smile at each other.

"Just so you know, I really like how Jane is handling our advertising work," he says. "That was a good move, promoting her into Shirley's position. Looks like you're all doing well."

"That's because clients like you hung in and gave us a chance to prove ourselves," I say. "I'll always appreciate how you kept Shirley out of the way so that Jane and I could sort out a few things on the sly."

"My pleasure. I just wish I could have seen her face when you fired her."

"It wasn't pretty."

He laughs. "I can only imagine."

"Drinks?" An astonishingly thin waitress with purple spiked hair hands us menus. "Special today is Tony's pepperoni with double cheese." She stands, pencil poised, waiting for our decision.

"Let's live dangerously Molly. Chianti on a workday?" Alex grins as I give him two thumbs up.

The waitress sashays toward the bar, her short tight skirt riding up as she walks. Alex's eyes follow her. "She is so *thin*! Do you think that's normal or what?"

I shrug, "Who knows?" But I picture her eating nothing more than a lettuce leaf for dinner, and it makes me sad.

He watches me with concern. "So, how are you doing, *really*?"

"I'm *really* okay."

I wonder if I appear as fragile as I sometimes feel. "Come on, don't keep me in suspense, Alex. Tell me what you have in mind for the magazine."

He grins, his creamy, straight teeth testifying to the years they spent enduring the trials of orthodonture. I wonder if their roots are worn down from all that wired pushing and shoving, like my client Rachel Rose's. She told me that by age fourteen, she'd already lost thirty percent of her roots. No one warned her parents that it could happen. Instead, the sleazy orthodontist kept silent and made thousands of dollars on a second round of braces. Of course, her family was furious, but the damage was done. Rachel said that she's been compelled to floss like a fanatic ever since.

"Where are you?" Alex waves a hand before my eyes, but his smile's taken flight and his eyebrows are knitted together.

"Not too far away," I fib, fearful at not knowing how long my mind wandered. "I was just trying to imagine what kind of interesting project you have in store for me."

Relieved that I seem okay, his smile returns. "In our weekly brainstorming session, we came up with the idea of flower arrangements made—"

The waitress plunks down our drinks. "Do you guys know what you want yet?" She uses a high pitch whine, like a bored child.

"We haven't even looked at the menu." Alex's eyes beam her a warning. "Please give us at least fifteen more minutes, okay?"

"No problem." She saunters off on stilt legs that grow out of flat, sensible waitress shoes. Her feet look huge.

"You want me to do a piece on flower arrangements?"

"We want you to do a piece on *dried* flower arrangements." Alex leans back in his seat as a bus boy pours water.

My heart droops. "Dried flowers?"

"Yup. Show our readers how to dry their home grown flowers and arrange them into unusual, contemporary dried flower arrangements." He searches my face. "You'll work with an expert arranger. We'll do a photo layout of you being taught how to do all kinds of stuff. You'll add witty captions the way you like, and throw in a little Molly magic here and there, you know offer a little earthy wisdom."

A sudden wave of weepiness has to be fought off.

"What is it? What's wrong?"

"Alex, I appreciate your offer, but dried flowers ... dead flowers ... I just don't know."What's wrong with me? Here's an editor who has actually thought up an assignment for me, and I'm *complaining?*

"It never occurred to me that this would remind you of, well, what you've been through with Bob. I'm sorry."

"You've been kind, as always." I hold back the deluge that threatens to drown me. "These days I'm just—"

"You guys want the special, or what?" The waitress taps her pencil against her order pad, and raps an Olive Oyl foot against the floor. She stares blankly at Alex.

He speaks in a quiet, level voice through tight lips and clenched teeth. "Can't you see that we are involved in serious conversation here? Let *me* flag *you* down when we're ready. Okay?"

"Jeez! I was just checking," she snorts, before flouncing off.

With eyes bulging and mouth dropped, Alex looks apoplectic. "Where the hell do they find these people?" he rasps.

I stop myself from wondering what her family's like, or

if she even has family, or if she's lonely, afraid that Alex will catch me lost in thought again.

He's peering across the room. ""Look at her now."

The waitress stands flirting with a man at the bar, her hand resting on his shoulder, her well-shod foot laid firmly on the rung of his chair, her skirt shifting up to alarming heights. She doesn't budge when the man's eyes slowly survey her spindly raised leg from ankle to thigh, where they rest awhile.

"There used to be a thing called training. Obviously, that went the way of the dinosaur in this place!" Alex harrumphs like an old politician, his schoolboy face a sea of pink, dotted with pale, sandy-island freckles.

A loud giggle breaks its way out of me, shocking us both. "Sorry!" I hold my hands over my mouth. "I just don't know what's gotten into me today." But I can't stop. Despite quieting the chortling sounds, my shoulders shake.

"I can't blame you for laughing, it's pretty stupid around here," he frets. "I'll be glad when we're back to doing breakfasts at the diner. Although, when I think about it, they ignore us there."

"That's true, but it's somehow less annoying," Still giddy, I snicker.

"I suppose it is." Alex eyes me warily.

I caution myself, and sip my drink.

He sighs. "Okay, no dried flowers. But then, what?"

Speaking with a confidence I don't feel, I throw him my best pitch. "I promise to come up with something soon. Okay? You know how I am with deadlines. Remember the tomatoes piece? I had it in at the last minute but you loved it and so did the readers. Remember the 'Bee Flashy' piece?

Same thing!" I sit on the edge of my seat. "Alex, I've never let you down and I won't start now. Let me mull it over for a while."

He puts his elbows on the table and rests his chin in his palms. Minutes tick over but I don't break the silence. Finally, he gives me a wry smile and says, "It's a damned good thing I trust you."

I feel warm all over. "Thanks Alex."

He puts a good-natured grimace on his face, as if to say he is in deep trouble now. "At least there's plenty of time. I need your ideas by mid January at the latest. We have an early March deadline for the finished piece."

"You won't regret it, Alex," I say, hoping this proves to be true.

After clinking our glasses together to seal the deal, he picks up his menu. "All of this hard work has given me an appetite. How about you?"

"I'm famished."

My menu opens to a list of pizza topping options that I pretend to read with interest. I glance across at Alex, who's busy reading about the restaurant's many offerings, his finger holding his place on the page.

"Wanna have the special?" He does a wicked mimic of the waitress's monotone, high-pitched voice.

"Sounds fine to me," I grin, keeping a close check on my sorrow, giggling, and mind wandering urges.

Alex's eyes search the restaurant. "Now, if I can just find that annoying woman."

21

The night before Thanksgiving Day, I have an upsetting and puzzling dream. I'm holding a small girl's hand. We're watching overcast skies cast long, dark shadows across a dying flower garden. Nearby, a Victorian house sits stark and dilapidated against a neglected landscape. Dull paint peels from rotting, carved wood. Elaborate rooflines tilt this way and that with tiles worn or missing. We walk toward it.

Wearing a shabby satin wedding dress, I creak open the front door and we step into the dusty foyer. Standing in the dimness. I feel a flame of fear lick at my back. To my left, attached to the wall, a staircase leads up into blackness. Covered in worn carpet that runs up the center of each step, it tilts precariously to the right. There is no foundation, nothing built beneath to save it from falling down altogether.

Reluctant feet carry me to the first step. As far from the edge as possible, my back pressed hard against crumbling walls, I hold tighter to the girl as we begin to climb. Heart skipping, I inch around the landing as it turns to the right. The staircase groans and shudders. Standing still, I peer upward and think: Why am I doing this? But I will not say.

The staircase stops in front of a rickety door that closes off the attic. I feel ill with fear and stand gulping air. There is something on the other side that I need to know about. Clasping the doorknob, I will myself to open it, but don't dare.

I wake up in a panic. What was waiting for me in that attic? Friend or foe? I sense it was something important, something I need to know about. My head won't let the question drop.

•

On a large, white, oval platter, a nicely browned turkey leg rests beside hills of sliced white meat and fragrant sage stuffing. Buttery mashed potatoes, sweet potatoes, green beans, cranberry sauce, and creamed corn lie in covered bowls. Before the Thanksgiving gravy can congeal in its boat, Jane has organized the leftovers, packaging bits and pieces of this and that, storing them for a later feast.

Bernie and Bernice are busy clearing the table and rinsing dishes before loading the dishwasher. They laugh and flick water at each other, playing as they work, leaving Jane and me to finish our coffee and pumpkin pie in peace. My brain starts sifting through bittersweet memories.

It's this time last year. I'm standing at our patio door,

watching Bob walk Bernice to Mount Everest, bending over to chat with her along the way. Bernice carefully operates her feet, carrying her small tray of vegetable peelings with both hands. Bob looks like a friendly giant, big and dark next to her little five-year-old strawberry blond self. (My eyes prick at the memory.) After she properly admires his compost creation, Bob gently lifts her up so that she can tip her tray's cargo right on top.

Jane is quietly refilling my coffee cup. She pours in a splash of cream.

I'm ten years old, watching my mother lift the Thanksgiving turkey out of the oven. Much to my delight, Dad struts into the kitchen, elbows sticking out like bony wings, head bobbing back and forth as he walks.

"Gobble, gobble, gobble," he twitters, looking perfectly ridiculous.

My mother shakes her head. "You're acting like a big turkey," she announces, her voice cheerful.

"I will admit that Turkey-osity is a problem today." Dad proclaims, before strutting around the kitchen even faster.

"If you keep this up, I might have to go to school and study Turkey-ology," I add, trying not to sound gleeful. My parents look at me approvingly, which delights me even further.

Dad struts over to me. "Young lady. The philosophy of turkey-ism requires more than just study. It's a way of life."

"Rubbish!" Mom keeps a straight face, "You have a simple case of turkey-tosis. It's a disease, not a lifestyle."

We all fall about the kitchen laughing. My mother manages to gasp out her usual comment, "A limited knowledge of words equals a limited ability to think. Right,

Molly?"

My heart squeezes tight whenever I think of that day. It's such a pity that most of the time they never got along like that. Usually there was a palpable tension between them, their voices tight, their faces stiffened by pretend smiles.

"It's been years since I read dream interpretation books," Jane says loudly, as if to wake me up. "I gave them all away, and don't know if I can remember enough to decipher yours."

"Just do your best," I say.

"I do remember that the child represents the dreamer as well as the adult. The house represents you too. In fact, many things do."

"Me…a dilapidated Victorian house?"

"The wedding dress must indicate marriage," she adds.

"Sounds like it's about my shabby marriage to Bob and his Victorian ideas on how to treat women," I huff, feeling strangely miffed.

We sit quiet for a minute. Jane murmurs, "Do you know that in one sentence Queen Victoria taught her daughters all she thought they needed to know about sex?"

"What did she say?"

"Close your eyes and think of England." She does one of her heart-stopping laughs, a loud guffaw that unexpectedly belts out unchecked. From the kitchen Bernie and Bernice join in at the sound of it.

I laugh too, but then wonder, shockingly, if Grandmother Victoria did the same as the queen and her daughters before putting my grandfather out of the house, or if my mother, Victoria, closed her eyes and thought of Canada during her couplings with dad.

Whenever Bob reached for me in the night, his arms encircling me in love, sweeping me away again, I never closed my eyes and thought of England, Canada, America, or any other geographical location. I thought only of us. Surely that meant something?

At once, I feel warm breath on my cheek and hear his whispers. My heart lurches in fright. My brain races back into my puzzle of a dream. "What about the dying flower garden?"

Jane hesitates, serious now. "Well…it's probably another dream metaphor showing how you, the dreamer, see yourself and your life." She sees my unhappy face and adds quickly, "Rightly or wrongly."

My throat is swelling. I gulp coffee, "What about that staircase tilted to the right, and the landing turned to the right? "

She brightens. "I think your climb was leading you in the *right* direction. Attics represents the conscious mind, so your climb up the stairs shows your desire to face your fear, step by step."

"It sounds really stupid, but I felt embarrassingly un-courageous after seeing myself in that dream. After climbing all that way, I didn't dare open the door at the top."

"But you wanted to, Molly. You just weren't quite ready."

•

Signs of winter are on display wherever my eyes wander. Trees stand like dark, fanciful skeletons against pale gray skies. Brittle ferns, their lives saved for next year in roots deep underground, face the coming challenge. Mounded, empty flowerbeds hold silvery pockets of powdery snow in freezing, bare soil. Chill winds buffet the house, making its bones creak. Inside, the fire roars and snaps. Not caring that it's not quite noon, I pour a glass of Bordeaux and watch the flames.

No Voodoo Woman worth her magic would have left her husband's closet full of stuff to evoke memories of his deceptions, like ghostly weapons of torture. In fact, it wouldn't surprise me to learn that Madame Marie Laveau's husband's clothes went missing even before he did. It embarrasses me to think that Bob's things loll behind closed doors and lie at rest in unopened drawers, yet the idea of handling his clothes fills me with dread. What else might I find? Today, almost four months since his demise, I'll fearlessly face the task.

A log bursts forth with a loud crack, shooting sparks out onto the hearth and bringing me back to the present. A camel waits to be tied. I top up my glass and start trekking up the stairs.

Weak, wintry light pours in through the bedroom's wide windows, offering no warmth at all. I imagine Bob preening in front of the mirror, fussing with his tie, making sure his shirt is perfectly ironed, wanting to create the right impression for his latest conquest. "*Master* bedroom," I snort and shake my head.

Plunking my glass down on top of his dresser, I deep breathe and get myself focused. Today, I want everything of Bob's that remains in the house brought out in the open and removed from my life and home. Then, I'll be able to think more clearly, my creativity will unlock itself, and I'll come up with the great idea I need for Alex.

In Bob's closet dress shirts hang benign, all pressed and clean on wire hangers. I gather them up and then fold and stack them into two high piles on the bed. His shoes, lined up along the shoe rack like sentinels, are placed alongside the bed, a big packing box beside them. A long row of suits, all dark and conservative, describe Bob to the nth degree. Those with dry cleaning tags still attached are left on their hangers and laid next to the shirts in a neat pile. After downing my drink, I pack everything into large, dark green garbage bags and sturdy cardboard boxes and cart them into the garage.

Two suits remain. One of them, I don't remember which, was worn on the 13th August, the day Bob bopped Mary or whomever at the O-K Hotel. It will have hung neatly on a hanger, a witness to the shameful event. God knows what's in its pockets.

The first suit produces only a clean white handkerchief and a neatly folded note that says, *"Pick up shirts and dry cleaning TODAY!"* I place it on the bed. Every single pocket in the last remaining suit comes up empty. Feeling relieved, I pack them both into a large box, along with Bob's belts, ties, and collection of t-shirts. His folded sweaters go into two large garbage bags. These too are dragged down the stairs and hauled into the garage. Although this is hard work, its lack of shocking materials has made it a lot easier than expected.

Bob's dresser is all that remains. Placing a packing box beside me, I start at the bottom. His striped pajamas and matching cotton robes are meticulously folded, a glowing testament to my perfect, wifely ways. I rub my eyes to block out the picture of Bob standing at the kitchen sink making us coffee on Sunday mornings, his pajamas rumpled and hair standing high on one side of his head. My body starts to weaken, my heart melting like snow caps in summer.

A whisper floats down from the ceiling. "You can make your own coffee," says Grandmother. "Better than he did," adds Mom.

Brought to my senses, I yank open the middle drawer where his underwear and t-shirts appear innocent and clean. "Liars," I sputter, rooting around under and over them, expecting to find proof as I lift them out.

The top drawer opens onto chaos. Bob's socks aren't arranged in their usual neat rows having been tossed about willy-nilly. I pick them out one set at a time, handling them as if they're poison. At the bottom of the drawer are two odd socks. One of them—black patterned with tiny red dots—is particularly scrunched. I lift it out for closer inspection. It's tied into a knot at the heel. Something hard and round is hidden in the toe. It feels like a circle with a hole in the center, a letter in the shape of an O.

My brain flashes with images of Voodoo circles and O negative blood. A chill hits the back of my neck. I think: *Bob is haunting me again.* Fright lifts me off the floor in one movement. Clutching the red dotted sock in one hand and my wine glass in the other, I rush blindly down the stairs.

After dropping both things onto the kitchen counter, Magic Molly and I exchange shocked looks. I hoof over to the bar, take a slug of wine right out of the bottle and carry it back with me. I wonder what people would think if they knew about the secret me, the haunted Molly Makepeace who likely (albeit inadvertently) Voodoo'd her husband to death, and is now suffering the consequences. Then I quickly untie the knot and give the sock a good, hard shake.

The tinkle of metal landing on granite rattles my ears. A flash of gold dazzles my eyes. Bob's wayward wedding ring rolls across the counter and off the edge. I watch it bounce against the floor before continuing its journey toward the patio doors and away from me. It spins, tips over, and rolls around in fast, tight circles before finally coming to rest.

When Dad first met Bob he told me, "That man's going to run circles around you." The zillions of circles Bob's ring just made as it rolled and spun makes me think that Bob is showing me Dad was right.

I think his ring might have landed where it did to relay a message to me from Bob. It's touching the patio doors. Look through them and I'll see where his ashes are supposed to have been scattered, in circles, around the bases of trees.

My stomach swirls and snakes. I remember my Victorian house dream and think of how I catered to Bob and neglected myself. I feel as if he has haunted me since the day we met. And now he's doing it from the *urn*.

I imagine his unboxed ashes, slowly rising up from beneath a mountainous pile of letters and parcels in the dead letter warehouse. In human form he hovers near the rafters, a see-though, shimmering ghost. "Which way," he growls, "is Woodside from here?"

"You're not getting the last word on me any more, Bob," I shout to the empty room, scaring myself even further.

I puff myself up and mutter, "He's got a lot of nerve. Since he preferred to bop his way through a line of sorry women rather than act decent toward his wife, he should've just moved his ass out of here. He pushed me into

Voodooing. A loving wife can take only so much."

But my cheeks are burning, and I can't help thinking that if I hadn't stayed with him, I would never have gone to buy Voodoo supplies, would never have given him that tiara of a pinning, that aneurysm in the making.

I think again of my Victorian house dream. I've already climbed the stairs. The next time that rickety attic door presents itself, I'm going to fling it wide open.

22

My father hasn't called me since the day after Bob's memorial. All he's done is send an October postcard from Sydney that highlights the harbor and opera house. His spidery writing scrawled on the back told me that he wished I were there, or that he and Denise were having a great time, or some other mundane sentiment. So, on December 23rd, when I open the door to find him standing on the front step next to his suitcase, I gape in astonishment. It's the first time I've seen his face in five years. His warm breath hits the icy air in a cloud. "Denise left me," is all he says.

"Merry Christmas, Dad." It's out of my mouth before I can think.

He stands in silence, staring at my face. "You look beautiful, Molly."

I sigh and roll my eyes like a child. "Yes, of course.

Flattery will get you everywhere. Right?"

He smiles sheepishly and shrugs. His hand rests on his suitcase handle ready to roll it in. "It always works for me."

"Really? So where's Denise then?" Seeing the pain in his eyes, I immediately regret my spite. "Sorry, Dad." I give him a stiff hug. "Come on in."

He keeps hold of me, his back ridged, his breath uneven. "The last time I stood here I was with your mother," he says. "I miss her right now."

My mother lies curled in her hospital bed, moonlight surrounding her like a halo. I don't recognize her at first, this skeleton with tangled blond hair and yellowed skin and square white teeth too big to be real. Dad leans against the wall, his eyes on the door. "I'll be back shortly," he says, before walking out.

"It's okay, Dad." I pull away and swallow hard. "Come on. Let's get in front of the fire." I turn to walk up the hall, afraid to see that he's on the brink of crying. My brain does a jig. What am I supposed to do with this man I hardly know? For a long time now I haven't even liked him.

Her brilliant blue eyes flicker toward the door. She's trying to hold on until he gets back. Her breath rattles louder in her chest. I cry, "Don't leave us Mom," and hold her hand as she dies. It's another hour's wait before he wanders back in.

I try to blink away the images.

Dad's suitcase trundles across the slate foyer and onto the hallway's wood floor. "I should have called," he says, looking so mournful even his ears seem to droop.

I open the hall closet. "Give me your coat, and let's go sit in front of the fire. You look cold," I say.

I take a deep shuddering breath. My dad is distant, selfish, unkind, thoughtless, hateful, loving, entertaining, charming and witty. Who can figure out such an infuriating person? Who wants to?

"I stood outside ages before daring to ring the bell," he says, softly, a tear in one eye.

"Why?"

"I know I've treated you badly. I've neglected you."

"That's certainly true." Disarmed by the truth, I smile when I say it, and then want to kick myself. Dad is up to his old tricks, weaseling his way in, earning my forgiveness by pretending remorse. "Did you fly into O'Hare?"

"Yes. I caught a cab right outside the doors and came straight over. The roads aren't too bad."

"I would have come to get you." Once more, I stop my foot from turning against me. A Voodoo Woman will not offer her services to someone who doesn't deserve them.

"I was too embarrassed to ask you to pick me up."

I'm nine years old and kneeling on the couch gazing into the street waiting for Daddy to get home from work. I'm wearing my new dress, the one Daddy likes the best. It's white with tiny red flowers on it and has a big bow tied in the back. He said he'd pick me up and whisk me away to the movies, just him and me.

He looks at the floor. "Nice finish," he says. "It's lighter than when your mother and I visited you." As a former hardware store owner, Dad always notices things like this. "In fact, the whole place looks different. Lighter."

"We had a lot of stuff done last fall. It was time for an update."

Mommy is gently tugging me off the couch. "Come on Molly, you've waited for Daddy long enough."

Dad takes in the room, nodding appreciatively. "Nice. Very nice."

"No!" I cry. "Daddy said this was our special day. He told me if I kept looking up the street, I'd see him coming."

Taking his arm, I walk him over to the fireplace and settle him into a large, red leather armchair. "Tea? Martini?"

With exaggerated seriousness, he nods once and says, "Yes."

I suppress a smile. "Okay, one tea, one martini. How about a snack?"

His voice booms grandly, "Thank you, but copious amounts of liquidity will do for the moment." He's going for the giggles, knowing that he can break through ice with his humor.

I get busy in the kitchen.

I'm thirteen years old, setting the table for Dad's favorite birthday dinner. Mom is lifting the roast out of the oven, her eyes on the kitchen clock. My stomach is knotting up. We busily mash potatoes and drain the vegetables and make the gravy and heat the plates. Now there's nothing left to do. I pick up his unused silverware and casually throw it back into the drawer. Keeping our eyes to ourselves, Mom and I sit down and eat.

He smiles across the room at me, his frown-lined forehead shining in the light from the window. The Australian sun has browned his skin, making him appear older. His thick hair, cut short and trendy with a bit of a quiff sticking up in front, seems whiter than I remember. But he's still a handsome man. My mother once told me, "You have his bones, those high cheekbones and that straight nose. If he lives to be one hundred, he'll still think he looks good." I never quite knew what to make of that.

"Where are you?"

"I was just thinking about Mom."

He nods. "I do that sometimes."

"You always imagine the worst from me," he yells.

"You break your promises all of the time," Mom yells back.

I pour the tea and place it on the tray next to our martinis while I examine this idea. "You think about Mom?"

"Sometimes."

On doddering legs, I walk toward the fireplace, tray balanced in both hands, hard eyes fixed on him. Who is the real Hugh Makepeace? I place his tea on the coffee table and hand him his drink. He averts his eyes and gives a world-weary sigh.

"How are you doing these days, Molly?"

"I'm angry."

"Because Bob died?"

"Because Bob lived!" I blast, sounding like a bratty teenager.

"What do you mean, sweetheart?" He leans forward in his chair, hand outstretched, ready to offer solace.

'Just forget it.' I snap. There's something about Dad that reminds me of Bob, something that makes me feel as if I'm in the midst of a terrible bout of déjà vu.

"Jeez! I was just trying to help." With forlorn face and plaintive tone he looks every bit the pious martyr.

Poor, poor Dad. He's such a great guy and yet has to put up with unreasonable me. "Don't go there, Dad. Don't try it."

"Try what, sweetheart?" His eyebrows pull together as one, like a dark, furry, familiar caterpillar.

"Don't try all of that old stuff on me. That stuff you did to Mom. Don't try it on me." Primed tears want to run in torrents, but they will not, *cannot* be given to him.

He presses his lips together, looks at the ceiling, and shakes his head. He drinks his tea and stares loftily at the flames.

I curl into a ball, pull the covers over my head and try not to hear any more of their fight. The back door slams. The car fires up. He's going out again.

"I'll get the teapot," I say in my Jackie O way. Then my feet propel me toward the kitchen like two synchronized machines.

In the morning, I overhear Grandmother say, "Women grow nothing but pain living like this."

The fire crackles and sputters. A log rolls off the grate and hits the fireguard. Dad gets to his feet and begins to rearrange the wood using the stacking method he taught me when Mom was alive. As I watch him work it seems that despite his large frame and wide shoulders, he looks unguarded and fragile.

Mommy's face frightens me. She's staring off at nothing, looking as if she has something in her mouth that tastes bad. I feel like I'm shriveling up. I curl up in my seat to hide as much of me as possible.

"So what will you do now, Dad?" I mumble, my voice thick.

He puts the fireplace tools back in their stand before returning to his chair. As I place a fresh pot of tea on the coffee table, he flops down hard and runs his hand across his eyes. Counting off points on his fingers, he lists, "I'm sixty years old. I've sold my store. I'm comfortably retired. I don't want to waste any more years. I want my daughter to admire me. I want Denise to come back." He drops his chin to his chest and gives a long, forlorn sigh. "I guess that means I'm prepared to do whatever it takes to be happy."

He looks anything but happy as he leans forward to grasp my hand. "Look Molly, I came here to sort this all out with you. I figured I should start by admitting that I was sometimes unkind to you and your mother."

I think: He's fixing things up again. He meets my stony gaze for a second or two, before his eyes lower.

My new bike is red and chrome and twinkles in the Vancouver sunshine. "I love it," I squeal, not wanting to remember that he didn't show up last night and take me to the movies like he promised.

Dad is tapping the coffee table to catch my attention. He tops up my tea and passes it to me. He quips, gently, "Your ears are like flowers. Cauliflowers."

I groan and shake my head at him. "Your teeth are like stars." I grow a smile. "They come out at night."

"Your eyes are like pools. Whirlpools."

We giggle like children.

'You have outstanding green eyes, Molly."

"You're only saying that because they're just like yours."

"True," he admits.

"You have, or should I say, you *had* outstanding black hair, Dad."

"You're only saying that because it's just like yours."

"True." I give a solemn nod.

We exchange smiles.

"It's been a lot of years since we played those games," he murmurs.

"Lots of years."

"It is probably hard for you to believe, Molly, but I don't like it when you're hurt."

My chest tightens and I forget to breathe.

His face looks pale and drawn, which sets me afloat on a surge of guilt. "How long will you stay, Dad?"

"Well, I thought perhaps you'd put up with me until New Year's Day."

I manage a smile, realizing for the first time that he's afraid to be alone at the Holidays with nothing but his memories for company.

"You can stay as long as you like," I say, just like my mother.

23

I lie in bed, my brain doing somersaults, my stomach slipping and sliding. Across the hall in the guest bedroom, Dad is already snoring like a bull with sinus troubles. God forbid *he* should lose sleep over anything.

I'm having my usual delayed reaction to a traumatic event. Lying on my back like one of Bob's extra starch shirts, both feet are tapping back and forth like they belong to a rock band's drummer. I'm so damned angry I want to get out of bed and hoof it over to the Old Town's Spiritual Magic Shop to search for a Dad look-alike doll and a box of the longest pins known to mankind.

That noisy, sleeping man refused to inconvenience himself by coming here to be with me when Bob died, yet when his wife walks out on him, he dares to show up at my front door unannounced, and at *Christmas* yet! After five years, does he think I've nothing better to do than cater to him? I was all set. I was going to spend my time alone resurrecting my tossed aside writing career. How am I supposed to do that now?

He is here five years too late. But I bet Dad never imagined that I might not want to see his uninvited face dropping in on me, no matter what he blabs to the contrary. The man actually expects to be welcome wherever he goes. (He is after all, a bit of a charmer.) He thinks he's got me all figured out.

I curl up in a ball to contain my fury.

It's ten o'clock in the morning. After showering and getting dressed, my feet refuse to take me downstairs. Dad has been in the kitchen for fifteen minutes or so, banging about in cupboards and drawers, seeking mugs and spoons and breakfast stuff. Now, the aroma of fresh coffee is in the air.

"By the end of the night," I groan into the telephone, "I was actually laughing, and letting him weasel his way in again."

"He took you off guard, Molly. You were in shock," says Jane.

"He uses humor to disarm me."

"I know. He has that dangerous charming way about him. When he was here with your mom, he used humor and his funny words to make us all laugh. People like that facet of him, and he knows it."

"He ingratiates well."

She sighs. "I never saw either of them again after that visit, Molly."

"You didn't see *him* again because he never came back

after Mom died. When I finally stopped going to see him in Vancouver, I never saw him again either."

"I'd be upset too, Molly."

"He's setting off these flashbacks…and they're all about things that need to stay in the past. I don't want to re-examine my mother's death. I don't want to see that exact moment…the split second she left. I saw it once. That was enough."

"Sometimes it's good to get that stuff out more than once."

"He says he thinks of Mom sometimes. Too bad he didn't think of her when she was alive."

"True."

"And then he acts like he's always been available to me. He stares into my eyes to fake me out, acting like he has this impeccable honesty, this perfect unassailable character. It's a complete contradiction to what he does when I really need his support."

"He's clever, all right. But you get it now, and that's good."

She's right. I'm beginning to understand something about my training ground at home. I think it might have led me to a man like Bob. "If I ever decide to let rip on Dad, he'll never forget it."

"It might just do you a world of good."

I stammer, "I couldn't…I mean…he's my dad…it would be cruel."

"Might just do him a world of good," says Grandmother from somewhere near the window. Mom nods. They're agreeing again.

Suddenly the intercom system blasts out with Christmas

music playing at full volume. "Jeez!" I shout, my heart in my throat. "He's put the frigging radio on in the kitchen and it's blasting right through the house. So far as he knows, I'm not even up and dressed, I'm still sound asleep in bed. He is so goddamn *selfish*."

"Hang tight, Molly. In a week he'll be gone." She has to yell this twice before I can make out what she's saying over the din.

Dad is sprawled on the family room couch reading his latest copy of *Hardware News Canada*. I switch off the radio with an angry flourish.

"Hey!" he complains, "I was enjoying that Christmas music."

"Well, I wasn't."

He sits up and gives me a cold stare. "What is the matter with you?"

At this moment, I can neither move nor speak. I'm locked in a time warp. "What is the matter with you?" says Bob, mimicking Dad's question, looking at me with that same disgusted expression.

'I have to run into the office,' I say.

"I thought it was closed until after the New Year."

"It is. I just have to tie up a couple of loose ends. I'll be home by six."

I open the closet door, grab my coat, and power walk like Mary Murphy out to the car.

•

I park at Chicago's Belmont Harbor and stare out at the water. What the hell do I do now? I can't face the empty office. Jane and I have worked day and night at the agency in preparation for this time off. I've had enough of it. I suppose I could go over to her house, but that hardly seems fair on Christmas Eve. She and Bernie are preparing for the big day tomorrow. As they do every year, to satisfy both sets of parents—hers are Episcopalian, his are Jewish—they've put up a "Chanukah Christmas tree." They plan to decorate it this afternoon. Jane and Bernie and Bernice have to be allowed to enjoy this time as a family.

•

The shops in Chicago are overheated and packed with last minute shoppers, mostly men, it seems. I stumble through the doors of Water Tower Place into the surging hordes, and then push my way straight back out again. No way can I suffer that.

"Well if it isn't my good neighbor, Molly Makepeace," a man says. I turn around to find Mary Murphy's husband walking toward me, his face all lit up.

I think: How does he know I'm using my own name and not Jamison? Then, I ramp up my most confident of smiles. "I haven't seen you for a while, Ivan."

"We've been away quite a bit. Went to Jamaica for a couple of weeks as soon as Mary was pulled together. Been working hard. The usual stuff."

I check my watch as if I'm in a huge rush. "My Dad's visiting over the Holidays. I've left him sitting alone at home."

"We've got the entire clan over tomorrow," he says,

cheerfully. "They'll all be getting on each other's nerves in no time at all. I haven't even finished shopping. It's such a pain in the ass." He grins. "You don't look too successful at this last minute stuff."

I'm suddenly aware of my empty arms. No bags or packages in sight. "Hopefully, there's still time," I say, feeling nervous. I hope he doesn't invite Dad and me over for a bit of Christmas cheer.

"How about letting me buy you a Christmas drink, Molly? There's a cute bar around the corner. I'd love to catch up with you, see how you're doing."

I freeze. He must not know about his wife's fling with my husband. "Thanks Ivan," I say, "But I really do have to get going." And I quickly walk away.

•

I sit in the art film movie house watching some black and white French concoction. According to the English sub-titles—which are difficult to follow since the black letters often get lost in the black background, leaving many words with big gaps in them—it's about a woman whose husband is screwing around with their next door neighbor, an outrageously curvy blond with a big round ass, not unlike Mary Murphy's, only smaller. I spend two long hours shoving popcorn into my mouth by the fistful, nibbling strings of liquorice, and chomping on chocolate covered peanuts. All the way through, I want to shout, "You bastard," at the actor.

But I know that my fury is really directed toward dear old Dad.

•

I cannot stop myself from walking into the house at exactly six-o'clock, as promised. From the couch, Dad says, "Welcome back. Want to have a martini with me?"

I yell, "After leaving me to get through Bob's death without any support from my family, *such as it is,* you have the nerve to show up here the minute your wife runs off rather than stay alone and deal with it for one goddamn week!"

He looks as if he's been hit. "There's no need for this, Molly. What is wrong with you today?"

"What's wrong with *you*?" I yell. "Not that you'll address *that* question, mind you. So, I guess I'll have to explain the obvious to you over and over again, in every way that I can think of, as if you can't figure out for yourself what is cruel and what is not. Then, when I'm exhausted and can't think of any other way to explain your bad behavior to you, you'll tell me that everything I've said is wrong." I smack the coffee table top with the palm of my hand.

He startles. "Molly, I—"

"Then, when I'm in a helpless rage over your stone-walling and your unwillingness to work with me in resolving anything at all, you'll tell me, or at least imply, how ungrateful I am to think so little of such a great dad."

"But Molly—"

"Then, when I get even angrier, you'll walk away."

He crosses his arms and shuffles in his seat. "Molly—"

"Even now you're not listening. You're just waiting for me to shut up so that you can tell me how it really is. How it's me who has the problem and not you."

He jumps to his feet and heads toward the coat closet. "Well, if that's how you feel about me, I'll leave right now," he shouts.

"Fine!"

He thrusts his arms into his coat sleeves like they're a set of pistons. He wraps his scarf around his neck like he's twirling a lasso. He snaps on his gloves like an emergency room doctor during a busy spell.

I watch in silence, eyes flashing, both feet tapping out a drum solo. He can get out of here and never come back for all I care.

At the door, he stops, no doubt realizing that all of his stuff is unpacked and upstairs. "This is ridiculous," he mutters.

Back at the coat closet, he pulls off his gloves and hangs things back up. "Okay, you win," he says.

I resume where I left off. "I've learned how to play your game, Dad. I know how it works. You know why? Because I spent nine long years with a man just like you, and he wore me out with his game playing. I didn't understand what was happening for such a long time. Didn't understand that he was just like you, and would only be nice to me when it was convenient, easy, beneficial, comfortable. *I'm glad he's dead!*"

Dad sits down and nervously hands me a tissue from the little travel pack he keeps in his shirt pocket. His hands shake. But for once, he stays. And then he says the right thing. "Go on, Molly. Get it all out."

I blow my nose.

"This game has played throughout my whole life. Now I've changed the rules. I'm not going to allow anyone to do this to me again."

He hands me another tissue. "I never did like Bob," he mutters, looking away.

"*This isn't just about Bob*," I blast. "It's about you and Mom, and Bob and me. *Why* did you choose to make Mom miserable? *Why* did Bob choose to make me miserable? What do you get out of making others miserable? Above all, *why* did I choose a man like you to marry, when I should have *known* it was guaranteed to make me miserable? Why was I so eager to do that?"

Dad's sorrowful green eyes seek to again disarm me. "Probably because without realizing it, I helped train you to expect that as your lot in life," he says, meekly.

My jaw drops. Then, I become wary. "What's the catch? There must be a catch."

"There's no catch, Molly. Really."

"Are you actually admitting you've played this cat-and-mouse game with Mom, and me?"

"I suppose I am." Slumped in the chair, he looks at the floor.

"Sorry Dad, but I think you're just saying this to lower my guard, to make me stop this tirade. You're charming me with a piece of honesty as part of your winning strategy. I've seen you do this before. Bob did the same thing."

He gives what's left of his martini a slow stir, watching the olive's wake shatter the still surface. Eyes lowered, he sighs. "In Australia, when Denise was surrounded by her family for twelve weeks, she began to think differently."

"Oh?"

"When we returned home, just before Thanksgiving, she told me she was going to see a psychologist. She said she used to feel really content and happy with me, but that it's worn off. I really don't know what the hell she means, but I'm trying to figure it out."

Striving to remain skeptical, I picture a row of tied-up camels.

Dad lifts his empty glass as though it weighs a ton. "Do you mind if I help myself to another?"

"I'll get it for you." I need time to think. He's admitted more than ever before, but the stakes are higher now that Denise has left him and I'm not playing peacemaker. I think he might just want to ratchet up the drama with a boatload of carefully selected shocking truths mixed in with his usual lies. To calm things down and get things back to how he likes them, he needs to confuse me enough to make me question my own judgment. Then he can relax and carry on as usual, with me playing the good daughter, no matter what. Rummaging through this familiar predicament, I want to shout to the rafters, "What's true and what isn't true? Just look at me. In no time at all he has managed to throw me again."

Dad sits watching. He doesn't speak until I begin pouring his fresh drink.

"When Denise left, she told me she still loves me." He shakes his head. "And then what do you think she said?"

"I don't know. What?"

"She said she needs to love herself too. She said she deserves to be happy."

"Well, she's right."

He hesitates. "Yes, she's right."

I try to shut up, but can't. "I can still see Mom begging you to talk to her, to treat her with a modicum of respect by acknowledging her existence. You would ruin her day and then comfort her until she'd rallied enough to feel hopeful about the two of you. And then you would do something else to ruin her day, like not show up for dinner when you knew she had made your favorite meal." I stop for air, holding up my hand to stop him from speaking. "This was Mom's *life* and it went on and on and on like this. You even left her to die without you. All she had was me."

I press my thumb and forefinger against the inner corners of my eyes to stem a potential flow. It's good that I've managed to define something to myself that rings so true.

Dad hangs his head, "I admit, I didn't always handle things right."

"*Why* wouldn't you cooperate? All she ever wanted to do was to please you. We could have all been happy." I wait for his response, my eyes on his face.

He unwisely decides to take his typical defensive action, his voice loud and belligerent. "Well, I was unhappy too," he pouts. "Your mother was a good woman, but not perfect."

"Somebody hold me back." I yell an appeal to the ceiling. "I didn't say she was perfect. Nobody's perfect. You're switching things again. Taking us off track."

"What do you mean?" He speaks softly now, and wears Bob's puzzled look, his eyes seeking my own as though trying to read them for a clear answer to this sorry maze of a puzzle.

I temper my voice to match his. "I mean that you're still just playing your game. Now you're blaming the victim. Acting innocent. You're trying to manipulate me against Mom. You can be so awful, Dad."

"That's not fair." Belligerency rises again.

"I'm not going down that road again."

"There's no such road to go down." He sounds petulant, like a falsely accused child.

"Now comes the big sulk."

"You're being very unreasonable, Molly."

"Now you're making it my fault."

"No, I'm not."

"Now you're denying the obvious."

Stymied for the moment, he looks away and shakes his head.

"I warned you Dad. I know your game."

He shrugs and sniffs, "I don't see it quite the way you do."

"Or the way Mom did. Or the way Denise does. Are we all wrong Dad?"

Eyes flashing, he fumes, "OK. You're all right and I'm wrong." He leans closer. "Does that make you feel better?"

"No! You don't mean it. You're just trying to make me feel guilty. You'll say anything to end a game you're losing."

Finding himself at a dead end, his face takes on a pale, frozen look. He tries a different tack. "Does it surprise you to know that at one time, the mere sight of your mother walking into a room made my knees weak?"

"It surprises me since I think you wanted to destroy her."

"Why would I want to destroy your mother? I loved her." His voice trembles.

"You tell me. Why did you?"

He adroitly switches strategy. "I'm glad Bob didn't do that to you."

"He nearly did. I put an end to it."

Dad stares at the fire. "I guess I don't blame you for feeling bitter."

"Good."

"But I hope it passes, Molly."

"It's on my list of things to lose."

He pats my hand with small, uncertain taps. "I want to say I'm sorry, Molly. I'm going to improve."

"Me too!" I shoot back, "I don't want to keep making the same stupid mistakes for the rest of *my* life."

"In that case, Molly, let's be patient with each other." He lifts his glass and clinks it gently on mine. "We'll get through this, Molly. You'll see."

Solemn faced, I nod and clink my glass back onto his. Dad thinks he's gotten away with something. Like Bob, he's managed to avoid answering me whenever I've asked him *why* he was so cruel to the woman he claimed to love. That's the question I want the answer to. But there will be other opportunities. For tonight, I'll let it rest.

Dad stands up, stretches, and heads toward the downstairs bathroom. "What's for dinner?" he says.

24

Christmas Day dawns crisp and cold. A pale sun struggles to shine across snow-patched lawns and trees. Gusty winds push against the house. Turning to survey the family room, my eyes catch sight of the bright row of cards that decorate the mantelpiece. Reindeer pull Santa Clauses on sleds through starry skies; quaint towns stand dressed to the nines in Holiday regalia; untied camels stand in front of stables; fancy red and gold letters convey cheery seasons greetings. Not that I care. This year, nobody has received a card from me, no tree stands decorated by me, not a single door or wall is embellished with a hand-made festive wreath. Voodoo women do not do anything that they are not in the mood to do.

Last night, as I laid out thick, red, festive bath towels, and rooted around the linen cupboard for soaps that Dad didn't think were as girly as the ones in the guest room bathroom, ("Jeez, Molly, you've got me scented up like a flaming diva."), he announced that he would phone Denise sometime this morning. "I'm finally learning a few important things about love and marriage," he said, "and now I need to make sure that I still have a wife to share them with." I wonder what Dad thinks he's actually learned about love and marriage since, so far as I can tell, he doesn't seem to recognize what it is he needs to fix.

With elbows resting on the countertop, I sip a strong, rich Sumatra coffee and consider what Bob would have done if I had up and left him instead of trying to fix the unfixable. Shirley Bills or Mary Murphy would be sitting here right now I imagine. Bob would have just let me go.

"A penny for your thoughts, Molly."

Dad stands in the kitchen doorway wearing his old red robe and wool socks, the ones with Santa Claus faces all over them. His ridiculous outfit and hangdog look make me want to set off crying. Instead, I start to blab, shocked to find that the ring story has been waiting in my mouth, priming itself, demanding an airing, and preparing to get one with or without my permission. "I was just thinking about something Bob did before he died."

"Want to share it?" He plunks himself down in Bob's chair, eager to hear all.

Wishing I had kept my mouth shut, I try to sidestep. "How about a cup of coffee? It's fresh."

He waves his hand to stop me from getting up. "No problem. I'll get it myself when I'm ready." He studies my face and waits.

Bob's humiliating, winning move is supposed to have remained my secret. I can't tell anyone about the ring thing, least of all Dad. Until last night, we've never talked about anything remotely personal.

"By the way, how was the weather when you left Vancouver?" I wax cheerily, revealing the dismal levels of my current critical thinking capacity.

"Same as it always is at Christmas." He shuffles over to the coffee maker and fills a red mug patterned with white snowflakes right up to the brim. Back in Bob's old seat he prods gently, "I'm all set and I'm all ears. Now talk."

I'm nine-years old. My mother stands stone-faced, gazing out of her kitchen window at her small vegetable garden and the myriad flowers she grows for cutting. Her hands grasp the counter in front of the sink as if to help her stay on her feet. Silent Dad sits straight in his kitchen chair, his nose held high, his jaw set. She asks again, "I want you to talk to me about why you didn't come home until midnight last night." Without a word, he gets up and stomps out of the room. Mom glimpses me huddled beside the back door. She drops her head and sighs. "Go outside and bring me a nice bouquet," she says. "You can decide what to put in it." I wander amongst her flowers for ages, unable to cut any of them down in case I hurt them.

It now dawns on me that this worrying of mine might have sneakily transferred itself away from flowers and onto people. I've rarely been able to cut people down, no matter how much they deserve it. Even Bob was spared my true wrath. Of course, that was before red polka dots began appearing, and before I found his brazen, rolling wedding ring.

Dad pats the counter in front of me. "Come on Molly, quit the silence. Out with it."

When she died, my mother had lived with Dad's silences

for over twenty-seven years. My heart clenches like a fist at the scope of it. I say, "Silences are often easier than other options, aren't they?"

He places his hand on mine. "Sometimes, silences can be deadly." I wonder if Denise told him that. We drink our coffee and consider awhile.

I once read a newspaper report about a woman who, after twenty-five years of marriage, shot her husband dead while he sat on the toilet mulling over his latest copy of the *New York Times*. She told the arresting officer that she did it because he refused to speak to her. He hadn't spoken to her in weeks, which she said was not unusual. I showed the article to Bob and he looked at me as if I were a murderess myself. He knew his silent games made me feel crazy-angry, because he never left the bathroom door open after that.

I wonder what happened to the poor, demented woman after she shot her silent husband right off the toilet and into oblivion. Was she thrown into a prison cell for the rest of her life, her days used up from marriage to death because she made such bad choices? Did she know now that had she matched his indifference with a greater indifference of her own, if she had walked out of his life forever, she might have been happy by now? Why had she stayed? Why had her husband wanted her miserable? It makes no—

"Share your story with me, Molly," Dad says. His skin looks too tight. His eyes flicker across my face before dropping to investigate an imaginary floater in his coffee. He seems more nervous than he was last night.

I think: He's practicing being a good dad. And then, I can't stop myself from blurting, "I went through Bob's closet and drawers. I wanted to unload his clothes, give them to the Vietnam Vets organization, you know?"

"Good idea." Dad nods his approval, leaning toward me, wanting to miss nothing. "You've put them to good use."

"That's when I found his wedding ring. It was tied up in the toe of one of his socks. He put it there the night he died."

Dad's eyebrows almost meet his hairline. "Jeez! Why would he do a thing like that?"

"That's what I want to know."

His arms lift his hands palms up. "There must be more here. What ideas do you have on this?"

"For years, I accused him of bopping the paid help, one woman in particular. Of course, he always furiously denied it. But then I found out *for sure* that it was true, and read him the riot act."

Dad drawls, "Oooooooh." He stares at the air, no doubt hoping to avoid continuing this conversation. He plays for time, nibbling his upper lip, shaking his head, acting as if he cannot even imagine the ring thing in the first place, let alone explain it.

"Well?" I pressure, my annoyance growing. "You wanted to hear this. Now you have to respond." I watch him going through all of his silent histrionics, and bet he's thankful that I don't know what he got up to.

"Okay," I snip, "Two questions. One: why did he lie about wanting to stay married if he didn't care about the marriage? Two: why did he hide his wedding ring? Why not just throw it at me, or say he wanted a divorce, or say he didn't love me?" I blot up angry tears with a paper napkin before they can hit my cheeks.

Dad sits with one hand holding his coffee mug, the other stroking his chin. Both elbows rest on the counter. He closes his eyes, sucks in a loud breath, holds it for a few seconds, and then exhales just as loudly. "Look, Molly, I know that in his own weird way, he did care about you and the marriage...the way I cared about you and your mom. It was just one of those guy things with Bob."

"What?" I'm dazed by the truth in his answer.

His gaze remains firmly fixed on the refrigerator as if the answers to life's questions lie on its surface. "If Denise read the riot act to me, I would probably act defiant and pretend that I didn't care about the marriage either, to save face." He takes a drink of his coffee, embarrassment hot on his cheeks.

Astonishment replaces my hurt and anger. I bet that Denise has read the riot act to him.

"Bob was an idiot," he says, shuffling in his seat.

"You're too, too kind!" I joke, rescuing him from further painful introspection and then regretting it. This is the perfect time to push for an answer to the acid test question, so I'd better use it well.

He heads over to the coffee maker and holds up the pot, "More?

I nod and watch him pour. "Since you seem to understand this stuff," I say, carefully, "why do you think that Bob cared about me, but acted as though he didn't? He knew that when he made me miserable, we would both be miserable. Why not try to make it work? Why not choose to be happy? I just don't get it."

"Was it that Shirley Sheila woman?" Dad shouts, startling me so much I slop fresh coffee onto the counter.

"What?" I dab at the bottom of my mug with a paper napkin, confusion throwing me into a fluster.

"That flashy, blond piece of work! Was it *her?*"

"Yes," I stammer, "At least, she was one of them."

"One of them?"

"She was the worst."

He looks murderous, his green eyes glittering like well cut emeralds. "At least I never did anything like that."

I can see them through the store's front windows. She is young with sleek black hair and small frame. They're laughing and leaning toward each other across the counter, Dad's hands are jiggling her breasts.

Dad picks up his coffee in trembling hands.

"So, how did you get that idea about Bob and Shirley?" I ask.

"It was her manner … and his."

Humiliation threatens to blind me. "You met her once, when Bob showed you and Mom around his office, and you could tell by their *manner*?" Was there anyone except me who hadn't known, who hadn't been able to tell just by looking? How many people believed their own eyes, while I believed Bob's lies?

"They were altogether too familiar with one another. And she was smug and superior with you. At least, I thought so."

"I fired her."

Dad chokes on his coffee, then throws his head back and hoots laughter. He rests his face in his hands. He clutches his stomach. He gasps for breath.

How can I help but join in? "Why are we laughing like this?" I giggle.

"Because you fired her."

"Why is that funny?" I giggle louder.

"Because you're too much, Molly. You're the best thing since sliced bread."

"That's funny?"

"Yes. When you're a proud father, that's funny." He takes a deep breath and passes me the Kleenex.

These days, I shed a few tears at the least bit thing. A huge pressure is being slowly and carefully released, so as not to have me explode into a ruined heap like our back yard's Mount Everest.

"I'm glad you're proud, Dad."

"I wouldn't trade you for millions of dollars, Molly."

I wonder if he knows that I'm so bedazzled by his unexpected burst of love, I no longer have the heart to persist in asking him why he thinks Bob set out to make me miserable. I've asked him a question he won't answer. Dad is still playing the same old game.

25

Heading for the city on dry roads bordered by low snow banks, we sit comfortable and cosy in the leather bucket seats of my tiny Triumph, its new heater blowing hot air around our feet and faces. Taking the Spitfire was Dad's idea. He loves old restored sports cars, especially mine. I think of my mother, who was always filled with warnings about danger. "Be careful. Those semi drivers can't even see that car. It's not much bigger than a tin can. Make one mistake, you'll be crushed like a bug." Grandmother said that Mom's security had been shaken loose of its base when her father deserted her. "This is why she's such a worrywart," she told me, "and it's why she struggles to be happy."

Dad fiddles with the radio until he manages to tune in the Oldies station and his hero, Elvis, who is soon found wrenching out his sorrowful "Blue Christmas." Turning up the sound, Dad launches into his exaggerated Elvis voice, the way he did when I was little, wiping away pretend tears and saying, "thank you very much" whenever he can. It's guaranteed to make me laugh.

I tear onto I-94, keeping one eye on the clock. Since Voodoo Women prefer to make reservations rather than Christmas dinner, we are going to Stefano's for their two o'clock seating. We have only twenty-five minutes to get there.

"This certainly would have been a blue Christmas if I'd stayed home alone." Dad sighs and pats my hand as I shift gear.

"I imagine it would."

"By the way, Denise asked after you this morning."

I think that Denise should have asked after me over four months ago when Bob died, so I say, "Same here, I suppose," which goes right over Dad's head.

"She's staying in Seattle with her Australian friend, Justine."

"Who's she?"

"You met her once, when you and Bob came to our wedding. She's really quite nice. Very intelligent. Very attractive. About forty-nine now, same as Denise. Twenty-something years ago they both came over from Sydney together. Remember?"

I search my brain. "Is she a tall blond woman?"

"No. Short and dark."

"Oh."

It's Dad's wedding day. The guests stand under sunny skies on the broad lawns of Denise's lovely English garden smack dab in the middle of Richmond, BC. Her small square house is charming: two stories, brick painted the color of Devonshire cream, wood window boxes spilling out flowers in blues, reds, yellows, beautiful enough to make my eyes sting. Fifty people are here, including the bride and groom. With her dark blond curls, big blue eyes and slight build, Denise looks so much like my mother, sorrow nips sharply at me every time I look at her.

"Justine was married to the Episcopal priest who married Denise and me. Remember? The long, lanky guy with the comb-over?"

"Hmm, I can just about picture him, but not her."

"Anyway, he died a couple of years ago, so Justine had to move out of their house. It belonged to the church. Now she lives near the water in one of those cute Cape Cods."

Soon after the wedding, Dad phones. Denise has sold her house and now everything can be moved into his brand new one, a fancy place in West Vancouver that sits on a cliff overlooking the ocean. Mom hasn't been dead a year.

"Her husband died?"

"Yup! Only fifty-one. Heart attack. I tell you, it's scary."

"Bob was only forty-five."

He looks out of the window so that I can't see how much he doesn't care. "I expected less traffic today," he says. "You'd think that people would be where they need to be already."

"They're probably on their way to restaurants, just like us. Anyway, tell me about Justine."

He clears his throat. "Well, it seems she went a bit off the rails after Dean died. Totally off the rails really."

"She went crazy?"

"She went to town. Painted it red. You know, played it fast and loose."

"The *priest's* wife? Oh my God! What happened?"

"I think it was because of all those years when she curtailed herself. You know playing that pious role and pretending to be something she obviously wasn't. In the end, she just bust out. It was shocking. Floored everyone." Dad grins, relishing his story and my interest in it. "Not that I blamed her, mind you."

"She must have really hated being a priest's wife," I mumble. "It's exhausting to act like all is well when all is totally fouled up and smothering."

Dad checks out his fingernails. "I suppose so."

My voice rises. "I mean, she gave up her own life for him and their church, and then he up and dies and the church boots her out of her home, leaving her to her own devices. Great."

"Watch out, Molly, we're almost flying."

I lift my foot off the gas pedal and growl, "That's Justine's reward for enduring the wrong life. She was abandoned on all sides. Nice."

"She chose to be there, Molly." Dad pats my hand again. "Remember that."

"It's still pretty harsh. Besides, I bet she didn't know what she was getting into."

Dad gives me a playful punch. "But now she's chosen something else, Molly. She's having a ball doing her thing. And she's looking better than ever."

"I'm glad she rallied."

"Yup. Me too."

"It just proves that sometimes you really do have to blast your way out."

"If you look under 'blast out' in the dictionary, you'll see

Justine's face."

I grin and dead-pan, "Ha-ha-ha." I never knew that Dad loved to gossip like this. It's fun. "What did she do that was so wild? Give me all the gory details."

"For starters, she thoroughly enjoyed male attention. They lined up, young and old alike." He leans closer, "You know Seattle isn't like New York. It's not easy to hide in Seattle. Not that it mattered, because she didn't even try to hide."

"Really?" I'm starting to admire Justine.

"Nope. She was seen everywhere wearing plunging necklines and stiletto heels. Doing those jiggly dances too. Denise said it was something else." He smiles. "Lordy! I wish I could have seen that. She's a great gal."

I think: She sounds like a great Voodoo gal. But I say, "She is indeed." And then I wonder if Justine is giving Denise pointers on how to blast out from her life with Dad. "How long is Denise staying in Seattle?"

"She's coming back to Vancouver after the Holidays. She has to get back to school."

"Is Justine a teacher too?"

"Believe it or not, she's a psychologist. Of course, she didn't practice when she was the priest's wife. Now she works from home. Evidently makes a good living." Dad stares at the dashboard, a small smile playing on his lips.

I picture a multitude of unhappy women lined up outside of Justine's cute Cape Cod, huddled up against her walls, protecting themselves from gale force winds and freezing rains. They all want to know her secret. How did she do it? How did she manage to blast out so spectacularly, without a care as to what anyone thought? Would she have done it if her husband had not conveniently died?

I feel achy all over. Is it possible Dad doesn't understand that Denise really can leave him? In fact, she's likely discussing that very topic right now over Christmas turkey with her best friend, psychologist and Voodoo Woman, Justine. Does he still imagine that he can charm his way out of everything and so won't get dumped?

He glances out of the window. "We're here already."

Pulling up next to valet parking, I ask, "Are you hungry?"

"Starving."

I swing my legs out of the car and hand the keys to the slender young man in a long black overcoat and thick wool hat who's rushed over to collect them. Dad walks around the car and catches hold of my arm. "Molly my girl, you're a sight for sore eyes."

"Thanks, Dad, so are you." I'm surprised to find that I mean it.

Arms linked, we hurry into the restaurant.

26

D ad groans and lifts his silk Santa Claus tie, inspecting it for drips and crumbs. Satisfied that it has survived the meal, he lets it drop, leans back in his chair, looks across at me and crosses his eyes for a second. "Any sauce on my shirt?"

"No, although it's a miracle."

"You might be right about that." He gives a happy sigh and lifts his Elvis lip. "Thank you very much."

"Anytime."

He stretches his torso and moans, "Jeez, Molly. Did we have to eat *quite* so much?"

"Don't start with me." I tease. "Nobody forced you to have the double chocolate gelato."

He tugs at his belt. "I guess my eyes were bigger than my belly."

Seated in the cosy dining room at Stefano's, at a choice

table overlooking Michigan Avenue, we've just enjoyed perfect service and even better food. A sense of well-being has been sneaking into my psyche, chipping away at my anger, growing some silver. I look over at Dad's broad smile and all seems well with the world. I have to remind myself that in the past, after good times like this, he often followed through with a deliberate change for the worse.

Around us, people sit with their families, quietly chatting, letting their Christmas dinners settle, drinking coffee and sipping anisette, or crème de menthe or some other tummy soothing liqueur, their children deep into ice cream sundaes. I pay attention to all of the contented women (who must have happily relinquished their Christmas role of chief cook and bottle washer at home in favor of a good pampering at Stefano's) and wonder if they too have a touch of Voodoo in them.

Dad gives a satisfied sigh. "Mind you, they do know how to make a Caesar salad here, I have to give them that."

I forgot that Dad measures a fine restaurant's merits by the quality of its Caesars. He'll rant to anyone who doesn't know any better than to talk to him about such things. "Don't rave to me about fill-in-the-blank restaurant. I've had better Caesars in a diner. So far as I'm concerned, fill-in-the-blank restaurant is taking up a valuable space that could be used by a decent place." He can be so endearing, I think. That's what makes him dangerous.

"Yup. Stefano's Caesar is definitely the real deal. The best I ever had." Dad gazes upward with dreamy eyes. "And that veal. Where do I begin?"

"I couldn't possibly imagine, Mr. Gourmet."

He leans closer. "I thoroughly enjoyed our dinner, Molly.

Good call."

I consider his contented face and think that perhaps Dad secretly likes Voodoo Women. This morning he didn't want to go out for Christmas dinner at all, especially to an Italian restaurant. "A Christmas dinner is not a Christmas dinner if we don't eat at home, and if we don't have something traditional like turkey, or ham, or goose," he sputtered. "To have to go out for *spaghetti* instead of *turkey*." Red-faced, he threw his hands up, too upset to continue.

Although I felt like calling *him* a turkey, I kept my temper and spoke in an even tone. "Well Dad, let me ask you this. Which part of our dinner did you plan to make?"

"What?"

"And will you package up the leftovers and do all of the cleaning up? Because I don't plan to."

He stood as if his feet were glued together and his mouth was wedged open.

"Dad?"

"You're serious?"

"Dead serious." I raised my eyebrows and curled my Elvis lip.

Fighting a smile, he quickly relented. "In that case I have to say, you make a good case."

I clinked my orange juice glass against his. "I know."

"But you drive a hard bargain, girly. T'ain't natural," he drawled, like an old, gravelly-voiced cowboy.

"That would be *Ms.* Hard Bargain Girly to you," I retorted, making him laugh.

After that, he began treating the idea of doing Christmas dinner downtown as if it had been his own. "You know it never hurts to try new things," he advised.

I have to admit, he can turn on a dime.

At the coat check, Dad roots through his wallet. "You got a couple of ones, Molly? Or, should I just leave a five with it being Christmas and all?" Without waiting for a response he drops a five-dollar bill on the counter. "Merry Christmas, ma'am."

A slender, old woman dressed in a blood-red uniform, her long, silvery hair pulled up into a fat bun on the top of her head, struggles to deliver our heavy winter coats. "Why thank you. Merry Christmas to you too." When she smiles, impossibly white teeth shine out from her beautiful golden face.

"Didn't you have a package?" Her eyes twinkle.

"No. Not me." I stare at her as I button up. She looks a bit like Marie from the Old Town's Spiritual Magic Shop.

Supported on dainty hands, she leans across the counter "Have a wonderful New Year."

"Thank you. You too." Dad and I answer her in unison, smiling.

We turn to leave, still fastening buttons and organizing our scarves and gloves.

Her cheery, raspy voice calls after us. "Your daughter won't be playing with dolls much anymore, I imagine."

"Ha!" Dad turns to respond. "I wish I could go back to the days when she did."

I spin around to take another look at her, but she's disappeared. "It can't be," I mutter.

"Jeez!" Dad nods toward the deserted counter. "That little lady's quick on her feet."

I think: That was Marie. Wasn't it? How does she know we're father and daughter? Why did she mention dolls?

Since I don't have ready answers, I shove these questions to the back of my head to mull over later.

The doorman is holding the door open for us. Dad begins to examine it, feeling the edges, checking the handles and eyeballing the jamb from top to bottom. "I've seen great workmanship all through this place. Everything is top notch. You don't see too much of that these days." He slips the man a tip. "It does your heart good to see that some people care about how things get done."

I'm twelve years old, standing stiffly with Mom at the door of Dad's North Vancouver store. Behind the counter, Dad is dressed in clean blue jeans and a carefully pressed navy and white "Makepeace Hardware" shirt. We're waiting for him to close up. He's taking his time giving a pretty woman advice on what size nails she needs, and telling her why one hammer is better than another for her particular nailing project. "You want to do it right," he says. The woman is wearing a low cut sundress and high heel sandals. She's fluttering her lashes like a fool. I watch Dad's dazzled eyes. I think: he's more alive here with his stupid groupies, than he ever is at home.

"I love the smell of that store," he confides later, wanting me to understand why it comes first in his life. "Somehow, it got into my blood."

I smile politely and say, "I know." But I think: Why aren't Mom and I good enough for you? And I want to curl up and die at the shame of it.

In front of Stefano's, cold air cools our toasty faces. "Feels good out here." Dad inhales deeply. "Want to walk awhile? I can certainly stand to burn off a few calories, and it's been years since I've seen Chicago's Magnificent Mile."

I scan the clear, navy blue sky and the frost spangled

sidewalk. "That would be nice."

He takes my hand and links my arm through his. "Let's go, then."

Glittering, tree-lined Michigan Avenue lies before us, its summer flowerbeds now presented as softly lit showcases for winter's colors. Holly bushes, with bright red berries and deep green glossy leaves, personify the Holiday spirit. Red and gold geometric sculptures stand amongst sturdy fir tree branches that fall this way and that beneath a dusting of snow. Low wrought iron railings surround each bed in neat European style, keeping each rectangle perfectly defined. We head south toward the Chicago River, between trees decorated with tiny white lights, and festive store windows that illuminate the city's wide sidewalks in shades of gold and red and silver. In light traffic, cars cruise by, their sightseeing occupants straining to look up at sky-high buildings and rooftops lit up red and green.

"Wow!" is all Dad can say.

"Chicago is beautiful, isn't it?"

"So is Vancouver," he counters with exaggerated huffiness.

"Yup. So is Vancouver."

"Maybe you'll come back now?"

I squeeze his arm, touched that he wants me home, falling into old habits. "I'll have to think a lot about that. I love Vancouver, but I've lived here since the start of college. Almost half of my life has been spent here."

His face falls. "*Over* half of your life was spent at home."

"I know Dad. I know." I'm flattered by his persistence. But then, a loose camel trots by, and I start to think. Does he want me back in Vancouver in case he ends up alone there? Will he need my company only until he knows for sure that Denise is coming back, or that his Shirley Bills/ Mary Murphy backup is secure, or until he finds a full time replacement for Denise? After all, he has nobody waiting for him at home right now and—despite claiming to want to sort things out with me—that's really what pushed him here. If I do what he wants, I'll likely end up alone myself living his worst nightmare, and he won't care. I stiffen at his cheerful selfishness.

"Come on. Give Vancouver another try, Molly. It's home."

If I knew how, I would swiftly jujitsu him over my shoulder and into the holly bushes for a few sharp pricks. As it is, I'm limited to a defiant, "Nope. I'm going to stay put. I like Woodside now that I'm settled there."

"But why?"

"Oh my God!" I gasp, shutting off further discussion. Since we're both avid readers, we've automatically stopped to look in Borders' windows. Half a dozen Jonathan Wilson faces look back at us.

"What? What is it?" Dad gapes through the windows looking every which way for something shocking to latch onto.

"I know him."

"Who?" He puts his face closer to the glass, trying to catch sight of someone shifty in the deserted store.

"The man on the posters."

He follows my eyes. "That detective guy?"

"Yes." I'm trembling and wonder if Dad can tell.

"Who is he? How do you know him?"

"He's the detective who was assigned to work with me when Bob died. His book is published and on the shelves already. Wow! What an achievement."

"What do you mean 'work with you'?" Dad persists, sounding annoyed.

"Well, when someone as young and healthy as Bob dies without any apparent reason, the police may decide to investigate the case to make sure that nobody snuffed him." I avoid Dad's horrified gaze.

"Snuffed him! You mean, they thought you might have done him in?"

"Throughout history, there's always been the occasional wife who has 'done in' her husband, you know. The police just checked me out, that's all." Secretly delighted that Dad is upset on my behalf, I turn back to the posters. "Jonathan is appearing here January 5th for a reading and book signing. How great is that." A spark of excitement shoots through me at the thought of dropping in to see him.

"Humph!" Dad stands with folded arms glaring at Jonathan's innocent face. "Well, I think it's a lot of nerve. Checking you out."

I think: If you only knew the half of it. But I say, "It was just standard procedure."

Hooking my arm back through his, I pull him away from the window. "Come on. We'll get cold if we stand around too long."

We walk as far as the 500 North building before Dad breaks the silence. "I've been so wrapped up in my own stuff, Molly, I never really gave much thought about what Bob's death put you through. The police checking you out like that, and you all by yourself. I'm really, really sorry." He looks cold. I pull his hat further over his ears and rearrange his wool scarf higher on his neck.

"It's okay Dad. I'm glad that you came now."

He blinks hard and looks at the sky. We're nearly at the river.

"I was thinking, Molly. Since I didn't come to the memorial service, maybe you'd like me to come with you to see where Bob's ashes rest. What do you think?"

My heart rock and rolls. "Bob's ashes?"

"I know it's a little late, but I would still like to go."

In silence, we walk between the Tribune and Wrigley Buildings without even admiring their lights. On the bridge, we lean against the railing, looking east along the glittering Chicago River toward Lake Michigan and west at the river's ladder work of bridges, each one brilliantly lit from beneath. Jewel colored lights lie in strings along the riverbanks. All around us, the city's magical, elegant architecture shines against the sky.

I say, "There's something I have to tell you about Bob."

"This isn't about snuffing him, is it? Because if it is, I don't want to know," Dad banters.

I lightly punch his chest. "It's about Bob's ashes."

"What about Bob's ashes?" His smile has vanished and he stands straight. He seems to be steeling himself, waiting for me to reject his offer of contrition, preparing to be hurt. I get straight to the point.

"Bob's ashes are lost in the mail."

Dad looks dazed, his eyes squinting as he tries to focus on me. "I'm sorry Molly. What did you say?"

"I said that Bob is lost in the mail."

"In the mail?" His eyes narrow further as he tries to grasp the impossible news.

"Yes. Quite possibly, Bob is buried in some dead letter

office."

"Dead letter office?"

Something is not computing with Dad. I forge on with my explanation, hoping to make it clearer. "It's my own fault. Very embarrassing. I forgot to bring him home after his memorial. I left him on the display table."

Dad still doesn't move. I wonder if he's slowly freezing and begin to talk faster. "A new temp at the funeral home packaged him up with some of our CD's and photos and whipped them all in the mail. Evidently, he didn't know any better." My voice trails off. I shrug.

Dad is clutching his chest and making choking sounds.

"Dad!" I shout.

He falls against the rail.

"Oh my God!" Thinking he is on the verge of collapse, I grab his arm and try to hold him up.

His shoulders are shaking. He bursts out laughing like a hyena, shocking me half to death. "Sorry Molly. So sorry," he wheezes, "It's awful. Terrible." Leaning forward on the rail, he puts his head down onto his forearms and howls even louder.

"Dad. I mean…Dad, this doesn't seem right." Yet, even as I speak, that evil belly laugh, the one that has been plaguing me for weeks, begins to erupt like hiccups.

"It's not right," he pants, "not right." Then he hangs onto the railing and laughs so loudly it echoes along the river and back. He attempts to pull himself up straight. "Especially that bit about the—" He sets off again, wiping his eyes before tears can freeze on his cheeks.

"The bit about the what?" I unwisely ask. "The dead letter office?"

Dad hoots to the sky.

Behind me a deep voice rumbles, "Are you okay, Miss? Is this man bothering you?" A large Chicago policeman stands stern-faced, ready to sort Dad out.

"Thanks, but I'm fine. Really. This is my father. He's just laughing over a story I told him."

"Sorry, Officer," Dad pants, "I'll manage to collect myself soon. Which is more than her husband could do." Then he looks at me, and we both roar.

The policeman grins. "Well, that's a story I'd like to hear."

"Sorry," I manage to wheeze between giggles, "It's a family secret. Dust swept under the rug and all of that."

Dad covers his mouth and tries to stifle himself.

"Too bad." The officer groans, feigning disappointment, "That sounds like a real good one." He begins to walk north. "You two keep on having a Merry Christmas," he shouts, his right arm raised in a wave.

We lift our heads up from the railing. "You too, Officer," we manage to gasp.

The entire laughing episode has worn us out so badly, we have to cab it back to the car.

27

'm doing my thing in Jane's downstairs' bathroom when Dad shouts at me from along the hallway. "Your cell phone's ringing. Want me to get it?"

I hesitate, wondering who's calling me at eight o'clock on a Friday night, and not wanting to find out. "Okay," I shout back, feeling annoyed at myself. I think: Why do I still rush to cooperate rather than risk causing hurt feelings by just saying no?

Through the one-way mirror, Mom says gently, "Practice makes perfect."

By the time I fly into the living room, Dad has my phone to his ear and is listening intently. He glances over. "Molly just walked in," he tells the caller. Handing me the phone, he says, "It's Liz Cooper, your real estate agent." The words tumble out in a rush, question marks practically visible in his eyes. "Seems like your Hancock Building condo has just sold."

"Let's hope so," says Jane, holding up crossed fingers. Bernie sits on the edge of his seat.

Three pairs of eyes are now fastened on me; half a dozen ears are tuned in to catch my every word; and a trio of lungs holds its collective breath. I think about running outside for a little privacy, and then worry it will hurt everybody's feelings. Taking a deep breath, I say cheerfully, "Hi, Liz. What's up?"

"Good news, Molly," she bubbles. "A couple from New York just offered us the asking price."

"That's absolutely fantastic."

"They want to move in as soon as possible."

"That's great," I say, wanting to swoon with relief. "How quickly can we get things done?"

"I told them we can close in about four weeks," she says briskly, all business now. "I'll start writing up the paperwork right away."

When I get off the phone, I'm shaking all over.

Bernie holds up a bottle of champagne. Jane waves four glasses. "We have plenty of time for a celebration before dinner," she sings, happily ignoring the fact that we had two rounds of aperitifs before Liz phoned.

Dad asks, "Since when do you own a condo in the John Hancock Building?"

My cheeks flame. "The agency owns it."

"Why? Who used it?"

"Shirley-I-don't-pay-the-Bills," blabs Jane, who clearly needs to be cut off from her Holiday cheer.

Bernie sternly shakes his head at her.

"Sorry," she stage whispers, although she doesn't much look it.

Dad raises his eyebrows at me. "Want to explain," he says.

I miss another opportunity to practice saying no. Instead, I suck down a glass of champagne in one go and start to fill him in on the Pink Palace.

"What nerve," he steams. "What *goddamn* nerve."

"Damned right," adds Bernie, with fervor. He's starting to get into the swing of things. His wife is having a good time being outrageous, which always puts a smile on his cute, round face.

"Shirley Bills has more balls than the Illinois Lottery. But after Molly and I broke into that apartment, we soon got her sorted out."

I think: This champagne is shaking loose too many secrets.

Dad's eyes are like green and white dinner plates. "You two actually broke the *law?*"

"Well…we couldn't give her any warning, could we?" I huff like a teenager, champagne bubbles popping in my own brain. "Otherwise, what would be the point?"

He and Bernie exchange amazed looks, which makes me feel quite proud. Jane and I grin at each other.

She launches into an animated account of Cat Burglary Day, which, until tonight, is how she used to refer to it in private. She stands up to properly illustrate how we ran through the forty-fourth floor in our skirts and high heels (knees together, feet flying sideways). She performs her rendition of me clutching the repossessed files and banging like a mad woman on the elevator buttons to try and make it arrive faster.

I note that Bernie is enjoying her stand-up comedy so much, he's forgotten to plug up his ears to avoid knowing what we did that day. He and Dad are laughing so hard, I worry they might soon need resuscitation.

Encouraged by her appreciative audience, Jane presses her back to the living room wall, her arms spread wide. 'We tried to make ourselves disappear in the Hancock Building lobby,' she declares, as though presenting a serious documentary. Taking outrageously long and careful steps she starts sliding along like a wide-eyed vamp in an old-time movie. "Remember, Shirley was flying through the door in front of us."

Nobody can tell a tale quite like Jane, especially after a drink or two. Her ladylike manner, which she somehow manages to hang onto despite her antics, makes everything she does even funnier. Before she is done, we're wiping our eyes and begging her to stop.

From the corner, Jane and Bernie's Chanukah Christmas tree glows. Star shaped blue lights reflect against the silver Star of David on top. A collection of Santas hangs here and there alongside a variety of gaudy angels. From top to bottom silvery garlands encircle the lot.

"That's a wonderful-icious confection you've got over there," says Dad, as we help clear the table. "It's what you might call tree-mendous."

Jane whispers to me, "You know, he really can be sweet."

"I wish Bernice wasn't staying at her grandma's tonight," I smile. "*She's* what I call sweet."

Bernie starts shooing Dad and me out of the kitchen, and brings up the rear with a pot of coffee. "Sit, sit," he says, pointing us toward the armchairs by the fire.

A sense of well-being has seeped into my bones. I love being here in this cozy, rambling house with Jane and

Bernie, my friends who are like family. I glance at Dad, who is staring at the fire as though lost in its flames.

"I'm so glad that apartment sold," Jane is carrying in a tray of desserts. "And it didn't take nearly as long as we expected."

"How long was it on the market?" asks Bernie, taking a Christmas arrangement off the coffee table to make room for the food.

"Two months," I say. "Of course, that was after Shirley moved out, and the decorators went in. I had to get rid of that pink paint and fuss the place up first. It took a while."

"Jeez. After all you've had to do, you deserve a little fuss-ery for yourself," Dad mutters.

"Agreed," says Jane, giving me a wink.

"Fuss-eraciousness definitely has its place," I say, cheerfully, surprised that Dad's been stewing on my behalf.

"Those two characters were vicious," he murmurs to the flames. "Doing all of that rotten stuff to you."

Jane raises her eyebrows and gives me a look that says, "He just might be getting it."

I give her a look back that says, "Don't be too sure of it."

Dad turns to me and says, "So, where is that woman living now?

"Last I heard she's renting a place up on the north side."

"Do you ever run into her?"

"Nope. We heard through the buzz that she went after a couple of high-level agency positions, but didn't get anywhere."

"Her reputation precedes her," mutters Bernie.

"So we think she's still trying to launch her own company from home."

"Thanks to her stealing your clients, she can do that," Dad says softly. "You should have sued her ass."

"I would have loved to," I say. "But legal battles and scandals hurt companies. I wanted her out, fast. I had to keep the agency going. I couldn't have stood failing at that."

His eyes are shining. "I'd have been brought up for *murder* over this," he growls. "I don't know how you managed to keep your hands off them."

I lower my eyes and carefully choose a fancy Christmas cookie from the plateful Bernie has put in front of me. "These look delicious," I say.

28

t's New Year's Eve already, and I haven't had such a fun eight days in a long time. Dad loves being on the move. He whisked me off to see the Milwaukee Art Museum's fancy expansion, "Santiago Calatrava was the architect for gosh sakes, Molly. The design is incredible, but the *workmanship* alone is worth the trip." He waved the museum's "Fun Facts" sheet in front of my face. "Jeez! I can't believe you haven't been already."

As a treat, I let him drive us there in the Triumph. He walked around it admiring the paint job and checking the tires before dropping behind the wheel. He stroked the steering wheel and examined the new leather seats. He fiddled with the stick shift, and nodded his approval. He did a deadpan rendition of his old joke, comparing my car with the often-repaired, inadvertently brand new, antique hammer, knowing it would make me laugh.

He drove fast, reveling in the Spitfire's nimbleness, stopping in a rush at the expressway tollbooths and then revving up before tearing off again, grinning like a maniac all the way. At the sight of the white museum, which appears to float on the edge of Lake Michigan and looks like it might set sail, I was agog. "I told you," said Dad, his face jubilant.

He made me remember how much I like to get out of the house and into the hustle bustle, the sheer fun of Chicago. He persuaded me to spend a day with him and the fishes at Shedd Aquarium, and another with him and the old masters at the Art Institute. "I don't care if you went there years ago," he teased. "My God, Molly, you're already a reluctant tourist. Keep up this attitude and by the time you're my age you'll have taken root."

He's starting to say things I never dreamed I'd hear. Friday night, as we drove home from Jane and Bernie's he proclaimed, "Jane is the best person you could have picked to be your vice president, Molly. She's a nervy broad, just like you."

I should feel more pleased at the success of Dad's visit. But all week, it's been slowly dawning on me that Dad and I have a tacit agreement. We've been carefully avoiding the issues that need addressing. Even during our quiet evenings together, we read or watched movies instead of talking and clearing the air. Throughout our meals, we never *really* talked. Instead, we just chatted about our outings and such, and pretended that all was perfect between us. Tomorrow he heads home. I feel disappointed over missed opportunities, and—for some weird reason—a tad uneasy.

About the time I start cooking our New Year's Eve

feast, Denise phones to confirm that she'll pick up Dad at Vancouver International Airport tomorrow night and drive him home. He is elated, practically singing down the phone. "Thanks sweetheart. That's great. I can't wait to see you." Resting his head against the back of his favorite armchair, he smiles at the ceiling.

I wince at his confidence. Is he really thinking that because Denise has been staying with Voodoo Woman Justine for a few weeks, she'll have calmed down and pulled herself together? Does he imagine that she is meekly coming home to him? I suspect that she's made her stand against him, and he's done nothing at all to make her want to soften it.

My heart patters with dread over what might come next. Watching out of the corner of my eye, I see his mouth drop. "Not staying with me?" He sits up straight, his eyes rolling. "But why?"

I find myself wanting to shout, "Do you ever try listening to her? Because you never bothered listening to Mom." Instead, I busy myself with the vegetables and pretend not to hear, wishing I could warn him that he'd better slow down and think. He's falling back into old habits, making a bad situation worse.

"No, I really *don't* know why," he insists, which is consistent with the denial part of the game. Soon he is acting like the offended party, his face reddening, his mouth set in a tight, straight line.

"What do you want me to do, Denise?" he bleats. "I do everything I can. Why aren't you ever satisfied?"

She must have gone off like a rocket, because he spends the rest of their conversation trying to calm her down.

I could wallop him a good one myself. Instead, I walk over to the bar and choose a wine for dinner, as if oblivious to his sorry backtracking.

"Okay, okay, okay! I'll talk to you when I get there." Droopy-face Dad lugs himself up, trudges across the floor, plunks the phone back on the desk, and then drops himself like a delivery of firewood into Bob's chair at the counter. He runs his hands through his hair and produces a groan that could curdle milk. "I just don't know what to do with that woman," he sighs. Picking up his ginger tea, he swigs it down and reaches for my big box of Marshall Field's chocolates.

I grip the edge of the counter and ask the universe to give me strength.

"She is never satisfied. Never." He shakes his head. "I just don't know what to do any more to satisfy her." He chomps on his Frango Mint chocolate and pops in another.

I'm eleven years old, picking a chocolate out of a box. My mother is sitting at the kitchen table, her books and papers spread across it. She lifts up her adult education class homework and shows it to me with pride. I start reading it out loud. "Question: An eight-year-old student is joining your class mid-term. How would you help her successfully integrate? Answer: I would select from my class a friendly, responsible child to put in charge of showing the new student around, and to help her get to know her new classmates."

"That's really good, Mom," I say, awed by her cleverness.

"Molly, make sure you go to college right after high school," she advises. "I always wanted to be a teacher, but I had to work to put your dad through Business College. After that, there was his store business I had to help build up from scratch," she strokes her paper

lovingly. "Still," she says, almost to herself. "I'm doing it now."

We're preparing vegetables at the sink when Dad walks in. "What's this?" he says, picking up her paper. Mom and I grin at each other, and wait for his praise.

"Jeez!" He looks over at her. "This is really stupid." He tosses it down and then snorts as he walks out.

We stand with our vegetable peelers and potatoes. Mom's face twists and her eyes squeeze shut. My hands drip water as I reach for her, splattering her pretty red blouse with a pattern of dark red dots, like tears of blood.

"Why did you provoke and hurt Mom the way you did?" says my mouth, sending shock waves across my chest.

"What?"

"You know you did," I say, in that strange monotone that occasionally pops out of me nowadays. "Please tell me why. I need to know."

"Now just hold on a minute, Missy. I don't like what's happening here. We've had such a great week together—"

"Yes, we have," I say. "We've avoided talking about anything important. But I need the answer. I really need to know." I fill a pan with water and throw in a touch of salt.

Dad is looking around the room as if checking for the exits. He jumps to his feet and starts to walk away from me.

I follow him. "Why did you hurt her so deliberately?"

"I don't know what to say to you, Molly," he says, opening the door to the bathroom.

I stick my foot between the door and the jamb. "Yes, you do. You just need the courage to say it." I'm half in the bathroom and half in the hall. I stand defiant, tear open the bag of carrots I'm holding, and challenge his silence with my own.

Finally, he shrugs his shoulders and slowly raises his hands, palms up, in a helpless gesture. "Because she was a *nag*?" he questions, as if trying his best to be helpful.

I cannot speak.

"Now let me get to my business here," he says briskly.

I think I see a touch of triumph in the curl of his lip. He uses his foot to nudge my foot out of the bathroom and fully into the hallway. The door closes with a sharp bang.

Carrots in one hand, scraper in the other, I remain transfixed, astonished by his assessment. After the toilet flushes, I shout over the noise of the fan. "She was a *nag*?" I press my ear to the door to catch his response. There is none. His shoes slap against the tile as he stomps over to the sink. He turns on the water full blast, and washes his hands like a gardener who forgot to wear gloves while weeding in mud.

I think: He can take all the time he wants, I'm not moving from this spot.

The door swings open and he gently pushes past me. "Let go of this," he says.

"She was a nag?" I repeat. "That's your reason?"

"Well, I suppose it is." He walks into the kitchen and reaches for another chocolate mint.

My mother's stricken face rises before my eyes.

"Tell me what she nagged you about that made it okay for you to treat her so badly?" I take out two baking potatoes and start to scrub them with a ferocity they do not deserve.

"She never stopped nagging."

"What did she nag you about?"

"Everything."

"What do you mean, *everything*?"

"I don't know," he huffs, "*Everything!*"

I stab the potatoes with a fork as if to put them out of their misery, and slam them next to the oven. "Tell me what Mom did wrong. Otherwise, it sounds like you're blaming her for everything again."

"I was always faithful to her."

"Were you?"

"I don't know what it is you want from me," he groans.

"The truth, for once," I say, as a long buried memory once more jumps to life.

I can see them through the store's front windows. She is young with sleek black hair and small frame. They're laughing and leaning toward each other across the counter, Dad's hands are jiggling her breasts. Flinging open the door, I imagine what it might be like to break her in two in front of him, to snap her tiny pigeon skeleton to smithereens. She smoothes down her top and smirks at me. "Hi Molly," Dad says, with a smile. "What brings you here?"

When I shake my head and say, "Nothing," he doesn't blink.

Now, he acts like an innocent man before the gallows. "Your mother accused me of things I didn't do."

I think: You bastard. But I say, "Are you saying she made things up, or that she imagined things?"

He sighs like a badly-done-to man, and says with exaggerated patience. "I'm just saying that she accused me of stuff I didn't do."

"Maybe she was paranoid, just like me. "

"I didn't say you're paranoid."

"Bob did," I steam. "He said I imagined things. You say Mom imagined things. Are Mom and I alike, or are you and Bob alike."

For a second, his smug look drops. "I'm not like Bob."

"No? Well, maybe he was like you." I go back to the carrots and start to furiously scrape them. "Bob didn't come home. He drank." I stop scraping and stare at him.

I'm seven years old, sitting at the top of the stairs looking through our banister railings. Daddy just got home. He's wearing his best suit, and looks dizzy—the way I do after turning round and round in circles. Mommy is wearing her silky nightgown. She got out of bed when she heard his key in the lock.

"Where were you tonight? Who were you with?" She sounds so angry it makes me shake.

"Don't start," he says, shoving her aside.

"Mommy!" I cry, running down the stairs.

"See what you've done now," he yells in her face.

He stinks of beer and cigarettes and icky perfume.

"Do you think I never saw you pushing Mom around, or that I didn't see your boozing, or hear you blaming her for every rotten thing *you* did."

"Right now you sound just like her the way you imagine things," he says, sounding exactly like Bob again.

"I saw how you put her down. You say she nagged you. But that's not the point, is it? Lots of men could bully their so-called nagging wives the way you did, but they don't want to. Why did you?"

He sighs as if in great pain, and sinks all over.

"You have the answer Dad. Nobody else is inside of your head." I drop into a chair, exhausted. "Mom never got her teaching degree because of what you said to her. You treated her like she was your maid, and then complained that she hadn't done better with herself. You never made her feel beautiful. And about a hot minute after she died, *you had the nerve to marry a teacher who looked just like her."*

Dad's mouth twitches, and his face turns ashen. "Do you ever think about how I felt?" he shouts. "Maybe I needed a little more consideration from your mother."

"Dad! We always thought about you. That's about all we ever seemed to think about. You made sure of it."

Mouth open to speak, he raises his hand to stop me.

"Let me finish," I say, loudly. "This is important."

"No!" he shouts. "I don't have to listen to this. I didn't come here for this." He heads for the stairs.

My breath comes in gulps as I take off after him. "You made us both into a pair of pleasers. I still relive this stuff. It's been playing in my head for years. I want some answers. I deserve some answers!"

He rushes up the stairs, but I stay on his heels. 'Pleasing you morning, noon, and night. You made life hell.' I bang a big carrot against the staircase banister. 'But, we could never quite manage to please you, could we? You would never allow it. You didn't respect her, did you, Dad? Nor me for that matter. What do you think that did to our self-esteem, our boldness? After all of that indifference, do you think we had any?'

"Just you wait a minute, Missy," he growls. "I did lots of nice things for you mother." He does an abrupt U-turn and shoots past me back down the stairs. In the foyer, he detours into the living room.

"Oh yes, you did," I shout after him. "But that was just so you could get her back under your control."

Mom is wearing a dress as blue as her eyes. From her casually upswept hairdo a few long tendrils hang in lazy curls. Her skin looks luminous. I think: This gorgeous, sexy woman cannot possibly be my mother.

"We'll be coming home late, Molly," *she teases, happy now that Dad is wooing her back.* "Don't wait up."

Dad opens the door, links her arm through his, and out they go.

"You're a nice guy, Dad," I yell. "Except when you're not."

And then, from an information collection point at the center of my brain, a sudden buzz of understanding telegraphs itself along tightly wired nerves and a miraculous burst of knowing falls into place. Suddenly, everything makes sense.

I run into the living room where he sits in a huff on the couch. "That's it," I whisper. "That's what it's all about."

"What? What do you mean?" He actually looks interested.

"You upset Mom by doing something rotten." He opens his mouth to protest, so I raise my voice and calmly keep going. "Then, you deny doing it. Then you criticize her for daring to think such a thing. In fact, you attack her every concern with a denial until she's so confused she can't think her way out of anything."

It is the morning after one of Bob's binges with a boozy client or two, and Shirley. "I'm sick of this," *I shout.* "You did this same thing last month and promised, yet again, that it would be the last time you'd do it."

"Last month?" *His eyebrows rise.* "No I didn't."

I stop, and try to mentally flip backwards though the calendar. "Yes, you did," *I say, uncertain now.*

"Weren't we in Hawaii last month?"

I hesitate. "Not all month."

"When did I have time to get out last month?"

"Well…" I say, my brain still stuck in the calendar and not on his boozing.

He throws his hands up. "You see?" he shouts. "You don't even know what you're talking about." He plods toward the door. "Just for once," he moans, "I'd like to see you count your blessings instead of bitching at me."

"It's so wrong, Dad. Wrong, wrong, wrong! We don't have to take this any more. We've taken it long enough. *I'm sick of taking it!*"

"I was good to your mother," he moans.

"You really expect me to believe that you were this Mr. Nice Guy married to a miserable nag," I snort, "What a joke. She was your scapegoat. You got control of Mom by making your actions against her, her own fault."

"You're wrong, Molly. Dead wrong."

I think: No. Bob is *dead* wrong. But I say, "Mom let her career dreams slide and maintained a five star hotel lifestyle for you—she kept a clean house, cooked your favorite meals, washed your laundry, raised your kid, and hated every minute because there was nothing at the end of it for *her!*"

"Not true."

"And how do you think your kid felt, Dad?" I shout. "Do you think that your kid felt loved at all? *By either one of you."* I gulp down sobs, thinking that the knowing of this is sharper than any pin.

"A lot of it was her fault," he insists. But his eyes betray an uncertainty, and his lips are on the verge of collapse.

"You gave Mom the chore of fixing the unfixable, because you knew she would feel guilty at failing to please you. It kept her in line."

"She changed, Molly. It's true whether you like it or not."

"I loved my mother, and she had a lousy life. She kept on trusting you even when you made trusting impossible. She *believed* in you."

He shakes his head and views the ceiling, his mouth set just like Bob's.

"I think that you were so clever at the confusion game, Dad, you've managed to confuse yourself along the way. It sucks everybody in."

He sighs and looks away.

"There are no winners in your game, Dad. Not Mom. Not me. Not you."

"If I was that bad, your mother should have dumped me."

"You *knew* she wouldn't," I say, harshly. "She was frightened you'd disappear from my life like her own father did from hers. But you know something? She wasted her time. You left us even though you stayed."

"I never left you."

"Oh my God! After the way you've acted, who could believe that?"

Worn out, I trudge back to the kitchen, lean my elbows on the counter and close my eyes. I refuse to appear as upset as I feel. Minutes tick by, but I am not going to be the one who speaks first. He's not going to suck me into a new game. That camel is tied.

I'm shocked to hear his chair scrape across the floor. He's followed me back into the kitchen. "Oh, for God's sake," he says, "we should be able to talk, shouldn't we?"

I nod, speechless.

"All right. I know I have to change a few things," he sighs, and then switches focus. "But so does Denise."

I slap the counter in front of him. "As we speak, she and Justine are probably having their heart-to-hearts. She might find out she doesn't *need* you. In fact, she could end up like Justine, happier on her own. Will you feel like a winner then?"

Dad's face pales. "I'm not going to be *that* stupid."

I put my hand over his, and speak urgently. "Aren't you? How else do you explain why you set out to ruin the future before it even gets here? The way you did with Mom."

He withdraws into silence. But not that tormenting, impenetrable silence he used against my mother. This time, he seems to have forgotten I'm here.

Refusing to feel guilty over telling him how I feel, I leave him alone and get on with the dinner, pretending calm, seasoning our prime rib and setting it in the roasting pan, stirring horseradish and a dash of Worcestershire Sauce into a bowl of crème fraiche, washing salad stuff, and preparing vegetables. A pan of water receives sliced carrots and a sprinkle of salt. Brussels sprouts bob in another. Pressing fresh garlic, I scrape it into balsamic vinegar and oil and give it a haphazard stir, thinking that I'd better start timing everything out. The Yorkshire puddings have to go into the oven an hour after the beef, and I must not forget the gravy.

•

I can't believe I got all of that said to Dad. It's left me so shaken, I have to go upstairs and lie down. I'm asleep before my head touches the pillow.

I dream that Bob is curled in a ball inside of his urn. Shivering and shaking he calls out to me, "I'm freezing my ass off in here, Moll." I want to breath warmth into him but don't know how.

I think he's in Iceland.

Now I see him, martini in hand, seated at a bar beside a black-haired woman dressed in red satin. "He's with me," I whisper, feeling frightened and vulnerable. When Bob turns toward me, he has Dad's face.

Dad wakes me up. He's tapping at the door and slowly opening it. "Want me to set the table, Molly?" he says softly.

I rush over to hug him. When I let go, I see he has a beaten up look about him—bleak eyes, yet wavering smile. Something in him seems settled.

I wrap my arms around him, again. "I'm glad I was able to talk to you about this, Dad," I say, wanting him to know that in my book we're still okay.

He hugs me back, hard. "I'm going to fix this, Molly. I promise you."

Stepping back to give him the once over, I hold down welling emotion. "You look like a man who means business," I declare, "and it's a wonderful thing."

His face grows rosier, which melts my heart.

"There are things you got right, you know Dad?"

"I know," he whispers tightly. "I got you."

29

His suitcase is packed and Dad stands next to it in the kitchen, taking one last look around the place. He walks over to the patio doors and stares outside. "I have to say, Molly. I'm glad I came."

"You couldn't have come at a better time." It is true.

We watch a squirrel doing accidental acrobats as it attempts to reach a hanging bird feeder. Dad runs outside to shoo it away. The squirrel knows just how far to run to stay out of trouble's reach before it turns around, sits down in the snow and waits. Dad walks back to the house, the squirrel creeping along behind him, heading toward the bird feeder.

"Damn! It's cold out there." A bitter wind blows into the kitchen as he quickly slides the patio door closed.

"Look." I nod towards the bird feeder.

We giggle as the squirrel scampers back up the tree,

tiptoes along branches and slides down the long hook attached to the feeder. Upside down, it tries unsuccessfully to figure out a way to get at the seed. Twisting this way and that, it falls into the snow, shakes itself off, and stares over at us.

"He wants to make sure we're watching him," marvels Dad. "I guess even squirrels like to feel appreciated."

"Appreciation does a body good," declares Grandmother from the family room.

Arm in arm, Dad and I walk back to the island to drink mugs of hot chocolate and watch the time.

"Look at the state of this," he points at his stomach. "In one week I've grown a kangaroo pouch. God knows what's in there. I don't dare weigh myself."

"I know the feeling."

"Last night's dinner was mega-licious." He waggles his finger. "I had no idea you could cook like that. Your mother and grandmother taught you well."

I raise my Elvis lip, "Thank you very much."

"It's the truth, Ms. Clever Clogs."

"I'll clever clogs you in a minute."

We shake our heads at each other and chuckle.

"I have to admit it was a major miracle that the food was all ready at the same time, especially after drinking that martini you made me."

"It was a good one all right."

"My glass overfloweth."

We sip our hot chocolate, the house warm and cozy around us.

"I'm glad we talked, Molly."

"It's made a big difference," I say. "Next time, I hope

you'll tell me about your parents."

"Some things are best left unsaid."

"After last night's talk, do you still think that's true?"

He picks up his hot chocolate and examines it. "Someday, I'll tell you."

I picture Bob as a tormented little boy. My hand reaches for Dad's.

He sighs, "It's another new year, Molly. Pretty soon, I'll be an old man."

My heart squeezes tight. "You'll never be old, Dad. Besides, Mom always said that even if you live to be a hundred you'll always believe you're handsome."

He bursts out laughing, "Well, thank you, I think."

"You're welcome."

He looks at his watch. "I ordered a cab. It should be here any minute."

"I said I'd take you," I say, in astonishment. "Why did you do that?"

"Because, I'm sure the roads are packed, especially New Year's Day when all the big sales are on." He throws an arm around my shoulders. "Besides, these days you're hardly allowed into airports if you're not actually flying somewhere. Why drive all that way in awful traffic just to drop me off at the door?"

I think: He still thinks he can make my decisions for me. But I say, "It's not that far. I wanted to do it."

The doorbell rings giving my stomach the flutters. My grandmother died before I got the chance to see her again. Now, I hate goodbyes.

Dad gets to his feet. "Thanks for everything, Molly, and I mean, everything."

"Next time, don't stay away so long." Feeling sad and awkward, I lift the handle of his suitcase from beneath its Velcro tie.

He chugs what's left of his hot chocolate and grabs his overcoat. "By the way," he says, "I've decided to go with Denise to a marriage counselor."

I almost fall over from shock. "That's great Dad. That's wonderful."

Looking pleased, he sighs loudly, "The things a man must do to pacify two good women."

"Ha-ha," I tease. But I think: Pacifying beats abandonment. And then something awful jerks in my stomach.

Struggling to keep myself together, I follow as he rolls his suitcase across the floor. Dad's bravery is on display, his courage out in the open, receiving its proper exercise. For the first time in a long time I feel proud of him.

"Will you come and visit me this summer, Molly? It's been five years since you've seen sunny Vancouver."

I envision the city and the mountains and the coastline lying splendid beneath bright skies. A pang of homesickness sneaks up on me. "Okay, I'll come in July, to see you—and Denise, of course."

"I'm going to hold you to that, Molly."

"You can ink it into your calendar."

The doorbell rings again, causing us to jump. Eyes reddening, Dad fiddles with the lock and opens the door.

Mohammed, his face wreathed in smiles, stands holding a huge bunch of anemones, their bright faces looking this way and that as if seeking out the next fun opportunity.

"Happy New Year, Hugh."

"Happy New Year, Mohammed," Dad responds. "These

are perfect. Thank you for finding them."

My brain clashes about. Why is Mohammed once more standing on my doorstep? I try to remember where I put his business card. Perhaps I was efficient and fastened it into my old Rolodex under TAXI. Dad will have found it when he looked for a cab.

Mohammed hands him the flowers, pleased he's done a great job. "I am happy I found them yesterday afternoon, almost too late, in a big, huge, Chicago flower shop." Describing its size, he spreads his arms out wider and wider. "I tell you something else. When I took them home after work, my wife made trouble for me." He laughs and raises his arms in a helpless gesture. "She asked why I'm not bringing some for her. Now, I have to get her some too. She likes the colors and the way they turn different ways, wherever they want."

I hope Dad hasn't set off any trouble to brew for Mohammed and his wife—a person unwittingly smitten by flowers that might easily bring out the Voodoo Woman in her.

He catches sight of me and beams. "Happy New Year, Molly."

"And a Happy New Year to you too, Mohammed."

"You two know each other?"

I nix the Rolodex idea. "Mohammed drove me back from the hospital the day Bob died."

"And later, your friend, Jane."

"By coincidence," I say, "Just like now."

Mohammed clearly loves what's happening. "When I first brought your father here from O'Hare, we arranged this." His wide grin uncovers straight creamy teeth. "Hugh wrote down the flower name for me." To prove it, he pulls a clean square of white paper from his pocket. "ANEMONES" is written in large print along the top. "My wife copied it so that she would remember for sure," he adds.

I nod, unable to find words. Everyone I care about, including me, seems to be on Mohammed's pick-up route. I wonder if these are Voodoo Coincidences, and a part of every Voodoo Woman's life.

Dad hands me the flowers and hugs me goodbye. "I remembered these are your favorites," he whispers.

A pang of guilt strikes. Here he is with his flower surprise, arranged before he even arrived at my door. I would never have given him credit for such a thing.

Before I manage to speak, he pulls away. "Okay, Mohammed, let's get rolling."

On this first day of the new year, I stand on the threshold, holding onto my best-loved flowers, watching my newly majestic dad blow kisses at me as he rides away in Mohammed's purple chariot.

30

For the first time since Bob died the house seems empty and cheerless. Dad's personality took up a lot of space, his energy revitalizing my home's quiet corners, and me. Our battles were worth every second of upset. I'm amazed and gratified that our straight talk brought us closer. Placing my enormous bunch of anemones on the kitchen island, I consider a suitable vase and start to feel sorry for myself. Without Dad around, everything has taken on a sudden dullness. What do I do now?

Unwrapping the flowers, I fret about Alex Fox. He has waited so patiently for me to come up with a winning idea for my *City Gardener* article, trusting me to rise to the occasion and not let him down—although, I suspect it's taken all of his willpower to withstand the urge to phone me, to worry and nag at me, to put my feet to the fire. I should feel more anxious, frantic really, over my lack of creative talent. Yet I cannot muster up the need—which worries me a little. Something will come up, I assure myself. Besides, I still have a few days left to make it happen.

I lift my best and heaviest crystal vase from beneath the counter, open a packet of flower preservative and absently swirl it around in water as the vase fills. From the counter, anemone faces beam joy at me from curvy stalks, not one alike. I have it in me to be just like them, I muse. I know how to cheerfully seek a new path, take on an S-curve, make a zig instead of a zag, and act like the person I was meant to be. Trimming off lower leaves and re-cutting stems before placing each anemone in the vase, I check to make sure they have plenty of breathing room before clearing off the counter. Carrying them over to the round glass kitchen table, I position them on it, dead center.

Molly Doll shoots me a big smile. I deliver one back, make myself a cup of mint tea and sit down to have a good think. I am a flowering Voodoo Woman. I will come up with something special; I just have to apply myself.

The picture of Mohammed carrying my big bunch of anemones from Dad keeps playing in my head. But now I see him holding a flashy Persian Onion. It stands proud and very obvious, its purple star shaped flowers forming a neat four-inch ball held high above its clump of sturdy leaves, its pungent scent a down-to-earth language designed to tickle noses with savory truths.

A strong sense of expectancy settles on me, and even though I warn myself to stay calm and wait for whatever it is that's trying to reach the surface, I can't stop the jangles and jitters that run frenzied around my belly and across my skin.

I'm staring at the anemones, feeling that it's about them, about flowers, about their personalities, and mine, when inspiration rises up in full bloom, spilling out of me like pollen for the honey bees.

I think: yes, yes, yeeeeeees! My hands dance when I punch in Alex's home number. He must have been hanging by the phone, since he answers on the first ring with a cheery, "Hello."

"Happy New Year, Alex," I trill.

He laughs. "Well, Happy New Year to you too, stranger."

"I couldn't stop myself from calling you at home, even though it's a Holiday. Do you have time to talk shop?"

"Shoot."

"I've got it, Alex. An idea."

"It must be a good one. I've never heard you quite like this before."

"It's different. But, I think lots of flower growers and people in general will relate to it." I'm breathless, like a giddy teenager about to describe her new love. "It just hit me Alex. Today. Finally."

"Well hurry up Molly. Tell me." He doesn't sound relieved to hear that I've had a major breakthrough, he sounds delighted. Despite my writer's block, he's expected that I'll make the deadline, his trust intact all the way, his faith in me stronger than my own.

Suddenly shy, I stammer. "Okay. Here we go." and then my thoughts fly all over the place. What if I let him down now? What if he's forced to tell me this idea is not worth writing about let alone publishing? I envision an empty white *City Gardener* centerfold, the ghostly spot where my more-than-decent idea was supposed to have been.

"Will you just spit it out!" he roars, making me laugh in spite of my terror.

"Okay, okay!" I suck in two lungs worth of air. "This will be a thoughtful, yet fun, article. It will compare flowers with people. Real people."

"Flowers with people? I don't get it."

I dig up my confident sales person voice and pray for a miracle. "Picture a vase of anemones."

"Okay."

"I say that anemones are like people who like to live large, people we often call eccentric. Anemones are like the folks who cannot live the way others say they ought to. They are brave. They make their own rules. They strive to reach their potential by taking paths that others dare not take. Anemones go anywhere they want. Their stems usually grow in curves, or with only one big kink that sends them off in a completely new direction. They refuse to conform. Get it?"

"I think so," he drawls, clearly unconvinced.

I add a splash of verve to my pitch, my courage growing with the action. "What about the dandelion that grows through your driveway cement in order to be seen. That flower is perceived as a weed, a misfit, yet it has courage to burn. Vulnerability be damned! A dandelion will grow, it will survive, no matter the odds." I wait as the seconds tick off.

"Okay, keep going."

"Alex, how many articles have you seen about people looking like the dogs they choose? We all love being entertained with ideas like that, don't we?"

"Well, yes, I think that's true."

"Well then, why wouldn't *City Gardener* readers like to read about how flowers seem to personify people? I'll find, say, two or three people, and then match each one up with an appropriate flower. It'll work."

"How will it work?"

"We'll do a photo layout that's cute and funny, showing the visual ties that each person has to his or her chosen flower. We'll make it a Chicago story, and have maybe one offbeat person, one well-dressed business type, and then one ... whatever person. It'll all come together once I start writing. It always does."

"You just might be onto something, Molly." He speaks slowly, thinking it through in true Alex fashion.

"I *am* onto something, Alex. I haven't been this fired up in years."

Silence runs up and down the phone line.

"Say yes, Alex." I blurt, unable to use patience and wait. "It won't be a heavy, maudlin article. It'll be enlightening. Fun. Interesting. I promise." I am going to write this article whether Alex wants it or not. No Voodoo Woman worth her *Miracle Grow* would give up now.

"It's a different tack than we've usually taken in *City Gardener*, but certainly not out of the realm—"

"Come on Alex. Be an anemone."

"I'll have you know you're talking to a manly man here."

"All right then. Don't be a thistle."

He groans. "You know the readers have missed you and your quirky stuff."

"I saw the two fan e-mails you published on the 'Letters to the Editor' page. Thanks for doing that."

"There are more, and you're welcome."

Silence hangs about us. My heart thumps in my chest, and my hands sweat as I hold fast to the receiver. I know that if Bob were here he would tell me to keep my mouth shut for as long as it takes. I hold my lips together with my free hand and wait.

"I'll give it a try, Molly. Go for it."

"You won't regret this, Alex." I babble. "I'm going to write you a great article, one you won't forget."

"Remember, the deadline is mid March. No later." His serious tone reminds me of the space he's holding open for my article, the chance he's taking on me pulling this off.

"I'll have it ready way before that, Alex. It's a promise."

"Good luck, Molly. I can't wait to see it." I can hear his grin.

Giddy with my own power, I put down the phone and dance around the kitchen like a soccer player after the winning kick. It is official. I am back in business.

31

I stop the car and stare down the deserted backstreet that housed Chicago's Old Town's Spiritual Magic Shop. It is eerily quiet. Pressing gently on the gas pedal I drive slowly, looking for signage on either side and finding none. Yet, this is definitely the right street. I'm absolutely, positively certain of it.

Since Christmas at Stefano's, I've known I'd come back here. Tossing aside the old adage about curiosity killing the cat, I believe that an innocent trip to the Old Town's Spiritual Magic Shop for a few boxes of candles will give me the opportunity to discover more about Marie. Who is she? Where has she come from?

Stopping the car in front of a small shop window in the center of the row, I think that if this is the only retail store on the street, it must be the one I'm looking for. A printed sign is pasted on the glass. It is black with looping silver lettering written in an upward path.

RETAIL SPACE
1300 square feet
312-777-1313

I note the number of thirteens written on the advertisement. My nerves jitter. Fishing my cell phone out of my purse, I quickly dial the number before I lose my nerve.

An ancient voice creaks, "Good morning. VP Real Estate."

"I'm calling about the retail space you have for rent on Central Street," I say, thinking that this voice sounds a lot like Voodoo Priestess Marie's, and imagining what the VP in VP Real Estate might mean.

"I'm sorry dear, it's already gone."

"What happened to the Spiritual Magic Shop?"

"What shop?"

"The Old Town's Spiritual Magic Shop."

Seconds tick over.

"Do you know what happened to Marie?" I persist.

The silence holds.

"Is this a crank call?" she says, her voice smiling.

Afraid that it is, I quickly hang up.

And for the first time ever, I picture the two Victoria Plants and realize that they each share Voodoo Priestess initials.

32

S itting at the window table in her winter-white business suit and peach satin blouse, the mid-afternoon light bouncing shine across her red hair, Jane looks stunning. She dabs at her lips with a pristine napkin. "I love this restaurant," she announces. "Thank you, Molly. This is a real treat."

"You're welcome. It's a nice change holding our monthly meeting here, isn't it? Next month we should bring our new hire. Mike's done such a great job."

"Agreed." She stifles a yawn. "Oops! Seems a siesta is in order."

"I know what you mean." I stretch my torso, trying to give lunch a bit more space to settle into, and smile. Life is heading in the right direction. Our new senior account executive, Mike Downing, brought in White Teeth Centers and Sweet Garb clothing stores and, at a handsome fifty, his friendly confidence and vast experience immediately won over the staff. The agency is humming.

In December, *Crain's* published a flattering in-depth piece about us called, "Makepeace Makes Peace at Makepeace-Jamison," which set off a major market buzz. My desk now holds a stack of resumes from all kinds of talented people pushing to get in. Account executives promise to add clients to our client list. Media buyers boast of their expertise in making strategic local and national buys, and sing of their superior relationships with media representatives that are guaranteed to give us the market's best deals. Graphic artists have sent copies of their design work, and direct me to their web sites. Writers wax of unique concepts that rocketed their clients into the market's top slots. Executive assistants and budding receptionists present their assurances of competence and professionalism.

Without Shirley and Bob and their illicit sex agenda, Makepeace-Jamison Advertising Agency Inc. is hotter than ever, which makes me proud. Yet it's not enough to rid me of the gray and shadowy shame that still slinks behind my ribcage and drips sorrow into my blood. I push it away. Give it more time, I tell myself, until I can cope with it. All it needs is a little more time, and then it will leave for good.

"Hugh was right about the Caesar salad here," muses Jane. "It really is the best in town." She squints her eyes. "I wonder if Stefano will give me his recipe."

"I doubt that he'll hand out any of his *secret* family recipes, but you're welcome to give it a try."

"On the other hand, what's the point in eating out if you can fix things like Stefano's Famous Caesar at home?"

"I should have ordered it without the Fettuccini Alfredo," I groan. "These lunch specials are a killer."

"Yes, but who can resist?"

"Evidently, neither one of us."

Jane blasts out with one of her hilarious cackles, which sets us off giggling like a pair of kids. Still grinning, she stretches her neck to look across the restaurant. "If I see Stefano, I'm just going to ask him about his Caesars. The worst he can do is say no."

I look around and find that aside from the two animated men arguing politics at one of the two-tops along the wall, we're the only people left in the main dining room.

Jane follows my eyes. "Do you ever think about dating again, Molly?"

"Not really. Besides, who's out there?"

"Do you ever hear from Jonathan?"

My cheeks heat up. "Nope."

"He gave you that fun doll. They don't do stuff like that if they're not interested."

"I think he just felt sorry about my situation."

"How do you feel about Bob these days? How is the anger? Is it getting any easier?"

"Sometimes I wonder why I put up with him. I'm still confused, in two minds."

"I know how Bob was. It's a lot to sort out."

I nod, and glance around again. "The place is almost empty. Looks like it's about time we got out of here."

"I guess so." Jane reluctantly agrees. "Remember the day we came here for lunch and talked so long we stayed for dinner?"

"I and my waistline do indeed remember that day."

"Bernie called it undeniable proof of our impressive—what your Dad calls—'talkability' talent, and feels obliged to contact *Guinness World Records* to see about getting our names in lights."

"Tell him to mention that we also managed to solve the world's problems in under eight hours. That should do it."

The deafening hoot she lets rip floors the two arguing men into silence. Laughing at her, I lift my coat from the back of my seat. "Are you walking back to the office right now?"

"I am." Jane plays her usual sophisticated self, acting as if she has not just emitted a noise loud enough to create heart stoppages throughout the restaurant.

By now the men have recovered themselves, and guffaw in gamely fashion. The big guy shouts over, "Ever thought of bottling that?"

"I already have the patent," Jane grins.

The men share hopeful looks. "Can we buy you two girls a drink in the bar?"

"Sorry boys. It's back to work time."

"Too bad. We could show you girls a good time."

We laugh and wave and fasten up our coats.

"I'm going to stop at Borders to pick up a new book on Illinois garden flowers. I'll walk with you that far. After that, I'm heading home."

"Good thing those guys don't know you're about to become a hugely big-time writer," Jane teases. "They'd be tailing us right now."

"Ha!" I bet those two men are super salespeople, pushing through rejection after rejection, breaking through any and all barriers to reach the highest commission levels

and a welcome bask in the sun. They are a perfect pair of
dandelions.

"I'm looking forward to reading your new article. And
shooting the photos with you."

"Soon, I hope, since I've promised Alex I'd meet an early
deadline."

I assess tall, willowy Jane and picture the graceful, orange
sherbet hued lupins that towered in one corner of my
mother's front garden. Perhaps I'll ask Alex if he can add
more space to the photo layout. Or, maybe I should expand
my thinking into something book length. There are all kinds
of people to choose from, and loads of flower options, such
as weeds, wildflowers, exotic plants, and cultivated varieties. I
might even look up flowering cactus plants for more prickly
folks. My excitement percolates at higher levels.

At the door, Stefano sees me and rushes over with arms
outstretched. Grasping my shoulders, he gives me a loud
Latin air kiss on each side of my face. "Ms. Makepeace,
it's so good to see you again. Was everything excellent, I
hope?" With his dark blond wavy hair, deep brown eyes and
swarthy complexion, I feel inspired to research Northern
Italian flower varieties for something exotic, yet campy.

"As always, the food was wonderful."

"You tell me if you have any problems. I'll fix them."
He makes a sweeping gesture toward the dining room, both
arms rising up and out in graceful arcs. "Your father, Hugh,
he likes it here?"

"He loves it here. He especially likes your Caesar salad.
In fact, he's still singing its praises."

Stefano's hands cover his heart as if he might swoon. "My
grandmother would be so happy to hear this, may she rest

in peace." He gazes upward, as though expecting to find her eavesdropping from the ceiling.

I glance at Jane, intending to encourage her to take this opportunity and ask for the recipe, but the unflappable Jane seems quite flapped at the thought of asking Stefano for any information regarding his dead grandma's secret ingredients. She's inching toward the door, anxious to escape. In the foyer, she confides, "It's so silly, but I just couldn't bring myself to do it. It seems sacrilegious, somehow."

January winds howl across Michigan Avenue, forcing us to hang onto our purses and briefcases lest they take off like high-flying kites. On corners, it threatens to scoop up people and whisk them away. I make sure my sense of balance is right on target, plodding along solidly, combating the idea that I might easily find myself swept up to the rooftops on the crest of a treacherous updraft, a Mary Poppins in distress.

"These winds must be gale force," I pant. "I can see why Chicago is called 'The Windy City.'"

Jane tries to fasten her long, wool scarf around her head. "Actually, we got that name because of long-winded politicians blowing loads of hot air."

"No!"

"Yes! But you can be forgiven for thinking the other," she grunts, "especially in winter."

"Here's Borders." I wave and duck into the doorway, relieved to escape the buffeting. Jane pushes on, her coat flapping around her legs. "See you tomorrow, Molly," she calls, her voice barely audible over the roar.

The store is overheated. As I walk through it, I unbutton my coat and unwrap my long, red scarf, which, due to the wind, has tightened itself around my neck like a noose. On the escalator, I push my gloves into the top of my briefcase. Stepping onto the second floor, I run my fingers through tangled hair in a futile attempt to smooth it down. I don't look up until I'm in front of the poster.

"Oh God!" I whisper, my heart tapping out the quickstep.

Before me stands a line of people, all clasping books, all waiting patiently for Chicago author Jonathan Wilson's signature. At the front of the line, Jonathan sits behind a wide table. A plump, young woman is leaning over it, holding her book open with both hands. Smiling Jonathan says a few words to her before signing it.

Stepping into the nearest aisle, I resolve to hide out until I can decide what to do with myself. The store grows even hotter. I put my purse and briefcase on the floor and begin to fan myself by flapping my coat open and closed. What is the matter with me? The amount of stuff I forget is truly alarming. My flower project certainly isn't helping. Even Jane teased me saying, "I know your creative juices are flowing because you tune out more than ever." It cannot be denied. Whenever I switch on creatively part of me moves to another planet.

Displayed at the end of the aisle is an artistic arrangement of Jonathan's books. Like a thief's, my hand shoots forward with lightning speed to snatch one. Booty collected, I retreat to my stash of belongings and gather them up before searching for a place to sit. Around the corner from the restroom, and somewhat off the beaten path, a large blue armchair beckons. Soon, I have my coat off, my briefcase and purse tucked alongside me, and the book at the ready.

The View from the Roof has a red dust cover with an unusual cityscape drawn slightly off kilter in the center of it. Jonathan's familiar face graces the inside flap. A flicker of pride runs through me, making me feel ridiculous. Blushing like mad, I turn to chapter one and begin reading.

Halfway through chapter four, when the murder victim is finally identified, and it looks like the police are about to arrest the wrong man, I hear, "Molly?" It doesn't quite register. "Molly Makepeace Jamison? Is that you?" Still somewhat disconnected from the world around me, I raise glazed eyes.

"I'm glad to see that you read quality literature." Jonathan grins. "Please don't burst my bubble and tell me anything different. At least, not today."

I wonder what my face is doing, and feel the glow of heat on my cheeks.

"Are you all right?" He bends toward me, his face serious.

Embarrassed by my ditzy-ness, I pull myself together and tease him like a confident Voodoo Woman ought to. "So sorry Jonathan. But when I read quality literature, my habit is to tune out everything else. Naturally, it takes me a minute or two to come to."

His face retains its solemn look. "I understand the phenomenon."

The heat begins to smother me. Tapping my fingers on the book's open pages, I rush on. "You write beautifully, Jonathan. Your characters ring true. Your descriptions of Chicago are elegant. And, the story is compelling. It makes for a winning combination." I congratulate myself for sounding somewhat intelligent.

"Thank you, Molly. I take that as a great compliment." His gray-blue eyes with the gold flecks never leave my face. His lips look full and soft. I bet he flosses his teeth.

"You published earlier than expected." Heat threatens to overwhelm me.

"My agent told me to expect the absolute longest time, so I did. It was a big surprise to see it off the presses right before Christmas. I've taken a few weeks off work to get through this tour, not that I'm complaining, mind you."

"Sounds exciting. Your publisher must have high hopes for you."

"Yup. I hope she's right." He glances at his watch.

"Do you have another signing?"

"Evanston's Borders. Six o' clock." His feet do not budge.

"Wow! You'd better get rolling," I twitter, sounding like a fool who wants to get rid of him.

He nods, still smiling. "You look great, Molly. Are you doing all right?"

"Much better, thanks." I wonder why he didn't bother to call after giving me Magic Molly.

He glances up at the clock behind me. "I wish we could talk more, but you know the traffic."

"Rush hour especially." Maybe he felt it was unseemly to make a move on a recently widowed woman. But now, Bob has been dead close to five months. What is the acceptable time for a widow to behave the way Justine had? Not that I ever would, of course, although it might be fun.

He checks his watch again. "I hope you enjoy my book."

"I already do. Very much." Maybe he's not interested in getting to know me at all. A couple of times he asked me to call him anytime. But was that about police work, or something more personal? He might think that doing anything more might appear disrespectful.

"Great seeing you, Molly." He hesitates, as though wanting to say more. A few seconds tick over.

"Nice seeing you too, Jonathan. Good luck with the book." I blurt, and then berate myself for interrupting the silence, for not waiting to see what he might have said. When he walks away, I realize that I didn't update him on my change of name, nor did I pass him my business card. I couldn't forget more if I tried.

In a fog of steaming heat, I pick up all of my paraphernalia and pay for Jonathan's book on the way out. Putting the car away at home, it dawns on me that I forgot to ask him to sign it. Even more annoying, I forgot to pick up the new book on Illinois garden flowers.

33

It's a good thing we trusted today's accurate weather report. The sun is shining, skies are clear, and the January air is crisp rather than bitter cold. We have a perfect day for our photo shoot, which is more like a snapshots shoot since neither Jane nor I are trained professionals.

Mohammed has parked his taxi on my driveway so as to highlight its brilliant shine to perfection. Since arriving, he has not stopped smiling.

"This is most interesting," he says to Jane, who is peering through the lens of my camera at him. "I've never been in a magazine before."

"I just want to make sure we have a perfect composition before taking any pictures," she says, sounding excited.

"We need to show Alex the best possible angles." I watch Jane's hand signals and turn Mohammed slightly to the left. "He'll probably want to use his own photographers and take more, but it won't hurt to get these right and give them sparkle."

"Never forget," Mohammed warns, "the sun brings us warmth and brings us light. But it also brings us the shadows. And we must never get caught in the shadows."

"I think we're ready," says Jane.

Mohammed stands straight and proud next to his polished purple cab. In his pressed purple pants and white shirt, with his black hair combed straight back, he looks handsome and exotic. When I hand him his flower, he beams.

"Try not to freeze," I tell him, "This won't take long."

"Perfect," shouts Jane. "Hold still, Mohammed."

Against one thigh, in a sturdy white pot, he balances a straight and proud Persian Onion, its strong stem supporting its large ball of tiny purple flowers at eye level. He stares straight into the camera, his brown eyes gleaming.

Jane snaps away like a pro, occasionally moving slightly left or right. After about a zillion shots, she stops. "I think I missed my calling" she grins.

Mohammed looks like he's about to shiver. I rush over to him with his coat, and help him into it. After buttoning up, he shakes my hand, "This is a very good thing that you do," he declares, "a very good thing."

•

Alex Fox wants to know more. "Are these folks famous? Local? Both? What?"

"I'm thinking that they don't need to be famous, they can be regular or extraordinary people, just like in my *City Gardener* article. If I'm talking to someone who tells me that their Auntie Florrie reminds them of daffodils, I want to meet Auntie Florrie. The only requirement is, they have a flower soul mate, so to speak."

We are back in our old haunt, a window seat in the diner across the street from the *City Gardener* building, inhaling eggs and bacon and drinking the sort of coffee that puts lesser people into caffeine jitters for a day or two. Enclosed in a large, white envelope, my finished article lies in the center of the table, the ketchup, mustard, and other condiments on either side of it.

When I phoned to set up our breakfast meeting, Alex was delighted and astonished by my efficiency. "You are amazing! You've finished the article early, and you already have a book proposal in mind." His appreciation creates in me great waves of pleasure and a healthy confidence boost. I'm glad he's in my life.

A small, round waitress appears, her light brown hair tied back in a wispy ponytail. "More coffee?"

"Please." Alex holds his cup out for a refill. "Okay. Tell me more about Auntie Florrie. How do you envision that particular photo composition?"

"I see dear Auntie Florrie dressed in a bright yellow dress and one of those summer hats that's shaped like a long funnel thing."

Alex looks blank. "Long funnel thing?"

I search my purse for a pen and a pad of large sticky notes. "Let me show you what a funnel hat looks like."

"Oh, this should be good," he teases.

I sketch and then sketch some more, hoping to improve my hopeless rendition. By the time I give up, it looks more like a bumpy, morel mushroom cap than a hat.

He grins, "I rest my case."

"Her hat would look better than this. I'm not exactly Picasso, you know."

"Maybe you are," muses Alex, turning my masterpiece every which way as if he can't tell the top from the bottom.

"Picture this." I resume enthusiastically. "Auntie Florrie is wearing her bright yellow dress and her bright yellow hat. She's sitting in a big, comfortable armchair next to a vase of bright yellow daffodils. The size of the vase will depend on the size of Auntie Florrie. If she has a figure eight shape, the vase must have figure eight curves; if she is round, the vase must be round; if she is tall and thin, the vase must be tall and thin; and so on." I pause for air. "She will hold one daffodil in her hands pointed in the same direction as her hat." I can't help but giggle.

Alex rests on his elbows. He holds his coffee cup in both hands and takes little slurps, nodding once in a while. I decide to believe in the best possible outcome and forge on.

"Can you see how whimsical this is? How fun?"

Alex scrunches his eyebrows together and places a hand on his forehead as though having a torturous think.

"Alex!"

He laughs. "You know, Molly, I do think your book idea has potential."

"Really?" I can't suppress a squeak of glee.

"Tell me a caption about Auntie Florrie that shows her daffodil qualities."

I clear my throat and speak with exaggerated seriousness. "Auntie Florrie has a sunny disposition. Every spring, dressed in bright yellow, she emerges from her winter hibernation, spent underground in her basement apartment. Had William Wordsworth known Auntie Florrie, his famous 'Daffodils' poem would surely have included a golden reference to her."

Alex chuckles. "That's pretty good."

"Well?"

"Well…" he pauses. "Until I actually read your article, it's hard to really get a true feel for your book ideas. I don't want to get your hopes up and then have to take them away."

"I've included snapshots with the manuscript to give you a better idea about what you might consider for the magazine's photo layout. As agreed, my article focuses on me and two other people. I've chosen the taxi driver-slash-owner of JC Cabbs, a hard-working Persian immigrant who offers wise advice to one and all, and who is steadfastly upright. You're going to love him. And, of course, there's Jane."

"Let me see the results of this artistic brilliance." He grabs at the envelope, laughing.

"Listen, Mister," I throw him my Elvis lip, knowing he loves it, "I would prefer that you read the article in one shot. No distractions."

"Alriiiight," he groans with comic exaggeration, "I'll just peek at the photos then."

Holding my breath, I watch his hand disappear into the envelope. "Your photographers might have different ideas than we do when it comes to composition, but Jane did a great job," I babble, and then tell myself to shut up.

Alex is smiling at a photo of Mohammed. "What does JC Cabbs stand for?"

"That story is included in the article, and it's worth waiting for."

He nods his approval, "So far, I like this, Molly. I'm starting to get the picture."

"Are you trying to be punny?" I ask, and then ignore his moans.

Jane's photo comes next. She's elegant in a flowing green dress, her long legs bare, her pedicured feet in silver sandals. Her smile is confident, her gaze unwavering, yet there's a glint of mischief in her eyes. Above her right ear rests a very large and showy Southern magnolia flower, its waxy white petals and ovate green leaves luscious against her red hair and creamy skin. The *Magnolia grandiflora* is the official Louisiana State flower. I bet that Creole women, like Marie Laveau, wore big, bold magnolias in their hair. After all, it takes a woman with a certain amount of chutzpah to carry it off.

"Even though I took Jane's photo myself, I have to say I think it's pretty good."

"Not bad at all, Molly."

A snapshot of me comes last (taken by Jane, the *artiste*). Holding an armful of vivid red anemones—a secret homage for the Voodoo high priestess at the Old Town's Spiritual Magic Shop, and the two Victoria Plants—I pose in my red dress, in a red armchair against a cream wall.

"This is great, Molly. It really is. If your article is this good, we're definitely in business."

"Can you read the article later today?"

"It's Friday."

"Okay, when?"

"Not until next week sometime, oh impatient one."

"Monday?"

"Before Wednesday."

"Tuesday?"

"Behave yourself." He tilts his head, smiling.

I shrug. "Strike while the iron is hot and all of that."

"Nothing will cool off before Wednesday. I promise."

We sit quietly, drinking coffee and looking out of the window. In front of the diner, a woman in a white fur Russian hat, and long black coat starts to thump away on a parking meter, her back to us.

"Wow! She's having a bad day," says Alex.

My chest fills with dread. "Oh God. She's really losing it."

Alex searches my face, concerned over my swift change in mood. "What's next on your agenda, Molly?"

I tear my eyes away from the spectacle outside.

"Obviously, I'm *really* hoping you run with the article as is, but either way, I'm going to put together a book proposal based on these ideas. Your support would be encouraging though. I hope to have it—along with a fab-tastic blurb for my book's cover."

"Well, I certainly hope to give it. Based on what I've seen and heard this morning, it's likely I will. And I agree that you have to make your book a priority—once this article is put to bed, of course." He wags his finger at me. "I don't know how you're going to run your agency, write freelance, and complete this new venture at the same time. But, you have to do your own thing, regardless of what anyone else thinks. Who's to say you don't have a best seller coffee-table book in the works?"

Outside, a police officer walks toward the parking meters, her arms waving back and forth across great swaths of air, trying to attract the woman's attention.

I say, "I think it will sell well. People like whimsy. They enjoy having their days brightened. Look at that poor woman outside. She could use a laugh."

The woman doesn't see the officer. She gives the meter another good kick with her white leather, high-heeled boot without realizing she has company. Beside her, the officer stands akimbo, her face set in hard lines, her breath puffing out like a steam train's.

"Will she get arrested?" I have great sympathy for unhinged women and police arrests, believing that I barely avoided it myself in recent months. Suppose that meltdown woman is married to a man like Bob. Who can blame her for losing it with a parking meter that has, no doubt, stolen her last quarter without giving her a single minute of time?

"Probably not arrested. She'll just get a warning, I imagine."

My heart twists and turns. She's acting like a lunatic in the middle of the street, not caring who might see. She probably thinks she's losing her mind. I picture myself sticking pins into Voodoo Dolls, and my cheeks flush. It seems to me that if they start arresting women for occasionally acting like they've been pushed to the brink of lunacy, they'll have to start building new jails en masse.

Alex speaks gently, interrupting my thoughts. "I'll try to read your article over the weekend, Molly. No promises."

The officer is now tapping the woman on her shoulder. People across the street are pointing and laughing. The woman spins around, arms swinging. For the first time

I can see her anguish (ashen skin, screwed up eyes, twisted shocking pink lips). My eyes feel riveted, something awful in my brain clicking over.

"Oh my God," I whisper. "It's Shirley."

Alex and I stare at each other, our eyes and mouths O-shaped.

34

The red dot light on the phone flashes and excitement zips through me. Perhaps another article is accepted. Maybe my *Flower Folks* book proposal has interested that important agent Alex knows. It is late May already. For months, at night and on weekends, I've worked harder than a navvy on the railroads. I've made lots of writing headway. Is this call the big payoff? I drop the grocery bags onto the kitchen counter and run to the desk for a pen and paper.

Nervous, excited and fully prepared to write down the minutest details, I press the Play button and listen to the recorded message. "Hello, Ms. Jamison. This is Brian Blackstone. I have excellent news. Your husband's ashes are found. Please call so that we can set up a time for me to bring them home to you. Isn't this wonderful?"

Mr. Blackstone, it seems, loves performance, loves drama-drama-drama to such a degree, he never considered how the recipient of his news might feel. Shock dizzies me. Falling into a chair, I struggle to fend off faintness. Bob is back. How like him to show up right about the time I've managed to cut in half my daily habit of stewing over him, his lies, and his traveling box of ashes.

I stare at the trappings of my busy new world. My two bags of groceries balance against each other on the kitchen island counter where manuscripts and lists of ideas lie scattered. At the end of the wall cabinets, my desktop hides beneath Makepeace-Jamison agency homework. Texts for writers, *City Gardener* magazines, and books about garden flowers stand in stacks at my feet—all of it scheduled to wend its way up to my spiffy new home office located in the back corner bedroom, overlooking the yard.

Over the past nine months my life has been slowly settling into a happier groove. How like Bob to spoil it. It used to be that whenever I had a smile on my face, he always found a way to wipe it off, garnering his strength by weakening me, stealing my power like a thief in the night. Has nothing really changed?

After calling Mr. Blackstone's direct number, I'm holding the phone so tight my hand hurts.

"Ms. Jamison, isn't this excellent news?"

"It's certainly a surprise," I answer, stiffly. "By the way, my name is now Makepeace." I slowly stretch my mouth into huge O's to help unclench and relax my jaw.

Undeterred by my less than excited response, he bubbles, "I can come over right now if you like." He is inches away from putting this extraordinary debacle squarely behind him. It's obvious that he can hardly wait. I picture him dancing in a chorus line, his long, plump legs in pink tights shooting up higher than anyone else's as he demonstrates his joy.

"Now is fine," I mumble, a headache forming behind my eyes.

"In that case, Ms. Makepeace, I'm on my way."

Needing to lie down, I move toward the patio. Perhaps sleep will come and carry me away, preventing me from feeling quite so undone by Bob's sudden appearance. Before collapsing onto the chaise longue, I leave the patio doors wide open so that I'll hear the doorbell. May's sunshine has warmed the air, spring wafts on the breeze, birds twitter and chirp. Within moments, I'm gone.

When the doorbell heralds Mr. Blackstone's arrival, I'm in the midst of a nightmare. Bob, Shirley and Mary hold hands, encircling me as I lie sleeping, their expressions joyous. "She's not long for this world," pronounces Bob. "Not long at all," echoes Shirley and Mary. Pouring evil into each other's eyes, they cackle with malicious laughter.

Fighting my way back into reality, I battle to understand what is real and what is not. The doorbell rings again. My eyes don't want to open. I blink hard for a while until I can let the sunshine back in. The bell rings a third time. Dragging myself off the chaise, I lumber into the kitchen and down the hall to the front door, telling myself to snap out of it and pull myself together.

On the doorstep, wearing an expensive black suit, white silk shirt, and black silk tie stands Brian Blackstone, his full moon face trying to find an appropriate position somewhere between delight and sorrow. He reminds me of those white-faced mimes whose mouths change from happy to sad with the up or down swipe of their hands.

Over his right arm hangs a large bag, which I imagine contains Bob's CDs and our photos. Against his chest, he holds Bob's brass urn, protecting it from further insult.

His face beams a hello. "Ms Makepeace, I'm so glad this turned out well in the end."

Still dazed and shaky, I am stuck to the spot, my eyes on Bob.

"Again, Ms. Makepeace. I'm so terribly sorry you were put through this ordeal." His face turns tragic as he tries to hand the urn to me.

"Would you care to come in for coffee, Mr. Blackstone?" I marvel at the good manners my mother instilled in me. Whenever I need to hide my true emotions and operate in Jackie O mode, they almost never fail to kick in—even though sometimes the effort feels too heroic and wears me out.

"Thank you, I would enjoy that. But I can't stay too long. I have a lot of work waiting for me. We're very, very busy these days." He smiles broadly.

I think: How nice for you. People must be dropping like flies. But I open the door wider and say in monotone, "I appreciate you finding the time to personally hand deliver my husband to me."

"It's the least I can do, Ms. Makepeace. I'm so sorry you were put through all of this." He looks bleak.

Bouncing back and forth between his up-and-down face and Bob's urn has made the world so bizarre I can't for a moment fathom any of it. I spout inanely, "These things do happen." Then I think: These things do happen? What the hell am I talking about? Who else has lost their spouse in the U.S. mail?

Mr. Blackstone walks along the hallway with dignified, slow strides, Bob's ashes held firmly in both hands like an offering on its way to the altar. I bring up the rear, lugging the bag.

Sitting at the kitchen island, Bob's ashes before him, he watches me shift the groceries over to the counter beside the refrigerator, and slide all of my papers into one pile that is pushed off to the side. He nods toward the desk. "You look very busy yourself, Ms. Makepeace." He admires the house, nodding and murmuring, "Beautiful home, very nice indeed. Lovely outdoor scene as well."

I switch on the coffee pot, take out mugs, the sugar bowl and creamer, reining myself in like a jockey on a runaway horse, doing my best to not bang things down or smash things up like a widow possessed.

"Should you need anything at all from me, Ms. Makepeace, just let me know. I stand ready to help in any way I can."

Sounding calmer than I feel, I ask, "Where was my husband and how did you find him?"

He hesitates, as if judging the safest approach, before proceeding matter-of-factly. "The post office representative said that the package showed up at the main post office in Chicago as if by magic. Someone set it on the floor next to his desk. He said he nearly fell over it. Seems amazing, I know. He said that disgruntled postal workers sometimes stash things away, play games, just to make mischief for their superiors."

Pouring coffee from a pot that shakes and trembles, I think: A disgruntled wife's Voodoo mischief sounds more like it. But I say, "That's not a very satisfying answer, is it?"

"No, not really." Mr. Blackstone stirs two heaping teaspoons of sugar into his coffee, creating a dark, sweet whirlpool. "But at least he's home now."

"Yes. At least he's home." I feel sick with fury, my stomach churning up pictures of things best forgotten.

"Tell me the truth about you and Shirley," I say. "This not knowing is making me crazy enough to leave you."

Bob breaks a two-day silence to quip, "Make sure the door doesn't hit your ass on your way out."

I lift a plate of quaking cookies and offer them.

"How nice." Mr. Blackstone ignores the dancing plate, chooses the cookie with the most chocolate chips in it, and glances at his watch. "I really must watch the time, Ms. Makepeace."

Scalding blood shoots through my veins and valves, an internal combustion firing up the engine, setting off a galvanizing call to action, and spinning me out of robot mode. I am not going to let him leave me here while he drives off into the sunset, a free man.

Conveniently forgetting that I'm not exactly innocent in this ashes scenario, I decide that because of him, his dope of a temp, and an errant mail carrier, my life is again turned upside down. Brian Blackstone owes me explanations.

"Why do people play cruel games?" I demand.

"Well, I don't really know for sure." Mr. Blackstone's long pale fingers stroke his jowls. "I'm guessing that he might have hated his boss and/or his job."

"I'm not just talking about the mail carrier," I sound a smidgen impatient, as if Brian Blackstone is the expert on all things human, an anthropologist-psychologist-guru with life's answers balanced on the tip of his tongue.

"Oh, I see what you mean." His calm, gray eyes stare at the air above my head while he carefully examines his expertise on this fascinating subject.

"Well," he sighs, after what seems like a week, "I suppose it's because they want to."

I gape in disbelief. "They *want* to? That's it? That's your answer?" This sounds altogether too much like Dad's, "because she let me," excuse. Life's answers are just not that simple.

"Well," he says gently, "They *do* want to, don't they?"

Stymied by what now seems illogical logic, I stammer, "Well, maybe they do."

He nods, wisely. "They do."

Collecting my wits, I manage a rally, "But *why* do they want to?"

Eyebrows raised high, he asks, "Does it really matter?"

"Does it matter?" I echo, aware that there is something very right and exceedingly annoying about his question. "Are you saying it shouldn't?"

Mr. Blackstone takes on a stately air, gracefully waving off my bewilderment, light glinting off his handsome ruby and diamond pinkie ring. "Sometimes, we just can't find specific answers to the 'why' questions," he proclaims. "People lie because they want to. They hurt others because they want to. They play games because they want to. We must understand this and act accordingly. That's all there is to it. I see it all the time in my business."

"Really?"

"Oh yes. The funeral business is an education to beat all others, if you'll excuse me for saying so."

"What do you mean?" I ask. But I think of my red dress

and the fiasco that was Bob's funeral. I can well understand if he considers that day part of his unbeatable education.

"Here's one example that I think you'll especially appreciate." Mr. Blackstone lowers his voice. "A few years back, I knew a dying Jewish man who wanted his remains cremated. His devoutly religious sister promised him that she would honor his request, even though she didn't believe in cremation for religious reasons. His big mistake? He knew who she was, but he trusted her anyway. He put her *in charge* of his vitally important, personal business!" He shakes his head, his eyes ablaze.

"What happened?" I gasp.

"When he died, she had him buried within twenty-four hours."

"No!"

"Yes! She waited until she had him in a position from which he could not defend himself, and then did exactly what she had intended to do all along. She betrayed him. Her brother should have known better than to trust her."

I say, "She was wrong to do that." But I think: Bob knew whom to trust all right, and it wasn't his sibling.

"She hurt herself the most though. No doubt about it."

"Why do you say that?"

He washes down his last bit of cookie with a dainty swig of coffee, making me wait for the story's grand finale. "She pretended that she had broken her promise to save her brother from a fate worse than death—told it to his friends, including me. That's how she lived with it, you see. She decided to believe herself a hero, which was the exact opposite of what was true."

"She lied."

"This time to *herself*. She betrayed herself in every way," he rasps. "There's nothing worse than that, is there?"

My stomach jerks as if on puppet strings. Resting heavily on my elbows, I look into Mr. Blackstone's sorrowful gray eyes. "No, there really isn't anything worse than that."

He drops his voice further. "In spite of Pastor Jamison's strenuous objections, you kept your promise, Ms. Makepeace. It was a matter of principle, wasn't it? As they say, stand for something or you'll fall for anything. You showed us all how important it is to hold your ground, even under the most upsetting circumstances." His eyes mist over. "Well done," he whispers.

I stare at him, speechless with astonishment, my emotions churning together a confusing mix of pride and shame and affection and sorrow.

He embraces my hands in his as he gets up to leave. "Well, Ms. Makepeace, I've enjoyed our talk, but I really must get going." He straightens his tie and adjusts his jacket. "Your husband's ashes are back and the circle is complete. That's so important, isn't it?"

I nod as if in agreement, even though the only circle I picture is the one on Bob's behind where it meets my foot.

"Thank you for your patience through this difficult time," he adds. "You've been a marvel."

Quirky Brian Blackstone is a wonder himself. On melting legs, I walk him to the door, wishing he had time to stay. With his duty complete and his mind at rest, he wears a kindly smile on his satisfied face. Before ambling over to his car, he shakes my hand. "I sincerely hope to see you again, Ms. Makepeace, under better circumstances, of course." At the driveway's first turn he gives me a regal wave, like he's the Queen of England.

Alone again, I trudge along the hallway. Late afternoon light pours in through the kitchen and family room's wide windows and doors, illuminating the entire area in a familiar celestial glow. No sounds from outside penetrate the house. For the first time in months, I stare at Magic Molly and wonder if this day is real.

Bob's urn glows dully, right above the chair where he's eaten many a casual meal and drunk all too many martinis. One of my long, black groans surfaces. No matter how much I've tried to prevent it, Mr. Blackstone's simple truths are reaching up to hit their mark. Did I place myself in a no-win position? Did I put someone untrustworthy in charge of my life, and then endure the result like it was my only option? My cheeks burn with shame.

The anger that helped fuel me over the past nine months had mostly dissipated—or so I thought. Now, from depths unknown, it is boiling upward. I think: If rage can kill, I will soon be dead myself.

I glower at the urn, hating the sight of it, wondering if Bob is gleeful at his power to torment me from the grave. Where has he been? In dreams or reality it's been impossible to know. I run my hand across the embossed brass, resentment streaming out of my pores. It is all I can do to stop myself from plugging in the vacuum cleaner and lifting the lid.

35

Eight years ago, when we first moved into the house and decided to work on our wills, Bob expounded at length on the disposal of his ashes. With his feet propped up on the coffee table and martini glass waving in the air, he cheerfully dished out his orders. "Do The Scattering at the bottom of the yard and make sure that you invite everyone to join you." He studied the ceiling and considered further. "Before you scatter me, I'd like everyone to have an opportunity to speak." Laying his head back, he closed his eyes, no doubt to better envision his clients and business buddies choking out their nice guy Bob tales.

I don't want their stories resurrected. I've worked to put the pain of them behind me, and still struggle with persistent snippets that have to be pushed down rather than felt. Besides, in the nine months since his death, most of Bob's drinking buddies have evaporated. To be fair, I suppose they might imagine that Bob's ashes were scattered in private; their mystery trip had, after all, remained a secret. None of it matters anyway. There'll be no invitations, no party, nobody waxing lyrical. This last act Bob and I will perform alone.

His urn remains on the counter, brazenly flouting itself, stirring up old angers, taking a chance that I won't accidentally-on-purpose tip it over the edge. Since its arrival, I've repeatedly weighed the vast discrepancy between my devotion to Bob's happiness versus his devotion to mine. The fury that followed crept up on me, taking me by the scruff of the neck, practically frizzling my hair with its heat.

Aside from inheriting Mom's waiting gene, why did I stay with him? What made me think he was worth it? Surely there must be lots of reasons? Was I just too afraid to walk away from the big house, the expendable income, and the Great American Dream? I wish I'd asked Brian Blackstone to give me a simple theory on this one. Although, he would likely speculate that I stayed because I wanted to.

I remember that Bob once gave me an opinion on that subject. I put my face in my hands as it jumps to life.

We've not been married long. After driving himself home from an impromptu night out, Bob is staggering through the door on legs that barely hold him up. He tries to hug me as I fill a glass with water. Struggling to sit him down, I say, "Drink this, you'll feel better." I want the booze rinsed out of him and away from us.

He waggles his finger at me and slurs, "You don't know it yet, Moll, but I hold you back. One day you'll get it, and then you'll leave me."

A flash of fear hits. I snip, "You don't hold me back."

"See what I mean," he says.

I should have believed what he told me about himself. I should have left him then. A headache threatens. I rub my temples and the sides of my nose to knead out tension. I wonder if questions about Bob and me will haunt me forever. I told Dad he knew why he did what he did. Do I still believe it?

My insides ache and burn. That shameful thing that snakes around my gut and lurks behind my ribs has once more roused itself. Since Bob's death it just won't settle. A wash of exhaustion flows over me urging me to lie down and sleep away the day. Yet, last night I slept so soundly a rocket could have launched next to me and I doubt I would have stirred. You can snooze but you cannot hide, I tell myself. So, you might as well keep going and get it over with.

Tapping my fingers against the granite counter, I grimace and groan over the task that lies ahead. It's nine o' clock. I can be free of Bob in thirty minutes or less.

In the garage, I find our super long extension cord. Huffing and puffing, I drag it to the patio, attach it to a plugged in cord, and then unroll it across the lawn, past the site of defunct Mount Everest, and beyond my more discreet compost heap toward the bottom of the yard and the densely wooded area that surrounds our woodland oasis.

Our rectangular cedar picnic table has lived in its semi-shaded spot for the last five years. I sometimes retreat from the house to this private, peaceful place, where I listen to the trees and read absorbing stories. Today, I sit down to take inventory on myself. I feel used up, like a slave running around after the master of the house, doing his bidding even though he's dead, putting my own life on hold in order to take care of him.

A sense of dread follows me to the kitchen where Bob's old, deluxe boom box and his chosen music waits. Instructions for every aspect of his memorial and The Scattering have lain in our red DEATH file folder for the past eight years. Except for his marriage, Bob did nothing by halves. My heart weighs me down and my knees teeter. I wonder who'll find me should I die from distress today. Jane would soon realize something was terribly amiss. Would she and Bernie come over? Would she send the police instead?

I picture Jonathan Wilson finding me in a heap in the yard next to Bob's spilled ashes, his urn still clutched in my hands, my flesh munched on by maggots and bones gnawed on by rats, my eyes and mouth gaping, and my clothing torn here and there (hopefully not *there*). After witnessing my unseemly carcass, Jonathan's every positive image of me starts to flee right out of his head.

I swig down a full glass of water, splash my face, and cool my hands under the running faucet. I think: This is the time to back off. Nobody has a gun to my head. I can just throw Bob and his urn into the garbage. I don't need to put myself through this.

But I know that I do.

On mechanical feet, I load myself up with Bob's stuff and lug it down to the picnic table. From the safety of distance, I stare at the house, shaking so hard I can hardly stand up. I think: Nobody will know if you stop now.

But I know that I will.

Emitting black groans, I hoof it back to the kitchen to collect Bob's urn. By the time I step through the door, I'm determined to get The Scattering done bravely and without further ado. Solemn faced Magic Molly stares at me with thoughtful eyes. "Let's put this behind us once and for all," I tell her.

With grave determination, I lift up Bob's ashes. Immediately, I'm struck by the weight of them. A tingle grows in the nerves in my hands, and sizzles along the wiring within my arms and up my neck, lighting up psychic images. Visions of his and his shameless women's escapades batter my head and eyes: Shirley's meals at our house, Shirley's hateful ways, Shirley's glittering diamonds, Shirley's escapades with Bob in the Hancock Building condo, Bloody Mary's nooners with Bob at that cheap motel, Bloody Mary's gimpy leg—an unfortunate, lasting memento from that fateful bus-pinning episode at Bob's memorial.

The pain of Bob's betrayals wrenches me worse than ever. It's excruciatingly embarrassing to have been made an unwitting member of Bob's lack-luster harem. Such a sad flock of sheep, I seethe. They knew all along that he was nothing more than a randy ram, a serial adulterer, a colossal liar. At least I didn't know *for sure* about Bob's women until the big O showed up on his jockey shorts. Both of those women knew about me. They hung in with him anyway, each one believing that she could knock me out of the competition, each one working herself to death trying to please him, wanting to make him understand that she was the one worth keeping.

Walloping Bob's urn a good one, I drop it back on the counter and pump up my anger, hoping to keep it going, wanting to use its energy to make me hate him and all of his awful women. I whack the top even harder. "Why do I feel like crap when I didn't hurt anyone?" Picturing his lying face, I slap the sides of his brass urn, full force. "You *hurt* me!" I hammer Bob's urn with my fists. *"I hurt nobody!"*

But I know this isn't true.

From deep within something terrifying begins to rise. White-knuckling the counter I swallow hard, but whatever it is keeps coming. I press my lips together and deep breathe. Still it rises. I jump out of my chair and try to get to the patio doors, wanting to flee outside and feel the flower garden's comfort, needing to do it before this thing rushes out of me, unchecked.

But it is too late. Doubled over, my arms hugging me as tightly as they're able, I stand struck in a twisted, frozen pose. A low wail rises from my mouth, frightening me into silence, taking me back to the afternoon of Bob's memorial. I watched when Mary's pain was no longer willing to stay hidden in the shadows, lurking beneath her skin and bone and muscle and sinew, slowly weakening her entire structure. It spent its life waiting for an opportunity to break out and present that single, stunning moment of truth.

Have I really kept awful secrets from myself? Have I gone about my life making tacit agreements with Bob? Have I unwittingly shown him that I am a second-class citizen, just like Shirley and Mary and the others did? Surely not!

I try to push these thoughts back down, but my pain has seen daylight and will not turn back. It sends me pictures of the church where Pastor Bull Dog's fearful congregation shake in rows of wooden pews. "Endure my rules," Clarence storms, "or God will forsake you!"

My heart pounds like a jackhammer, drumming away my breath and leaving me gasping. I see myself clustered together with Bob's frightened, faceless women. "Endure my rules," Bob sneers, "or I will forsake you."

Shock skitters along tattered nerves, shredding tissue paper lies along the way. Bob felt powerful controlling his frightened flock. Exactly like Clarence. And I was a card-carrying member. Me!

I reel at the idea that Bob truly *wanted* to hurt me. Day in and day out he wanted to hurt me. He wanted to hurt me because it made him feel less afraid; made him feel better and more in control than when he treated me well. And I went along with it because I didn't know any better.

This was the answer to the question that Dad wouldn't address.

Unwrapping one of my arms from my chest, I give Bob's urn a sideways whop. "You and your brother should have learned to control *yourselves* instead of everybody else." My face glows like a beacon. A shocking heat emanates from it, warming my hands when I try to hide behind them, making me faint and woozy. I think: This is just how I felt when I discovered Bob's infidelity underpants, as if the ugly truth about us had not been in front of my eyes all along. I wasted years of my life pretending to be happy.

My mother's hopeful face comes into view. I watch her cooking roast beef and Yorkshire puddings for a favorite meal that will never be eaten. I see her ironing Makepeace Hardware shirts with one eye on the window to see if Dad is coming home on time tonight. Day in and day out, I watch her diligently performing the chores of futility, drowning in mind-numbing minutiae, following rules that require the relinquishing of her own desires and happiness, unwittingly teaching me to do what she herself did not want to do.

Hunched up next to her hospital bed, I feel abandoned and sick with fear. Right at the end, I whisper, "Please Mom. Don't leave ME!" She dies as she lived, without a fight. I kiss her hand and watch her go, and see in her face, a crucifying joyous relief.

That was more than seven years ago, yet it is only now that I discover I have a dam just like Bob's—the one he had to deal with when he was awarded a speeding ticket on the shoulder of I-94. When my dam breaks, the force of it pushes me to the floor. Torrents of tears burst upward from my gut, past a throat that can no longer tighten enough to stop them. They spurt like geysers from eyes that have given up trying to squeeze them back.

Salty drops splash onto the pale oak floors so loved by my sorry father, floors that once felt the softness of my mother's feet, floors surrounded by walls that have heard my mother's gentle voice, walls that held windows which saw my mother's sad eyes, windows that look out into a flower garden that once felt my mother's gentle touch, a flower garden that flourishes near a garage that houses a bright red Triumph Spitfire standing in lieu of my grandmother's cheery flash and boldness.

I roll onto my side and pull my knees up to my chest, trying to protect myself from the onslaught. Into tightly closed eyes pokes a view of Woodside Park, the clients, the striped tents in the Rose Garden, and the brazen, gooey-eyed looks Bob and Shirley exchanged over ten years ago. I see myself in pain, swallowing pride, turning a blind eye to their shenanigans, believing that I needed Bob more than I needed myself, abandoning myself in front of the three of us, putting up with their insults rather than lose him.

That was the day he left me, even though he stayed.

That was the day I started to act like an addict, always pandering, desperate to recapture that first six-month love fest, sucking up his love-lies the way a grateful addict's nose snorts cocaine. I was an addict. My mother and I were Dad addicts. I became a Bob addict. I fell for his toxicity and let it take over my life.

Grief kicks at my ribs. Tears pour. Shirley and her sly eyes were never the problem. Mary and her mega-ass were never the problem. None of Bob's women were the problem. Bob wasn't even the problem. *I was the problem!* I weep out sorrow with loud sobs, unwilling to stop, wanting to clear out all of the corners, telling myself that after this, there will be no more dams built.

Much later, I open my eyes and stare at the ceiling, taking in shuddering gulps of air, and shaking my head. You think you understand something, I marvel, you believe that you are enlightened, and that you get it. But when there is too much pain and anger filling you up, there is no room left to put the getting of a thing. So for the longest time, you don't get it. Even when you say things that are true, you still *don't* get it. You *don't* get it! You *don't* get it! And then one day you *do*, and it drops you to your knees.

I struggle to my feet and flop into my seat at the kitchen island. Resting my elbows on the gleaming granite counter, I sit for a moment struck by its beauty. I consider its strength and depth of character, and wonder how many years it lay hidden inside a mountain of its own making.

Drying my eyes with the sleeve of my t-shirt, I think in consolation that I could have done worse. I could have been like Bob, a perpetual combatant, seeing the enemy in everyone, destroying naïve people left and right. Naïveté is not the worst sin. Trying to make a futile situation better is not the worst offence. I would rather be the naïve woman on the floor than the man, or any of the women who worked to put me there.

A sense of well-being begins to take root. Knotted nerves start to smooth out. I remember my Victorian house dream and think that I've finally climbed the stairs, opened the door to the attic, and walked inside. I don't feel quite so alone. Half expecting to find a couple of friendly ancestors nearby, I sit up, nervously scanning the empty family room and kitchen for my mother and grandmother. Magic Molly gazes out from her perch on the window ledge, her smiling face a welcome sight. Like co-conspirators, we exchange a knowing look.

Having succumbed to the downpour, a defeated Kleenex lies at my feet. I pick it up and sniff my way across the kitchen to toss my tears into the garbage bin beneath the sink.

From now on, I am choosing to get through whatever faces me with courage, the way a true Voodoo Woman ought to. No matter the outcome, I will have no regrets.

It is noon on the dot when I check myself for damage in the bathroom mirror, holding iced washcloths over swollen eyes that shine clear and calm, the color of leaves brightened by heavy rains. I am ready for The Scattering.

Wearing my black robe, I collect Magic Molly from her kitchen perch. I position her on the picnic table propped

up against the vase of thirteen red tea roses that I took from
the kitchen table on the way out. A tiny pool of pleasure
seeps into my bones. The beauty of our huge backyard
with its pruned high hedges and mature trees reminds
me of Vancouver. The sensuous curves of my well-tended
flowerbeds wax glorious. Multitudes of red tulips, white
crocuses, purple hyacinths and sunny yellow daffodils revel
in their rebirth and scent the air. Amidst the magic of
nature grows a greater soothing of spirit.

I turn on the prescribed music, which is set to repeat
throughout the actual scattering of Bob's ashes. Willie
Nelson sings *Always on My Mind,* filling my ears with his
bittersweet words. I can't help feeling connected to these
lyrics of love and sorrow and regret. I just wish my husband
had been the man expressing them to me.

On the picnic table, Bob's brass urn shines and twinkles
in splashes of sunlight. Warm breezes gently ruffle through
branches and leaves, whispering their secrets. Placing my
hands squarely on each side of the lid, I gently pry it open.

There he is. Pure. Clean. Reduced to an almost white
ash. A lump forms in my throat as I lay my hands on him
and feel his powdery remains. This was my husband.

I swallow hard and begin to scatter handfuls of Bob's
silken ashes around his favorite stand—our nine ash trees.
"Scatter my ashes around the ashes," he once said, thinking
it such clever irony.

I think: We shared good times as well as sorrows. Like
the time we were waterskiing at Lake Geneva and his suit
fell down as he one-skied past a boat of cheering tourists.
Or like the time we walked across Atlanta airport attracting
everyone's attention. "Wow, they're noticing you today,

Moll," he said proudly, neither of us realizing until I sat down on a cold seat that the hem of my swishy skirt was caught in the waistband of my underpants. Or like the time we lay drowsing under the stars on Waikiki Beach and he said, "You're the best person I've ever known."

I wipe my eyes on my forearm, and then realize that I've been scattering for a quite a while. Given the size of Bob's urn, it contains a surprising amount of ashes. They're like the Biblical loaves and fishes; there appears no end in sight.

Feeling spooked, I begin to toss him out faster and less neatly. But as though in defiance, his ashes lift on the breeze, catch the sunlight, and spin away from their designated areas like small gossamer clouds. After hopping this way and that to avoid getting Bob on my hair, up my nose, or in my shoes, I'm forced to slow down and pay attention to his needs, which piques my annoyance.

"Don't start with me, Bob, or I just might betray you the way you betrayed me," I say.

Willie Nelson sings a gentle apology, his voice growing louder and more tremulous.

A pang of shame springs through my chest. Bob never experienced the fierce love of a true Voodoo Woman, just the infatuation of a silly young girl who took a long time to go through her metamorphosis. Then again, I've never known the love of a Voodoo Man. We both lost on that one, I think.

I begin to handle his ashes in a more loving fashion, picking up small amounts, bending over to sift them gently through my fingers, making sure they land perfectly on target exactly the way he envisioned it. Right away the wind settles and it's safe to breathe without fear of inhaling him. Like the hush of a cathedral, an eerie quiet envelops me. As if by magic, the birds quiet, the music softens.

I think back to when we built the house as newlyweds. It was Bob's pride and joy, his manly trophy. We drove to the lot every weekend to watch over the creation of it, making sure we got what we ordered. "Never give any builder the opportunity to screw you, because he will," was Bob's mantra for the entire year we watched it go up. During one visit, he patted two-by-sixes like a proud father. The next, he ran his hand over the walls like a detective looking for mischief. Each weekend brought something new that needed his scrutiny, and he loved it. "This is a quality house, Moll. Not like some of those flimsy shoeboxes we've seen going up down the road. This here is quality." I understood his pride. Our house, on its three acres of prime land was the perfect, tacit announcement to the world that he, Bob Jamison, was not a failure. People only had to look at his possessions to see that he made it pretty damn big.

Always on My Mind nudges me back into the present, its poignant plea giving my heart a painful squeeze. Even though he's gone, Bob wants my love and forgiveness. Despite behaving to the contrary, he has needed it all along.

I step back to survey my completed work. Sun, piercing between lacy leaves, sends brilliant rays to the ground surrounding Bob's ashes, illuminating him with steady, ethereal light. The sight of it sends a rush of disbelief rolling from my toes on up. My throat constricts, my eyes smart and I have to blink a lot to make sure they're not deceiving me. Each of our nine slender ash trees stands regal in its circle of silver.

I think: This is one ring for each year of our marriage.

How like Bob to get all romantic on the way out, to leave a message that just might soften me up.

Even so, my tears spill. He's left me with nine silver Os to help erase the memory of that awful dark red one.

I hold Bob's urn upside down and gently tap it against our oldest tree until not a trace of ash remains in it. After closing it and setting it back on the picnic table, I go back to the same tree and rub my hands against its cool bark, transferring to it any unseen speck of ash that's tried to cling to me. Then I shake out my robe and nervously wiggle my toes against each other, feeling for bits of Bob that might have succeeded in finding their way into my shoes. Within a minute or two I'm satisfied. After all of these years, Bob is finally grounded.

Turning to the chaise longue, I sit down slowly my legs and feet stiff and tired as if suffering from being cramped in a confined space. I watch sunshine stream across the lawn, warming the earth, encouraging healthy growth. Carefully stretching out my bare legs for a touch of it, I stare at the house. It looks vacant. My eyes close against the sight.

Around five, I collect everything up and put it all away. Since neither Bob nor I ever thought about what should happen to our urns once they were empty, his goes into the garage's built-in tool chest and sits on a shelf by itself. In my jewelry box, his gold wedding ring lies next to mine. For now it seems fitting.

Caught by another rush of tears, I dab at my face with the hem of my robe. I'm nearing the end of a significant transition, an unnamed rite of passage. My eyes feel overused and my nose resembles a shiny red stoplight so brilliant in color, it could warn drivers across a four lane highway that they'd better come to a halt. But I have a freeing sense of lightness and roominess. I think that there is now more available space in me for the growth of pure silver. I left more than Bob back in those trees.

A sudden observation presents itself. Firmly planted in his chosen territory, Bob has become a permanent fixture, like the electrical outlets, the plumbing, and the garage. In fact, long after the house is gone, he'll still be around. Thirsty trees will have sucked up ash-laden water, weeds will have used him to help fertilize their roots, worms aerating the soil will constantly weave bits of him in and around the garden. In no time at all, Bob will be all over the place.

I have brought him home. We have come full circle.

36

iz Cooper, real estate agent *extraordinaire* crosses her stocky legs, lifts up her teacup and smiles. "Spring is always the best time of year to put a house on the market."

"I hear that nothing much is selling these days, though."

"If anything sells, this house will," she says confidently, pushing the documents over to my side of the table. "Just sign here."

My eyes flicker around the kitchen and family room. I see Bob in his chair at the island, martini in hand, raising his glass to me, smiling. Dad stands by the fireplace. "This is a great place you've got here, Molly. Excellent workmanship." I glance out into the yard. Mom is in the flowerbeds picking flowers, her hair shimmering in the sunshine. Jane and Bernie relax with Bob and me at the dining room table, their brand new Bernice asleep on the couch.

We're whooping it up over Christmas dinner, and laughing at how the baby sleeps through the racket. We've had good times here. Lots of good times.

"Are you sure you're ready to do this, Molly?" Liz has her hand on the papers ready to slide them away. "You need to feel sure."

"It's time," I say. And then I pick up my red pen and do it.

37

After a quick client update meeting in the office with Mike Downing, I grab my red umbrella and head out for lunch. As soon as my feet hit the street, the glorious busyness of the city fills my senses. Michigan Avenue is alive with throngs of slow moving tourists eyeing their shopping agendas, while armies of speed-walking business people push their way around them. Here and there taxis honk, city buses pull away from their stops, and between them a zillion cars carry people-watching passengers. Shrouded in low heavy mists, tall buildings appear to have lost their tops. Trees and flowers smile through the drizzle. On the breeze, layers of lunchtime aromas tantalize noses and tease empty stomachs. Umbrellas keep off the rain, but not the dampness my skin so enjoys. I wonder what my hair is doing, and picture each strand working its way into a happy, crazy coil. There's no point in worrying about it.

Heading north I spy Jane just ahead. "Hey! Where's the fire?" I call.

She turns and grins, "I thought I was going to keep you waiting. My dentist was running behind."

"An okay check up, I hope?"

"They're all still there and doing well."

The rain has reduced itself to a fine mist. All around us umbrellas are shaken off and snapped shut.

The mischievous, young doorman at Stefano's holds open the door, eyeballing us with deliberate failed discretion. "Well, hellooooooooo ladies," he flirts, enjoying our laughter as we swoosh by, his eyes still roving as if they're loose in his head.

Settling down at our favorite window table, we order wine and put our menus aside, sighing with pleasure over what promises to be a leisurely Friday lunch.

"Liz phoned this morning. She says she expects to have a spiffy penthouse for me to look at next week. Terrace, city views, lake views, the lot. It's supposed to go on the market Monday."

"Sounds fabulous, Molly. I'll keep everything that's crossable crossed for you."

"Who could have expected the house to sell in three weeks? Not that I'm complaining, mind you."

"If need be, put your stuff in storage and stay with us until you find exactly what you want. Wait for the place that's perfect for you."

I feel a rush of affection for her. "Did I ever tell you how much I appreciate you, Jane? Bernie and Bernice too."

"Ditto," she says softly, her eyes glistening.

The waiter brings our wine, glances down at our unread

menus, and glides away.

"It's so quiet in here today." Jane stiffens. "Oh my God. Look at that."

Expecting to face a horror to beat all horrors, I turn to look across the room toward the object of her distress. In front of the corner booth, a woman attached to a mammoth ass bends over to swing her packages along the bench seat. A cascade of straight, blond hair that almost reaches her waist falls down her back like a satin sheet.

"Oh-oh," I whisper, "Is that who I think it is?"

"Is there any other ass quite like the one we're viewing right now?" Jane whispers back.

Mary Murphy straightens up and adjusts her watch. A tall, athletic man with shiny chestnut hair creeps up behind her. Grabbing her around the waist and hugging her like mad, he gently rocks her from side-to-side and nuzzles her neck. She turns to face him, laughing.

"Look who she's with," Jane sputters.

My heart bumps and grinds. "They say that leopards never change their spots."

"I feel bad for poor Ivan," she hisses. "I don't think they live grand enough for her tastes. She always seems to want more."

I breathe in deeply. "At some level, I imagine Ivan knows what's going on."

Jane snorts without taking her eyes off the scene in the corner. "What a sorry sight."

Sporting silly grins on their sneaky faces, Bob's dear old friend, Shirley's likely lover and my wannabe lover, Doctor Jim Burdick, positions himself across the table from Mary. He reaches for her hand.

"Do you want to get out of here?" Jane asks in a voice that hints, "Don't do it."

"What do you think?"

"Just checking."

Consternation strikes. "You know, I was an inch away from reliving the same scenario with the same two women and a near identical man to Bob."

"Not *that* close," she says firmly. "You left that Zeno's restaurant a winner."

"It was a damned close call."

"Those two deserve each other," Jane says, still glaring at them. "In fact, since Shirley is likely in the mix, those *three* deserve each other. I can hardly wait to see them see you."

I prickle at the notion that I once thought I deserved Bob. "Poor Mary," I say magnanimously. "She's in for another rough ride. No pun intended."

"I have no sympathy."

"What if she too ends up trying to murder a parking meter?"

"Shirley and Mary are spoiled gold diggers. They didn't give a damn about what they did to you."

"True enough," chorus Mom and Grandmother from either side of me. I gasp in shock. It's been a while since I heard from them.

Jane stares at me. "Oh my God, Molly. You must hate seeing that woman again. Especially like this. And here I am rattling on as usual. I'm sorry."

I wave off her apology. "Mary Murphy and Shirley Bills don't matter," I try on a smile and it holds firm. "I know now that they never did matter."

"I'm glad you feel this way. I'm not sure I would."

"After all of her public histrionics at his memorial, Mary soon got over loving Bob, didn't she?" I say softly, "Not one of us loved him, not really."

She stares across the table at me. "Are you sure you're all right?"

"I'm sure," I nod. "Positive, in fact."

Jane tilts her head. "I must say, Molly, you've got one helluva lot of chutzpah."

"I've just learned a lot. It helps."

Her frown suddenly drops replaced by an innocent wide smile. "Jim's just seen us."

Since I'd have to turn slightly to monitor the love doves, and wouldn't want them to imagine that I have the slightest interest in them, I need Jane's running commentary. "What's his face doing?"

Like a professional private eye, Jane appears to be looking at me while watching them. "If I didn't know better, I'd think he's actually blushing."

"Are you sure it's not just ambient light from her trained to flame cheeks?"

"Hard to know."

"Has *she* seen us?"

"She's gabbing away, no doubt being sexy cutsie-cutsie," she says. "Oh-oh, he's getting up."

"No!"

"She's not happy."

I sit frozen, watching Jane watching them, her eyes appearing to stare at me.

"Here he comes," she says, just like she's talking about today's luncheon special. "He's heading this way."

"Hi Molly. Hi Jane. It's good to see you."

We both look up and smile like we're surprised to see him.

"Hi Jim," we chorus back.

He is indeed blushing. "Mary and I just ran into each other. She was shopping. I was shopping."

"How fun," says Jane, sounding bored.

"We hadn't seen each other in, well, I don't know how long. Anyway, I thought it would be nice to catch up. You know? See how she's recovering from that awful crash."

"How thoughtful," murmurs Jane.

I can't stop smiling. "You're looking well, Jim," I say, suppressing the urge to giggle.

"We'll have to catch up ourselves," he says, blushing furiously now. "It's been ages since we talked."

Jane gives off the slightest of snorts.

"You must try the Caesar," I say like a restaurant hostess, "and the Fettuccini Alfredo. They're both excellent."

He stares at me with liquid eyes. "You look as if life is agreeing with you, Molly."

"It is, Jim. It really is."

Jane points toward the corner. "I think you're wanted over there, Jim."

Mary is sitting straight-backed, staring hard at him, her face flaming. A waiter stands beside the booth, looking uncomfortable. His eyes scan all three of us, before landing back on her.

Jim sighs. His perfect teeth peek over his full lower lip and hold onto it for a second while he ponders his next move.

"Oh, I get it now," says Jane. "Mary is making the waiter wait for your order."

His eyes do an ever-so-slight roll.

"Enjoy your lunch, Jim," I smile.

He nods, and then slinks back across the floor.

Jane and I stare at each other. Her mouth is pressed shut but her shoulders are shaking. Then, one of her outrageous laughs peals out of her, shocking everyone around us, setting me off on a giggle session that threatens to end in tears. She fans herself with the lunch menu and gasps for air. I'm already wiping my eyes.

"There they go," she manages to squeak, nodding toward the door.

We watch from the window as Mary and Jim scurry toward the traffic light. They cross the street and disappear in the crowd.

38

Before taking off my business suit and flopping onto the couch to tackle a tall stack of mail, I pull my travel itinerary from the desk drawer and pick up the phone. I'll arrive in Vancouver July 18th for a ten-day holiday, as promised.

Dad is thrilled. "That's fantastic. I can hardly wait to see you, Missy. I've got lots of great stuff planned, right down to a day on Granville Island. We might even want to go more than once. We'll visit the art shops and market, and do lunch at Bridges for your favorite fish and chips. We'll pick a good weather day so that we can eat on the deck overlooking False Creek. I remember how you love to watch all the water traffic and the views." His voice softens. "Denise is really looking forward to seeing you too. Says she always wanted to get to know you better."

"You two seem to be doing well," I say, pleased.

"Well, we still have our moments, but at least she's come home now and I suppose she'll stay as long as I keep my nose clean."

I can hear his grin. "I'll bring you lots of hankies."

"Thank you very much," he says sounding more like Elvis than Elvis. We both giggle.

I feel encouraged at the way my life wends its way toward the direction I choose. It's made me understand the importance of heeding my dreams and weeding my garden. I'm choosing well for myself and my sense of security has steadily heightened. It's reassuring to know that there's something magical at work in me.

As Dad rattles on about Granville Island's many attributes, I pick up my Voodoo Woman's List of Goals and place in on the counter in front of me. I started it right after The Scattering, and review it every day, adding new stuff whenever I think of it, and checking off my accomplishments. My eyes start scanning.

- *Get to know Dad and Denise better. Grow good relationships with them*
- *Set up a cozy guest room for Dad and Denise in my new place*
- *Visit them in July as promised*
- *Keep on writing*
- *Be open to dating (write up a list of requirements)*
- *Appreciate learning (even when it's rotten)*
- *Appreciate the agency staff*
- *Appreciate my friends and family*
- *Appreciate me (shouldn't I be first on this list?)*

Now my hand rests on the page, pen at the ready, its point pressed against the top line where a small dot of red ink collects and grows. It seems safe to place a check mark against: *"Get to know Dad and Denise better. Grow good relationships with them."*

"So what else is happening, Molly?"

I hold off on the pen check. "Well, this week I sold the house."

"Jeez! That was quick. Jeez! It's such a great house on such a gorgeous big lot—"

"I've outgrown it," I snip, unwilling to add that Bob's ashes are probably closing in on the patio by now.

"I know. I know."

Regretting my tone, I become conversational. "I've looked at a few condos in Chicago, but nothing that I want has popped up yet. Liz has more lined up next week." I wait through the pause, hoping that he's not developing a lecture on my current house and investment security and whatnot.

"Well," he pauses, and then clears his throat. "Your grandmother always wanted your heart to sing. Isn't that what she used to tell you?"

I feel touched that he remembers. "Yes, she always told me that. She told me lots of things." I could have added that she still does, through memories and dreams and magical coincidences. I'm not afraid to listen for women's voices, ancestral wisdom rising from their graves. I've learned a lot from them.

"When do you have to get out of your house?"

"Mid-August." It is actually August 17th, the one-year anniversary of Bob's death, an interesting coincidence that makes the move feel especially right.

"Jeez! That's just a few weeks away and you're coming here in the middle of it. What will you do if you haven't found anything by then?"

"I'm not worried. Jane and Bernie are standing by."

"Maybe you'll find something here?" He chatters happily. "Wait until you see the fabulous new condos facing the water and Granville Island. Get the right one and you can even see the Coastal Range." Dad's expounding on Granville Island is sounding more and more like one of his endearing Caesar salad rants.

"You already know that I've made the decision to stay here, Mr. Persistent-atious."

"Illinois is as flat as a pancake." He sulks shamelessly. "Why would you want to stay there, Ms. Stubborn Chops?"

"Stop it, Dad," I laugh. "You know I have the agency business to consider. Besides, my writing career is finally taking off. At least, it looks that way."

Looking around the kitchen and family room, I consider the artwork, furniture, color schemes and window treatments that will be needed for the new place. I want to travel light, give myself lots of space, and have room to breathe. "We can visit each other often. My new place will have two bedrooms and an office. So, I'll have a comfortable guest room ready and waiting for you and Denise."

"How do you know you'll find that?" He pouts.

"Because I won't settle for less. I've learned that I'm not happy when I do."

I wait through the silence.

"I guess I can't argue with that." He takes a deep breath. "Do you remember the time you took your mother and me to the Hancock building? It was a gorgeous day. We went all the way up to the observation deck."

Tears well up. It was eight years ago, a few months before my mother died. My parents were amazed that they could follow the pattern of its pyramid-like walls all the way down to the ground. Gazing up, all three of us admired a collection of cotton ball clouds as they sailed across brilliant skies, casting their shadows like floating navy inkblots across Lake Michigan's silvery, turquoise surface.

"Yes, I do remember that day. It was very special."

"Your mother said, 'I think that if I had come home to a view like this every day, it would have been a comfort to me.' Remember?"

I do. It made me wonder at her life and what it must have taken away from her. "You can still do that, Mom," I answered, knowing how she feared change ("Better the devil you know than the devil you don't know."), none of us knowing that it was too late for her to change anything.

Without waiting for my response, Dad continues his reminiscence. "I've thought about that day a lot lately. Your mother always loved a wide view of the water. We could have had that in North Vancouver. I just never offered it to her. Even at the end."

Using the sleeve of my new silk blouse, I damp mop memories from my face. I too want a view of the water and the city skyline. I too dream of wraparound windows and a large terrace or balcony where I can grow tomatoes and anemones in huge, clay pots in summer. I think Mom will be pleased to see me get it.

"Hindsight is always painful, Dad."

"*Regret* is always painful."

"Yes."

He pauses to steady his voice. "Do whatever makes your heart sing, Molly. And do it now."

39

In my dream, the walled garden is a square shaped sea of flowers standing tall beneath vivid skies. Wearing a flowing red robe, I stand at the center. Now I can see dead, gray blooms hiding behind the living, restricting them from embracing a wider stretch of earth. I bend to weed them out.

Nearby, a white house with large polished windows sits on top of a grassy slope. Now I stand in the foyer gazing up at brightly colored ceilings painted in perfect and intricate patterns. A central broad staircase leads to higher floors. Pure white empty rooms stand in pristine beauty. Clean kitchen cupboards await my utensils and foods of choice.

My hands hold a crystal vase filled with clear water and anemones from the garden. I place it on the round glass table that has materialized on the large stretch of floor between the front door and the staircase. Radiant anemones greet all who enter my house, alerting new arrivals as to who lives here, granting them the wisdom to watch their manners.

•

Saturday morning, from the kitchen window ledge, Magic Molly's green eyes survey me as I sweep by her on the way to the laundry room. The dryer buzzes harshly, as if impatient. I open it up and lift out my lacy black lingerie, lay it on top of the washer, and think of Jonathan Wilson.

Since the day Bob died, Jonathan and I have twice run into each other by coincidence: first on the expressway when he caught me singing in my car like an imbecile; second at his book signing, when he caught me sitting in an armchair with my nose stuck into his novel. Unless coincidences come in threes, Jonathan will never again pop back into my life.

He predicted the same about Clarence. After thwarting him at Bob's memorial, we were sitting with Jane and Bernie in the Passages room, both of them still buzzing about the ashes confrontation and the potential backlash that awaited me. "Pastor Jamison lost his blood connection to you when your husband died," Jonathan said. "Chances are, you really have seen the last of him." So far, it appears he was right. Last time I checked, his website *Pastor Clarence's Boot Camp for Sinners* showed him alive and well. Yet, he hasn't come back to bother me, which seems a minor miracle. In fact, it seems too good to be true.

I begin to transfer a new load of damp clothes from the washer to the dryer. I press the start button and glance through the dryer's glass door as my jeans and t-shirts start rolling over and over inside.

I think: What would Clarence do if a bus should roll

over me tomorrow, killing me outright? Come back here to even the score? Give me a Pastor Clarence burial? He might show up in August when Bob's one-year memorial hits, and start badgering me into crossing out "cremation" from my will and writing in "Christian burial" above it.

Despite the unlikelihood, I can't help but shudder. Being buried underground, trapped inside a box is one of the worst things imaginable to me. When I die, I want to rest on the earth like my mother and grandmother, or float with the tides, or take flight in high winds. I don't want to have some nosey anthropologist dig me up one day and strip me bare in front of the world. I don't want the Chicago River to flood so badly it pops my coffin out of the ground like a champagne cork from a bottle.

The mere idea of Clarence interfering with my cremation has me envisioning tri-colored candles, long sharp pins, and tall thin Voodoo dolls in austere black suits. After all that's happened, it's surprising that this is the solution that has come to mind. I try to shake it off. I think: I'll never flirt with Voodoo again ... so long as Clarence behaves himself.

Gathering up my black lacy lingerie, I move toward the kitchen and resume speculating about Jonathan. Since seeing me that day at Borders, he has neither shown up nor called. Yet he has always acted pleased to be around me. Hasn't he? Questions about him bounce through my head. How successful was his book tour? Is he working hard on his new novel? Has he read my highly touted article in *City Gardener?* Is my writing inspired? My thinking inspired? My anything at all inspired?

I seriously doubt that he will call me now, even if he is interested. He wouldn't want me to think him pushy or disrespectful. I am a widow, perhaps still in mourning.

But does he know I care about him?

It occurs to me that a true Voodoo Woman would not hesitate to find out. On my desk, Jonathan's business card lies in plain view. I consider that I might as well see if he would like to go out for dinner sometime to catch up. The worst thing he can say is no, and I should be able to survive that. Besides, for all I know, he might live with someone, or date someone special. He might even be married, although I've never noticed a ring.

I'm ready to start dating. If I want to know *for sure* that my interest in Jonathan is returned, I'll have to contact him and discover it for myself.

I've never done anything like this before. Dropping my freshly laundered clothes on the kitchen counter, I hover by the phone for a few moments and consider the importance of tied up camels. Then I pick up the receiver. When my fingers lift up Jonathan's business card, I take deep breaths, and remind myself of the need for courage. Then, even though my legs feel wobbly and my insides quiver, I punch in his number.

"Molly! It's great to hear from you. I'm so glad you called."

"You told me to let you know if there was anything at all you could do for me," I banter, in hopes of camouflaging a bout of nerves. "I hope you meant it."

"I like to keep my promises," he says, softly.

Goosebumps blossom all over me. I think: I believe you do.

"Let's have dinner one night and talk about writing," I say, calmer now.

"Are you sure—?"

"Yes."

"I'd love to." He answers quickly, his voice betraying his excitement. "When?"

I inhale the deepest of breaths, and answer him slowly. "How about tonight?"

Feeling happy and slightly dazed, I sit like a lump at my desk and hope I've done the right thing. Perhaps I've misread Jonathan's interest. Maybe he agreed to see me because he still has questions about Bob's death.

"That man is perfect for you," Matchmaker Jane said last week, having taken it upon herself to get me out more. "Bernie agrees," she added, proudly.

But Jane and Bernie don't know the whole story.

Sunbeams begin to dance through the patio door's vertical blinds and shimmer in dots across the floor to my feet.

An ancient voice whispers, "Understand your powers. Know yourself."

I rush to tear the blinds wide open.

There, through the mist, three shrouded figures appear amongst the flowers. My heart is racing. For a split second, I catch sight of my smiling mother and grandmother standing hand-in-hand with a woman who looks like Voodoo Priestess Marie from the Old Town's Spiritual Magic Shop. They're all dressed in red.

Tears on my cheeks, I yank open the doors. But they're gone.

Before me, a watery sun burns through the clouds. Behind me, red-robed Molly stands strong. I have taken control of my life. I've completed my own circle and I'm starting the dance.

Like a true Voodoo Woman, I have set myself free. ●

Author's Note

Marie Laveau was a powerful New Orleans Voodoo high priestess. Although dead for almost 130 years, she continues to attract followers, many of whom travel great distances to visit her crypt in New Orleans Cemetery Number One, where they pay homage, and ask for favors. Much of what I've written about Marie is true. However, in the interests of storytelling I have also embellished. The same can be said for the Voodoo descriptions in *Pins*. Creative license was embraced throughout.

About the Author

Christine Todd was born and raised in County Durham, England, but lived most of her life in the American Midwest, most recently Chicago. She graduated from Concordia University–Wisconsin, and worked in advertising. Her short fiction and articles have appeared in various US and UK publications.

Visit her website at: http://christine-todd.com/

READING GROUP QUESTIONS

1. After Bob's death, Molly starts to examine her life more honestly. She says: *"What happened to me? Where was Molly Makepeace? … Was she all used up? Long since gone?"* Why didn't Molly notice the loss of herself when Bob was alive?

2. When Molly learns of Bob's infidelity, and tries to figure out what to do, she says: *"My mother would tell me to keep trying to work things out. My grandmother would advise the opposite. … I could rarely please one without disappointing the other."* What contradictions did Molly attempt to believe in throughout her life so as to try to keep the peace and please others?

3. In death, Molly's mother and grandmother form a solid support system for her.

    a. How does this differ from their support of her when they were alive?

    b. Do you think Molly is imagining this partnership between the two Victoria Plants so as to move forward in a way that grows her strength? Or do you think their presence is real?

4. *Pins* is tied in with the idea of Voodoo pins. But the word "pins" is also used as a metaphor to describe Molly's life.

    a. Where do you see this metaphor at work in her life?

    b. Do you ever feel pinned down, or see pins in the lives of others?

    c. What other metaphors do you see repeated throughout *Pins*?

5. Molly discovers that facing ugly truths is better for her than believing in pretty lies. Do you think that people who choose to believe lies can ever expect to achieve true happiness and contentment?

6. Jane is a loyal and supportive friend.

    a. How important do you think she is to Molly's growth?

    b. Do you think women tend to be this supportive of each other in general?

7. When Molly meets Bob at her first advertising luncheon, she thinks: *"He was everything I was looking for ... He was Prince Charming to my Cinderella."* Given her own significant accomplishments:

    a. Why do you think Molly sees herself as Cinderella and Bob as a prince?

    b. Do you see the Cinderella factor still running strong in the culture? If so, where?

8. Molly says of her mother: *"I watch her diligently performing the chores of futility, drowning in mind-numbing minutiae, following rules that require the relinquishing of her own desires and happiness, unwittingly teaching me to do what she herself did not want to do."* Why do you think Molly's mother trained her to be a traditional wife when she herself did not enjoy that lifestyle?

9. Molly ultimately describes her painful relationships with Bob and her father as addictions that have to be kicked. Do you know anyone who seems addicted to another person? If so, what behaviors do you see in her/him that are similar to Molly's?

10. Do you think that Ralph Makepeace and Bob Jamison are addicted to women who allow them to behave badly? Would Bob have behaved honorably if Molly had refused to put up with bad behavior, or was he simply the wrong choice in the first place?

11. Do you think Molly's dad is "cured" of his selfishness? Will he succeed in his marriage to Denise, and in his quest to win back his daughter?

12. Molly's grandmother advises: *"If you always do what you always did, you'll always get what you always got."* Molly takes her at her word, and does something entirely out of character in order to break out of her unsuccessful mind-set. Have you ever acted in a slightly mad or offbeat way, only to find that it was the right thing to do?

13. Can you see Molly doing another Voodoo dabble someday? If so, whom might she target, and why?